A

# ALIEN APPEAL

## THE CLAIRE TRILOGY – BOOK TWO

## TOM McCAFFREY

Black Rose Writing | Texas

Third printing

This is a work of fiction. Names, characters, businesses, places, events, and incidents are either the products of the author's imagination or used in a fictitious manner. Any resemblance to actual persons, living or dead, or actual events is purely coincidental.

ISBN: 978-1-68433-840-5 (Paperback); 978-1-68433-868-9 (Hardcover)
PUBLISHED BY BLACK ROSE WRITING
www.blackrosewriting.com

Printed in the United States of America
Suggested Retail Price (SRP) $18.95 (Paperback); $23.95 (Hardcover)

*An Alien Appeal* is printed in Garamond

*As a planet-friendly publisher, Black Rose Writing does its best to eliminate unnecessary waste to reduce paper usage and energy costs, while never compromising the reading experience. As a result, the final word count vs. page count may not meet common expectations.

Cover art by Richard Lamb of Inspired Lamb Design

Edited by James Fronsdahl

*This novel is dedicated to my dear friends James and Kathy Fronsdahl, without whose invaluable assistance and support I would not only never have published The Wise Ass on time, but I would never have written An Alien Appeal in such a timely manner. Jimmy edited my work as it was written, which made the later revisions easier, and Kathy provided me with the iconic Claire photo which appears on the cover of The Wise Ass and is incorporated into Richard Lamb's amazing cover of An Alien Appeal and will hopefully make its appearance on the cover of KMAG, the final installment of The Claire Trilogy. Thank you both. Enjoy Idaho.*

# AN
# ALIEN APPEAL

# CHAPTER ONE
## (THE TIES THAT BIND)

I thought it would be easier. I mean, after all she was my sister. I guess it was the guilt which now came flooding back through my veins and caused the flush to rise above my collar line. My selfish conduct had led to the deaths of our three brothers.

I stood staring across the bobbing heads in the crowd of other arriving passengers effortlessly connecting with their loved ones at the gate, but I could not bring myself to do anything to catch the attention of the two women holding the hand drafted sign on a rainbow background that read: "BROTHER—DON'T KNOW HIS NAME—HE'S A YANK IN THE WPP!"

I placed my suitcase on the floor and let the other passengers from other flights roll past me like I was a protruding stone in the middle of a gently flowing stream and watched as the two women nervously scanned the advancing waves of faces for that spark of recognition as their eyes made momentary contact.

Thirty years is a long time. When I last saw Bonnie, we both had matching, thick, dark brown hair. The two petite women holding the sign were blondes, with streaks of grey highlights. I was bald. Not that chrome dome with the fringe of fine hair around the periphery, or the desperate comb-over. Once I realized that my hairline had retreated too far from my eyebrows to see both at the same time in the car rear view mirror, I made the conscious decision to shave it completely. The first few times required a lot of styptic and toilet paper, but after a while I got it down to where I could shave my head faster than my face. You see, gravity favors the dome, not the jowls, so my head could be completed smoothly with one hand, the face, which required manual manipulations to work around, required two.

My sister's spouse, Tessa, gave up her watch and began to whisper nervously in her companion's ear, while Bonnie gave the replenishing crowd one last sweep, just as a gap in the human herd opened around me. She stared long and hard in my direction, finally locking eyes with my pair of matching blue. And then she smiled.

"Brother," she shouted with the polished accent of a BBC newscaster. I grabbed my bag and used my best New York crowd dancing moves to slip through the masses that were coagulating at the gate. Bonnie, on the other hand, left Tessa holding the sign and carved a straight groove through the crowd on her end. I quickly learned that the years had not diminished Bonnie's strength; when she embraced me in a bear hug that took my breath away and lifted me to my toes. I held my suitcase over her head, which was buried in my chest, until she finally released me.

"Where's your hair?" she said as she took a step back and gave me the once over.

"I left it with my other hat," I replied, drawing that delightful laugh I had not heard in ages. Her blue eyes sparkled.

Tessa arrived, and Bonnie quickly introduced her. "Jimmy – it's still Jimmy, right?"

I nodded and she continued.

"Jimmy, this is T, I mean, Tessa De Mille" Bonnie said, giving Tessa access to the space she had just occupied.

T effortlessly pulled me down to her height and planted the double European kiss on my cheeks. Before I could say "nice to meet you" she wrenched my suitcase from my hand and with a firm "follow me," led us through the rest of the airport to a waiting black cab just outside of the arrival area. As we followed, Bonnie grasped my hand for dear life. We did not speak but kept stealing glances at each other as we walked along. We were instantly transported back in time to the front of the family pram in McCoombs Park by Yankee Stadium in the Bronx. I laughed as I thought about how she still had the strongest grip in the family. My dad certainly would be proud.

The ladies sat together on the back bench of the cab and I sat facing them on the kind of fold up jump seat that I had not seen since the last of the Checker cabs left New York in 1999. T called out an address on Regent's Park Road, Primrose Hill, and the cabbie nodded and merged seamlessly into the traffic flowing out towards the airport exit. I recoiled briefly until I remembered that we were supposed to be driving on the wrong side of the road.

"You're taller than I expected," T said, her deep brown eyes studying me for some conversational opening.

"He was the runt of the litter," Bonnie chimed in, "at least among the boys."

I laughed. At five foot ten, I was the smallest of the male pack, who all were over six feet tall by their teens. Growing up, that disadvantage forced me to rely more on my wits than stature for survival. The irony was that I was now, by default, the tallest and last man standing.

"You don't talk much." T continued. She turned to Bonnie. "You told me he was the chatterbox."

"I'm sorry," I responded, "It's T, right? Just a bit jet-lagged."

"Bonnie says you were some kind of mafia lawyer." T countered, deadpan.

"Wait – What –" I stammered.

"T! That was not for public dissemination," Bonnie responded sharply. "And anyway, that's all in the past. Isn't it, Jimmy?"

I quickly turned to check on the cabbie, who seemed to be distracted listening to the Cricket scores on the radio and oblivious to our conversation.

I leaned forward, and stage whispered, "I was a government witness in a federal criminal matter." I could feel my face flushing. "But that's all behind me now."

"Oh, yes. And what do you do now?" T said, undeterred.

"He's a day-trader," Bonnie said, then changing gears as she saw my rising discomfort. "How's Gina. It is Gina, isn't it?"

"Yes, Gina." I said, my eyes still engaged with T's. "She's doing great. Sends her love." I thought about how Gina told me before I left not to worry about calling her, that she would be busy with her projects around the property, and I did not want to be chatting at weird hours given the time differences. I waited another long moment before adding a placating, "to both of you." T smiled at that. These simple questions kept reminding me how much we had missed in each other's lives.

"Bonnie, are you still the Headmistress of that posh school?" I asked my sister, seizing control of the conversation before T got to follow-up with another question.

"Oh no, we've been retired for years." T answered, tenaciously engaged.

"Yes, T and I packed it in about five years ago." Bonnie said, reaching over and squeezing T's hand.

"Spend most of our time at our home in Salisbury." T continued. "But we still keep our place in Primrose Hill. We come in for short stretches for a little culture booster."

As I listened to T speak, I tried to get a fix on her accent. It had the same patina of BBC newscaster that Bonnie shared, but there was a tiny plumy lilt. I was about to mention it when the cab pulled up in front of a stretch of creamy Victorian row houses with white trim, and the cockney cabby called out, "home sweet home, ladies and gent."

The cabbie retrieved my bag from the boot of the cab and settled his fare with T, who waved me off when I offered to pay. There was a stone wall with a wrought iron gate segregating their home from their neighbor's, and their front yard consisted of a meticulous small green garden on either side of the short path leading up to their front steps. The buildings along their block looked only forty feet wide and were each uniformly three stories high. Some had French doors opening onto small balconies with overhanging gardens on the upper floors and I could see that their rooftops also served as outdoor living spaces.

Across the winding street was a lush green park, with rolling hills and flagstone paths littered with old fashioned benches, the kind that Central Park once proudly displayed before New York fell.

"Remember when Spaghetti dragged that bench home from Central Park?" Bonnie reminisced from somewhere beside me.

I laughed at the memory of my grandfather, who returned from his job as an upper east side doorman one night dragging the cast iron sections of a Central Park bench. It had been replaced on its spot on Fifth Avenue by a more modern version, to keep the local Brahmans happy. The workers were a couple of micks from "back home" that were more than happy to shift the burden of disposal of the original bench to one of their countrymen. Each section was at least fifty pounds. Spaghetti was built like, and had the strength of, a lowland gorilla, so he was more than willing to take it off their hands.

We were all playing tag in our backyard in Riverdale when we spotted him carrying the pieces, two in his right hand, one in his left, up our driveway. He had carried them across the park to the upper west side and brought them with him north to the Bronx on the number one subway line. He walked the remaining mile from the subway to our house. In two days, he had replaced the missing wooden slats and it looked as good as anything I was now staring at in Regent's Park. That bench gave me my first set of six stitches shortly afterwards, when my brother, the Ginger, tripped me as I ran past him, my right eyebrow making solid contact with one of those large iron circles at the end of that bench. Nothing comes free, and New York City always draws its blood sacrifice. My father, as always, did a great job on the stitches. The scar is barely noticeable to this day.

"He still feels bad about that." Bonnie said.

"Who? Bad about what?" I asked, startled back to the present.

"Our Ginger." Bonnie said. "C'mon, let's get you inside and squared away with some breakfast and a kip." She smiled. "That's a nap to you Yanks." She turned and headed through the gate and up the stairs of the corner row house, where T stood patiently waiting with my suitcase.

I took one last look at the benches and turned and followed her inside, briefly wondering about the synchronicity of that last comment. If I had not been jaded by the most amazing year of my life, where life, death, the supernatural, and extraterrestrial all merged together, I probably would have given it more thought. As it was, I was feeling jet-lagged from the overnight flight, so I shifted my focus to the possibility of some breakfast and a nap as I followed them up the front stairs, before venturing any deeper into my family reengagement.

# CHAPTER TWO
# (TEA AND SYNCHRONICITY)

Where the exterior of their row home transported you to the era of Dickens, Bronte and Hardy, the interior of their row home was modern and sleek, with three floors of front to rear open floor plans, soft lighting, earth tone pastels on flawless walls and ceilings, and built-in storage spaces. It had dark oak flooring throughout, and unpretentious but expensive antique furniture. The kitchen was on the main floor and was large and open with a long center island and lined with stainless steel appliances bearing names like La Cornue, Sub-Zero, Wolfe, Miele, and Fischer. There were three bedrooms on the top floor. The master faced the front, and had its own large terrace overlooking Regent's Park. There was a large, four post mahogany king size bed, with a matching mahogany secretary's desk off to one side. A walk-in closet, filled with clothing from the shops of New Bond Street in London, and their *ensuite* had a floor to ceiling, slate walk-in glass shower with a bench and six showerheads lining the wall. A forty-inch rainfall showerhead above opened on the side of the common wall of their neighbor. The claw-foot porcelain soaking tub by the back window was large enough for my mule, Claire, to bathe in. In New York money this house had experienced a ten-million-dollar renovation.

T had placed my bag in one of the two matching guest bedrooms facing the rear of the building. Both opened up through sliding glass doors onto a single terrace that ran the width of the building and overlooked other similar terraces and gardens on the less expensive blocks extending away from Regent's Park. There was a small iron stairway that led to the roof on the end of the terrace. The only difference between my bedroom and its twin was that mine had windows that opened out on the quaint, curving side street that led away from the park.

Bonnie circled the room drawing the thick black-out curtains before retreating to the bedroom doorway.

"Get some sleep and then we can catch up properly over brunch." She said as she gently closed the heavy oak door to the bedroom. I leapt on the full bed in the corner, fully clothed, and was asleep before the echo of the door catch had dissipated.

I immediately entered REM sleep, which I had not experienced since I left New York as a dues-paying member of the federal government's Witness Protection Program. But it was restless and troubling, as my mind was filled with a series of zeros and ones that kept replicating in a repeated pattern. I could not force myself awake and the numbers began to emit a corresponding sound and the next thing I knew I was repeating the numbers while keeping time with the sound. It became comfortable as my mind gained control over the content. I did not know what these numbers meant but it felt eerily familiar. The pattern was finally broken by an external sound of gentle but repeated rapping of knuckles on solid wood, and I finally relinquished my sleep as the door of the bedroom cracked open and T poked her head through and said, "brunch in ten, Luv, downstairs in the back garden."

I rubbed the sleep from my eyes and nodded as she shut the door. The clock on the night table said twelve noon, which meant I had been sleeping for almost three hours. I stood and went to the small desk and retrieved a pen and some paper from the drawer. I wrote down the numbers with an astonishing full recollection, as follows:

```
01000101 01110110 01100101 01110010 01100101 01110100
01110100 00100000 01101101 01110101 01110011 01110100
00100000 01110010 01100101 01110100 01110101 01110010
01101110 00100000 01100001 01110100 00100000 01101111
01101110 01100011 01100101 00100000 01100001 01101110
01100100 00100000 01100001 01101110 01110011 01110111
01100101 01110010 00100000 01110100 01101111 00100000
```

```
01110100 01101000 01100101 00100000 01000011 01101111
01110101 01101110 01100011 01101001 01101100 00100000
01100110 01101111 01110010 00100000 01101000 01101001
01110011 00100000 01100010 01110010 01100101 01100001
01100011 01101000 00100000 01101111 01100110 00100000
01110100 01101000 01100101 00100000 01010000 01110010
01101001 01101101 01100101 00100000 01000100 01101001
01110010 01100101 01100011 01110100 01101001 01110110
01100101 00101110
```

When I finished, I could not begin to fathom what the numbers meant, so I folded the paper and stuck it in the back pocket of my jeans, then quickly washed my face and brushed my teeth in my small bathroom before heading down to brunch.

The bottom floor had a large, luxurious, Persian carpet running along most of its central flooring, with an oversized matching sofa, loveseat and two reclining chairs along its perimeter. There was a 98-inch QLED, 8K flat screen on the common wall and high-end PMC speakers dotting the four corners of the large open room. There was another guest bathroom tucked ergonomically under the stairway. The back wall was completely made of thick glass which filled the room with natural light and opened up though sliding glass doors onto a small, ivy-covered, walled-in garden. The high, green thatched walls provided a strong feeling of solitude and privacy. A capacious, ornate alabaster fountain against the far stone wall streamed clear, bubbling water from the mouth of the gargoyle situated at its peak into a large semi-circled pool embedded in the moss-covered earth below. The soft, gurgling sound was comforting and inviting. It reminded me of the sound that accompanied the numbers in my dream. I was distracted by what appeared to be a hummingbird as it darted quickly up from the water's edge and over the back wall.

In the small center patio sat my sister, engaged with her iPhone. Two fine china settings bookended a three-tiered, sterling silver lazy Susan at the center of the table, ladened with rich looking pastries. A matching sterling silver coffee pot, steam rising from its spout, completed the ensemble. Bonnie looked up from her cellphone, as I slid open the plate glass door, and smiled, pushing her thick glasses up the bridge of her nose as she stood to greet me.

"How was your kip?" She inquired, stretching up and kissing me softly on my cheek. "Ooh," she said, rubbing her fingers along my stubble, "someone needs a shave."

I returned the peck and followed her gesture to my place at the table.

"Sorry about that," I replied, rubbing my face with my palm. T made it seem like there wasn't time for a shower and shave."

I ran my hand over my face and head feeling the stubble. I was surprised to sense some roughness towards the front of my dome, which had been relatively smooth between shaves for decades.

Bonnie smiled and rolled her eyes. "Life with T, like the trains of yore, runs on an extremely strict, and tight schedule. No excuses."

"Where is she?" I asked.

"She's playing a round of golf with some friends at Highgate. She'll catch-up with us tonight at the house in Salisbury."

She slowly spun the lazy Suzan to give me a closer view of the delightful pastries. I snatched one of the butter-glazed scones and tore it open on my plate.

"Butter?" I asked, scanning the table.

"Try the Cornish clotted cream," Bonnie said, sliding over a small bowl of a thick, cream-colored, almost meringue, consistency. "T makes it herself fresh every morning."

I scooped some out of the bowl with my knife, slathered it on my scone and took a large bite. It was delicious. Another first for me.

"It's really a shame you don't have it back in the States," Bonnie added.

"Really? Why not?" I responded before stuffing the rest of the delicious scone into my mouth and reaching for the coffee.

"It's illegal to make it." Bonnie said, with a twinkle in her eye. "It's unpasteurized."

I did not even wait to add milk to my coffee cup before filling my mouth with its almost scalding liquid and swishing away any imagined microbes that could give me a dose of the European version of Montezuma's revenge. Bonnie watched me with amusement.

"Don't worry, it won't kill ya." She said, slipping back into her Bronx accent. I was immediately transported back to when she fed me a dog biscuit when I was five.

"C'mon," She continued, "you still haven't forgiven me for the Milk Bone?"

I paused my forceful, heated oral hygiene and swallowed my large mouthful of coffee while I quickly replayed her earlier comment about the Ginger. I stared across the table silently assessing this tiny woman with large coke bottle glasses and an impish smile. Under normal circumstances, I would have immediately gone for my tinfoil hat, but I had just spent the last year somewhere over the rainbow, so I knew anything was possible and I could recognize the real deal when I spotted it.

"Thank you, Nana Burke." Bonnie whispered as she gazed upward, placing her hands together in supplication.

I laughed out loud. "Fuck me." I said. "Is everybody in this world gifted, but me?"

"It's a female thing." Bonnie responded. "We can't all be perfect."

Suddenly, I was distracted by the blurred figure of the hummingbird circling around Bonnie's head. It was joined by another, and then another and then they began to hover in formation. She seemed not to notice them. I kept trying to get a fix on their obscured, gyrating figures.

"Those hummingbirds really like you." I said pointing. They seemed to shift laterally away from any spot my index finger was directed at.

"There are no wild hummingbirds in Europe." Bonnie replied. She held out her hand and the three shapes all descended on her open palm. They landed as one, and there, standing before me, were three, tiny beautiful young female, humanoid creatures, dressed in diaphanous, earth tone clothes. Each had a set of silver gossamer wings which extended from their shoulders to just below their hips, which they now gently folded behind them. Their golden hair mimicked glowing filaments that seem to dance around their shoulders. I could see tiny points of flesh as the end of their ears peaked out the sides of their heads. They were enchanting.

"These are my dear friends, the water Sprites." Bonnie said as she passed her free hand over the creatures. "Aine, Breena, and Cirrha." She extended her hand forward and they each curtsied *seriatim*. As they gazed up at me, each with whitish blue eyes, I could see tiny smiles forming around their mouths. One of them stepped forward and attempted to speak, but it sounded like the high-pitched chirps of a baby mouse.

"No, Breena," Bonnie answered. "Jimmy doesn't speak Sprite."

With a flourish Bonnie flipped her palm skyward and the three Sprites each spun upwards into synchronized, reverse backflips before morphing back into their gyrating blurs and heading as a group towards the fountain, chirping to each other as they went. Bonnie waved her hand to get my attention which was totally on the Sprites and then gestured towards my plate and food.

"Eat up, baby brother, we have lots to talk about and a two-hour road trip ahead of us."

# CHAPTER THREE
# (MS. MAGOO'S WILD RIDE)

Having showered, shaved, and repacked my bag, I joined Bonnie downstairs in front of the row house, where she waited by the curb with one RIMOWA carry-on suitcase. She was dressed in fitted, brown slacks and a tweed jacket with a beige cashmere scarf tied in that foppish way that my, once upon a time, legal brethren, Robert Meloni, liked to wear his, with a large loop at the neck opening of his jacket. Even though I never gave the feds anything on Robert, I marveled at how he had avoided going down with the rest of the Valachi family, and Lenny had told me Robert had changed his practice from criminal to entertainment law. Personally, I did not see much of a difference between the two.

I lifted the brown, Medianoche, wide-brim fedora hat from her head and tried it on for size. *Not even close.* I gently returned it to its proper place. She ignored me while she stared down the hill. She had replaced her reading glasses with even larger, thicker, driving glasses. When she finally looked up at me, she looked like a barn owl.

"So, what's the plan, sis? Another black cab ride?"

We were distracted by three quick beeps from an approaching SUV with another smaller sports car trailing behind it. They pulled up directly in front of us, and the driver in the first car hopped out and grabbed Bonnie's and my suitcases and slid them past the side-hinged tailgate into the back of the SUV.

"The keys are in the console, Miss." The driver said when he finished.

"Thank you, Spencer," Bonnie called to the young man as he waved back and slid into the shotgun side of the second vehicle, which immediately headed off and disappeared around the corner with a roar.

"C'mon then," she said, with her traces of Bronx accent. She marched over to the open driver door and hoisted herself into the seat. *What is it with tiny people and big cars*, I thought to myself, as I watched her scramble up the high step, supporting her body weight on the interior arm rest. I hesitated for a moment to get my bearings before sliding into the shotgun seat where the driver's seat should be. I did not even get my seatbelt fastened before Bonnie called out, "hang on" and took off around the corner.

It turned out that Bonnie's SUV was a 2020 Land Rover Defender X, and looked ready to take on an arctic expedition, never mind a trip to the country. It was metallic silver, with gloss black detailing to the hood, tailgate script and front grille, and a Narvik Black hood checker plate. It had twenty-two inch, five-spoke wheels, that could just about drive over anything.

"Who was the kid back there?" I queried.

"That's Spencer. He was a student in my school. He's on gap year so he looks after our property for us. We keep our cars in a private lot a few blocks away. He shuttles them back and forth when we need them. We let him use them as needs be. He maintains them lovingly."

I wondered what their other cars were like.

"I adore this car." Bonnie called out as she accelerated and intently followed the directions of the lovely British voice coming from her GPS, winding her way through the side streets of this beautiful section of London. I watched as her legs worked the gas-peddle and brake alternatively but in tandem, like an elliptical in a gym. It was a method that is an anathema to any Driver's Education teacher, but which my father, also short of leg, mastered effectively. Bonnie had moved her seat so far forward that her breasts were rubbing along the middle of the steering wheel which she spun erratically to pass any car that was in her way. Her magnified eyes peered intently over the top of the steering wheel and did not blink as they studied the road before them. She looked like the cartoon character Mr. Magoo and drove with the same faculty. Numerous cabs flicked us their two-fingered salute as she flew by. Finally, our British navigator politely pointed out that the entrance to the M25 was 500 feet ahead and Bonnie accelerated her approach, edging out a Mini Cooper that I did not notice until I heard its tinny horn when we were almost on top of it. Not yet acclimated to driving on the wrong side of the road, I propped my feet on the beautiful leather console and reclined my seat to provide whatever protection I could from an impact I knew was only one wrong move away. But it never came. To this day, I am not sure which of us sacrificed one of our nine lives making that trip.

"I hate driving in London," Bonnie muttered, as she nestled the car into heavier traffic on the M25 which forced her to slow down. The high barrier on the middle isle hid the oncoming traffic and reduced the sense that we were driving on the wrong side of the road. I could see the planes in the distance on final approach to Heathrow.

"Look, there's Windsor Castle," she said, pointing off to the side. I saw by the digital images appearing in the left-hand corner of the rearview mirror that we were heading West. After a while she worked her way across some lanes and exited onto the M3. I wondered where the Brits' fascination with the letter 'M' came from.

"Next stop, Salisbury!" She announced, recovering her BBC accent.

We drove in silence for a few miles past a couple of towns that both seemed to be "upon the Thames" and I lost myself in the surrounding beauty as we proceeded farther and farther west. Bonnie did not seem in any hurry to break the silence, so finally I did.

"So, tell me about Nana's gift."

"Well," she began, "I didn't go looking for it. It found me a few years back when my eyesight really started to decline."

Bonnie was the only one of us who wore glasses as a child. Hell, I did not don my first pair of readers until I hit 50, and I blame my legal career for that.

"What do you mean, it found you." I asked.

"Just what I said. I was sipping some tea in my back garden one early Spring in 2014, and the tiny finches I thought were inhabiting my English Ivy landed on the table and, bold as you please, introduced themselves."

"The Sprites?"

"The same." She drove a few more moments in silence and then added, "they told me Bridey Burke sends her regards and said 'Tag, You're it.'"

I grinned, thinking about my eccentric old Nana, who used to regale us all with her stories of ghosts and fairies when we were children. She enthralled us with tales of regularly spying on the wee folk during the twilight hours of dawn and dusk back in Ireland. She also could communicate with the dead, which made her a bit of a celebrity in Tuam where she often shared messages between the locals and those on the far side of the veil. She said she was the best *Cailleach* in Western Ireland. She also told me shortly before she passed that she was 'The Queen of Connemara.' To this day I believe her on both counts.

"Why you?" I finally asked, again jealous on not getting the golden ticket.

"Comes with the vagina," she said deadpanned. Two seconds later we both burst out laughing hysterically, and would have continued to do so, if it were not for the sound of the horn from an angry lorry driver who had to swerve to avoid hitting us as we drifted into his lane.

"Wait until he gets home and catches his Misses with his best friend." She said as she contritely waved as he passed us. I noticed the Land Rover did not shake from the pressure as the lorry hurtled onward.

"And you know that how?" I asked, remembering the answer the multi-generational witch, Bobbi Angelini, gave me to the same question back in Colorado.

"Not really sure." Bonnie answered, tentatively. "The easy answer is, it's the voices in my head. They shared earlier that you were thinking about Spaghetti's park bench adventure."

"Do you see ghosts as well?" I asked, thinking about our brothers.

"Better than I see you with these goddamn glasses." She answered. "And before you go there, yes, I've seen our brothers."

I thought about everything that had transpired over the past year, right up to my last meeting with my brothers on the other side. I rubbed the round scar over my heart through my sweater. It was my talisman.

"Oh yes," Bonnie said, "your Lazarus trick really impressed the shit out of them." She laughed. "But our Ginger said you really needed to lose a few pounds, or your next trip over may be your last." She quickly glanced at my stomach and scrunched her face. "He was being a bit harsh. You don't look bad at all."

I had been steadily losing weight through Gina's roadwork regimen and had been feeling rather good lately. The dead are a tough crowd to please.

I tried to distract my thoughts with the alliteration I spotted in consecutive signs for Frimley, Farnborough, and Fleet. I still felt the guilt over my brothers' deaths at the hands of my old boss, Tiberius Valachi, despite receiving absolution right from the source.

Before I made this trip, I had set up trust funds for each of my brothers' kids as well as regularly funded checking accounts for their families' day-to-day expenses. All coming from overseas corporations with considerable assets on the pretense of my brothers' past foreign investments. Not enough to wake the tax man but significant enough to keep them all in comfort.

"In addition, T and I paid off their mortgages, so their widows own their homes outright." Bonnie said, popping into my head. "We've arranged to cover their annual real estate taxes as well."

"Those are awfully generous gifts from a retired headmistress at a private school." I mused. "They must have paid you in gold bullion."

"I've done very well with my money, thank you very much" Bonnie countered. "Especially since Nana decided to share her gift with me. I've made a killing through my investment portfolio."

*Another gift I could certainly use, giving my day trading. Just have to continue doing it the old-fashioned way, through guile and luck.*

I thought about their beautiful rowhouse, the Land Rover and their other trappings of wealth, and tried to do the math that would allow for this generosity.

"If you must know, T has family money." Bonnie added.

"Must be quite the family," I said with a chuckle.

"She's a baroness." She said with a wink. "Wait until you see the country house."

We drove a while further and were exiting onto the A303 before Bonnie broke the silence.

"I was beside myself with grief when I learned of their deaths." She appeared to focus while she passed some road workers on a coffee break by the side of the road. "John came to me that morning. I barely recognized him."

"Was his hair grey?" I asked, always jealous of our youngest sibling's hairline.

"No, jet black," She answered. "Thick, as always."

"Of course, it was," I answered, burying my jealousy, and rubbing my hand over my bald scalp. *What were those new bristles I was feeling with my fingers?*

"I was worried sick about you as well," and then added sternly, "what were you thinking getting involved with the mafia?"

I searched my mind for a simple explanation of an overly complex, if not impulsive, decision I had made those many years ago. *It seemed like the right idea at the time*, did not appear to cut it.

"Well, don't worry yourself over it. It's all behind you now," she said. "Now tell me all about your talking mule, Claire," then quickly added, "believe it or not, Spaghetti made an appearance just to tell me about her."

Over the course of the next forty-five minutes, I told Bonnie about all of the amazing things that had happened to me over the past year, including meeting Claire, my lesbian friends that included a witch, and my interstellar neighbors. I closed by explaining how a number of shrunken bad guys ended up sitting in a Hot Wheels SUV at the bottom of Crater lake and how I came back from the dead. I felt like I had to speak faster than normal, if only to prevent Bonnie from looking into my head and finishing my sentences for me. In the end, it did not matter, because it was clear that she already knew everything. She also knew that my recitation was cathartic for me. By the time I had finished telling my incredible tale to my equally incredible sister, I felt as mentally exhausted as I did after taking my bar exam.

By then, we had followed the A338 to the A30, and finally to the A36 for the last leg of the journey and arrived at the exit for Salisbury. The autumn afternoon sun was beginning to fade into twilight. I spotted some signs on the road for Stonehenge and felt an odd sense of familiarity, like I had arrived home.

# CHAPTER FOUR
# (A SIMPLE COUNTRY RETREAT)

Our arrival in Salisbury seemed to have a calming effect on Bonnie's driving. It may have been that the town itself had a soothing energy about it. But I noticed a lot more pedestrian traffic as Bonnie insisted on providing me with a driving tour of the town, where she pointed out things like the ancient Salisbury Cathedral, Bishop's Mill, Queen Elizabeth's Gardens and Fish Row. We even crossed the Avon river, and I gave a silent nod to the Bard. The town had a quaintness that was earned over hundreds of years of history and not imposed by some creative zoning laws, as they like to do in the States.

If I had left a breadcrumb trail, I would not have been able to recreate the tour, as there were so many small streets with twists and turns and most of the buildings that lined the way had similar facades. There were also a lot of unexpected but delightful pedestrian walkways where some of the larger streets had once ferried flocks of sheep during the town's regular market days. It was quite beautiful.

At some point Bonnie circled back north onto A345 and after a short drive exited onto Stratford Road, where, after a few more minutes, she pulled up in front of a stately piece of property surrounded by a tall iron gate.

"Welcome to Potter's Mead." She said with a sweep of her arm.

She hit a button in the Land Rover and the large gates slowly opened to allow us access to a long gravel driveway that ended at a carriage house. The main house sat a few yards away in the center of the property and I could see high walls out back, extending towards the rear of the property, which I guessed totaled about 3 acres of land.

The front of the house was a two-story Victorian. It had a light beige brick façade, three large windows on the second floor and two even larger windows book-ending the tall center entranceway. Bonnie removed a key from under a faux stone along the walkway and opened the front door to let me pass, carrying our two suitcases.

The interior front of the house consisted of matching spacious, pastel-colored sitting rooms off an open center hallway. Each room had squared corners, high ceilings and blonde wood floors. Lots of natural light flowed through the oversized windows in the front, even at dusk. It actually looked like the furnishings had been staged by a realtor, they fit so perfectly around the rooms. But these rooms lacked the warmth I was expecting from a country home.

"Don't stop there," Bonnie said as she whizzed by me and continued past the center stairway to a hall in the back, "this part of the house is just for show. Follow me."

She led me through a doorway which took me architecturally back in time to the Elizabethan era. Bonnie stopped in a spacious open room and pointed to where this Tudor section of the house bonded with its Victorian descendant. This room held the kitchen, with an oversized fireplace with descending metal hangers for pots of all sizes, with an Aga tucked inside it. Directly opposite the fireplace stood a modern cooking island with stainless steel vents, with a built-in, 60-inch, Blue Star gas range. As with their London home, everything here was top of the line. A long farmer's table with ten chairs ran along the far side of the room and I could see a small stairway leading upwards in the corner.

The most impressive part of the room was the slightly undulating, hand crafted, whitewashed walls and the naturally aged, exposed, squared off wooden beams that ran the entire length of the ceiling being held up every ten feet by a series of equally immense, rough-hewn support beams. I reached over and ran my fingers along the walls, in awe of the many dead artisans that had performed all of this work by hand.

"That is the original wattle and daub, more commonly known today as clay and dung. And this wood is five hundred years old." Bonnie declared proudly.

"They say Shakespeare himself might have slept here when writing a *Midsummer's Night Dream*."

I peeked back through the portal into the Victorian section of the house and studied the opening above the doorway to see how the two, vastly different sections of the house abutted. It was a chimera. There was a distinctly different energy on either side of the opening.

"C'mon now," Bonnie said, opening one of the three door panels in her Fischer refrigerator, and removing two frosty bottles of Fuller's London Porter, snapping off the lids on a bottle opener on the edge of the island. She then led me out through large sliding glass doors into the back garden. I left the suitcases and followed.

Dusk was setting in, but I could still see fairly well. Bonnie handed me one of the bottles and we toast-tapped necks, before she drew a long sip from her own. I followed suit and was pleased with its rich and malty flavor. I studied the ten-foot high, thick, solid stone walls that ran the perimeter of this open rectangle of lush, green lawn. It provided a strange sense of privacy, as if there were no other houses in the area for miles. The garden was silent as a church. There were a few seasoned benches strategically placed under trees along the walls on either side. There was also a large iron based, glass topped, outdoor table with a half dozen matching chairs not too far from where I was standing. An almost empty bottle of wine and two glasses rested on the glass top next to a leather-bound copy of Charlotte Bronte's *Jane Eyre*. Off in the distance, a discarded croquet set, with mallets, balls and wickets lay in disarray in the middle of the lawn.

"You really are a Brit." I observed. "Spaghetti would cut your throat with his garden shears."

Bonnie laughed. "Spaghetti is one of my biggest fans. Stops by all the time to give me tips on gardening. Tells me some of his best mates on the other side are Brits, even a couple that he killed."

My grandfather never told us why he and his younger brother Barney left Ireland in the middle of the night in 1913, when he was just twenty years old, or why he never went back "home" to visit for the rest of his life. But whenever there were family gatherings around the holidays, or wakes, and the liquor loosened the tongues, there were always whispers among the elders about Spaghetti and his brothers' exploits during the Troubles. So, Bonnie's last comment did not startle me.

"Please give him my best the next time you see him." I said, as nonchalantly as I could. My life in Colorado had really jaded me.

I pointed at the thick group of tall shrubbery down at the far end of the garden that completely covered the last twenty-five yards to the back wall. It was so thick; you could not see into its mass and it was too tall to see its end.

"What's back there?" I asked, gesturing with my rapidly emptying bottle.

"That's what I wanted to show you, so come with me, before it gets too dark."

She took my hand and led me passed the croquet set. I went to reach for the red ball, and she forcefully pulled my arm. "Don't touch that, we are on an honor system here. T hates if you cheat."

Again, I marveled at the strength from such a tiny woman. Bonnie's paranormal gifts may have come from our maternal ancestors from the West, but the source of her strength was Spaghetti's clan in the North. She tugged me along until we reached the perimeter of the shrubbery, which rose uniformly over seven feet high, and then raised her finger to her lips and leaned in to listen. I watched her for a moment and then mimicked the motion.

"Listen," she whispered.

At first, I heard nothing but the loud buzzing of a nearby bee looking for the last sources of pollen in the fall. Bonnie squinted through her oversized glasses at the bee, which had now landed on the shrub right at Bonnie's eye level, and when she pointed silently back in the direction of the wine on the table, the bee flew over her shoulder towards that mark. Then I heard the faintest echo of what sounded like a children's chorus singing softly in a language I had never heard before. Bonnie took the beer bottle from my hand and gently placed it on the ground next to hers, then crooked her finger and stepped towards the shrubbery which appeared to part in response. I paused for a moment, staring at the shifting vegetation, before her strong hand reached back and dragged me into the brush. It was pitch black inside.

As Bonnie dragged me forward, the brush around us never made a sound and barely contacted our bodies as we passed. About twenty yards in I thought I could see a faint light close to the ground. The hum of the chorus grew stronger. I could see the shrubs ahead thinning to a clearing. Then Bonnie slowed and finally crouched towards the ground, pulling me down behind her. She pushed her hand forward and the brush opened around it to provide a small opening. Bonnie again looked back and raised her finger to her lips then pointed through the hole and shifted to allow me the view. I did not think anything else could amaze me, but I was wrong.

Within the clearing, which was about fifteen feet across and irregular, but whose top was enclosed as a canopy of vegetation, was a perfect circle of luminescent mushrooms of various shapes and sizes. The circle looked to be about six feet in diameter. I could not tell if the clearing was darker because of the tall, thick shrubs that enclosed it, or if night had taken a shortcut since Bonnie had led me into the dense shrubbery. I could hear soft fiddle music, and the sound of those high-pitched voices rising from somewhere within the dark center of the circle. The glow from the mushrooms barely lit the ground more than a few inches around their perimeter, and the contrast of their light to the darkness beyond made it hard to focus. It took a while for my eyes to finally adapt, but once they did, I saw them.

At first it was just shadows and movement. But as my eyes strained to draw in the faintest of light, the shadows sharpened into tiny figures, discernibly males and females by their dress, paired off and dancing with more flowing grace than the greatest human ballroom champions. Indeed, as the couples traversed the circle to my side of the clearing, I could see that their feet were not firmly touching the ground, but skimmed along with their toes barely making contact, the way that fingers over the side of a slow-moving motorboat skim the water. As my eyes further adjusted, I could see similarly dressed figures in the center of the ring playing their tiny instruments while others stood by them and sang with haunting voices. While they were larger than the Sprites, it was not by a substantial margin. And they did not have wings.

An older male sat on top of one of the mushrooms close to our vantage point. His hair was full and pure white and hung to his shoulders. His fine but antiquated clothes and a golden staff reflected a deferential rank above the others, which was confirmed by the respectful nods and curtsies of the couples that passed before him. A pulsating glow emanated from the bowl of an ornate, acorn pipe with a long stem, and he blew small jets of sweet smoke out of the corner of his mouth in time with the music.

Bonnie joined me by the opening, and I pointed in the direction of the older creature.

"That's the Fairy King," Bonnie whispered.

At that moment, the older creature turned his head in our direction, as if he heard her voice, and while I backed deeper in the shadows, Bonnie bravely stayed peering through our vantage point at the edge of the dim light and met his gaze. She nodded respectfully, and he returned a sparkling wink and tiny wave, before returning to watch his dancing subjects.

Bonnie smiled, rose, turned, then led me by my hand back in the direction we had come, while the thick bramble opened a new path to allow our passage.

# CHAPTER FIVE
# (WHEN TIME FLIES)

We were met on the outside of the shrubbery patch by T, who was holding two crystal wine goblets filled with Bordeaux. The sky was black, and the only light came from overhead stars and tiki torches flickering by the table closer to the house, which was now dressed in a white, linen tablecloth with three china place settings, the redundant chairs having been removed. I could see steam rising from a number of large serving bowls with oversized spoons on the far side of the table. A half-filled carafe of Bordeaux completed the ensemble.

T handed us the goblets and turned back towards the table, calling over her shoulder, "dinner is waiting."

"When did you arrive?" I asked T, as I fell into line behind Bonnie.

"Three hours ago." T replied. "When I found your empty beer bottles by the edge of the bushes, I knew you'd be awhile, so I unpacked the groceries and made dinner."

"Wait," I said incredulously, turning towards Bonnie. "We were only in there for twenty minutes, a half hour at the outside."

Bonnie reached into her pocket and removed her iPhone. The screen said eight p.m., four hours after we had arrived at the country house. That had to be wrong, so I removed my phone and checked its screen, which had automatically adjusted to Greenwich Mean Time. It confirmed my sister's.

"She didn't mention the lost time?" T asked, then without waiting for my response continued. "The Fae are not governed by human time. You are lucky Bonnie didn't take you into the clearing itself, or you would have been gone for years."

I looked at my sister and she nodded, sheepishly. "I would have told you, but I was afraid you might not have come with me."

"I won't step a foot into those bushes." T said. "Once was enough!"

"But you love the Fairies." Bonnie entreated.

"I don't mind the Sprites," T responded. "They amuse me. But I don't trust anything that can control my life like that. And besides, when you get to our age, time becomes a precious commodity, not to be trifled with through supernatural dalliances."

We arrived at the table and T directed us to our places while she served the food. She ladened my plate with an amazing steaming vegetable salad. The bouquet of garlic butter permeated the air around the table.

"Bonnie mentioned you are a vegetarian." T said. "So, I stopped by the green-grocer on the way in through town. It is all seasonal and locally produced. I hope you like it."

T placed two sirloin tips on her and Bonnie's plates, then added some of the garlic vegetables as sides. She sat in her chair, filled the empty goblet before her with Bordeaux, then raised her glass in a toast. "What shall we toast to?" She asked.

"To family reunited!" Bonnie saluted, clinking her spouse's chalice, and then turning to me, she clinked mine. "May we never be divided again."

The food was delicious, and I was ravenous, polishing off my first plate and going back for seconds. The conversation followed a comfortable course as T coaxed me to retell my adventures as a mafia consigliere. After a third round of Bordeaux, I gave her the abridged version, making sure not to share some of the more chilling moments I had confirmed to Bonnie during the drive. Whenever my memories drew too close to the darkness, Bonnie would reach over and gently squeeze my hand.

"So, tell me about Claire?" T continued, shifting gears.

I hesitated a moment, not sure how much of that I was willing to share. T put down her cutlery and took a long sip from her glass, her eyes engaged with mine over the rim. She gently returned the goblet to the table and wiped her lips with her napkin.

"You have just met our family's Sprites and Fairies." She said, refilling her goblet. "You're going to play shy about your talking mule? I mean, your sister has already given me the broad strokes, I'm just looking for the juicy details. Bonnie's family fascinates me."

I looked over at Bonnie. She opened her palms in supplication. "We have no secrets here."

T tilted the top of the carafe in my direction, and I lifted the glass and met her half-way. After my own long sip, I started to recount the tale of my life that began a year and half before, beginning with the night that the feds kicked down my door in New City, New York, and arrested me on federal R.I.C.O. charges. My story ended on the night, just one month before, when I died in Berthoud, Colorado. Woven throughout that tapestry was the central story of my meeting and adopting my loquacious, psychic, and fearless mule, Claire. The story was seasoned with a unique cast of other memorable characters that I now counted as family. My retelling their story made me miss them more.

"I can't wait to meet Helen and Bobbi," T said as she stood to gather up the plates an hour later.

"Everett and Michelle certainly top our Sprites and Fairies." Bonnie added. "What must it be like to travel through space?"

"Your own supernatural gifts have jaded you." T said with a wink at Bonnie. "I'm more interested in what it must have felt like for Jimmy to die like that. I mean, shot through the heart! I complain if I get a paper cut."

"Our brothers told me you were a bit hesitant on the landing over there, but you recovered quickly." Bonnie said with a smile, nudging me playfully with her elbow.

I reached beneath my shirt and touched the remnant of the scar on my chest. It felt thinner, and slightly diminished. I tried to remember the feeling of what it was like for the few moments I spent on the other side of the veil, what it felt like when I hugged the three of them that one last time, but all I could remember clearly was the consuming pain I suffered when I sucked in that first breath upon my return, and the relief on Gina's face when I looked up from the ground, my head spinning, my chest burning.

"I wish I could verbalize it for you." I uttered, suddenly very tired, the jet lag really kicking in.

"You don't have to," Bonnie said softly. "I got it."

T gave me the once over and proclaimed in a tone that would suffer no challenge, "you need to get some sleep. Come along, we can pick this up tomorrow."

We all grabbed the last of the table ware and returned to the kitchen, where, after being instructed to leave everything on the counters by T, Bonnie led me up to one of the guest bedrooms overlooking the Victorian front of the house. My eyes were closed before my head hit the pillow.

# CHAPTER SIX
# (T FOR TWO)

When I awoke, the house was silent. It was still dark outside and the clock on the bedside said three a.m. I lay there for a while, hoping I would fall back to sleep, but my mind was racing towards full consciousness trying to recover the traces of the dream I was having just before sleep ended. It was the repetition of those same numbers again. First slowly, then faster and faster, but this time my mind was able to keep pace with them, until they were passing with the speed of a rifling deck of cards, and I could see each one clearly. The speed of the accompanying sound increased apace until it almost sounded like Morse code. I hopped out of the bed and found the jeans I had been wearing yesterday and retrieved the piece of paper with the twelve lines of random, alternating zeros and ones from their pocket. Again, it meant nothing to me. It was frustrating.

I pulled on a sweatshirt, went down the stairs and through the time portal on the first floor from the Victorian to the Elizabethan section of the house. There, in its open kitchen, I made a delicious chocolate flavored latte on a Jura coffeemaker that did everything but tell me to 'have a nice day.' Not wanting to wake the other occupants, whose bedroom was somewhere above me in the rear Tudor section of this house, I carefully slid past the glass doors and wandered into the back garden. A waxing crescent moon offered enough light to make my way without stubbing my toes on anything. The icy October dew felt refreshing on my bare feet and shocked the last of the sleep from my brain.

I tried to distract myself by attempting to figure out how the game croquet was actually played and almost kicked the red ball from yesterday, but my attention kept being drawn to the small forest of shrubbery at the distant end of this country courtyard. Giving in, I placed my coffee cup on the garden table and walked the hundred yards to the thicket. I stood for some time before it, trying to locate the opening Bonnie and I had passed through but could find no signs of it. The foliage was so thick and intertwined I could not find a spot wide enough to insert more than a finger.

"I wouldn't go prodding that if I were you. Could lose that finger!"

I was surprised by the elevation of my leap, as at its peak, I saw clear over the tops of the shrubbery forest and was eye level with the top of the ten-foot wall twenty-five yards away. I was equally surprised when I landed without blowing out both knees. I spun and was face to face with T, standing in a fluffy lavender bathrobe. She was laughing hysterically.

"Bonnie told me her brothers were athletic," T said as she recovered, "but that was dunk worthy."

At my physical peak at seventeen, I was thrilled to be able to grab the basketball rim. That vertical ascent just now could have given me a nosebleed.

"Funny what a major dose of adrenaline can do to you." I offered. "Old ladies lifting cars. Old men dunking basketballs. You scared the shit out of me just now." I said with a soft laugh. I rubbed my legs through my pajamas and was surprised to feel some definition in my thighs.

"I got up to go to the bathroom and I saw you walking around out here from our bedroom window. I figured you might want some company." She said, adding, "and you don't want to go poking in those bushes. They only open up for Bonnie."

I turned back to the bushes and gave them a final inspection. She was right, they remained impenetrable.

"C'mon, I'll fix you a cup of coffee." T said, her posh accent giving way to my sister's influence, and turned back towards the house.

Once back inside, she directed me to the closest end of the farm table and went over to their amazing coffee maker. Within seconds she was back with two steaming cappuccinos.

"So, the hedgerow back there," I started when she had seated herself, "and the Fairies, did they come with the place?"

"God no." T said as she blew gently on her cup. "Bonnie found this house after looking at dozens in the area. Had to have just the right soil and water conditions, she told me. And privacy. That was the most important item on her check list."

"But then how did the Fairies get here?"

"Oh, those are part of a larger colony from Grovely Wood, about ten miles from here. It's not too far from the Witches' trees, off the Roman road." She said before taking a long sip of her cappuccino. "Bonnie just had to lift a few of those shrubs from around their colony and plant them out back. Evidently your grandfather has been helping her build up the area. 'Lots of extra space with an abundance of fresh horse manure,' is his mantra. It must work because it's come a long way in five years."

I had more than enough reasons for my jaded response to Sprites and Fairies, and even the presence of my grandfather's ghost, but could not figure out how anyone else, especially T, could be so nonchalant. Before I could ask, she continued.

"The Fairies showed up around a year ago." She said, rising and removing a loaf of bread from a nearby cupboard. "Would you like some toast? I'm having some."

I waved her off. "No, thank you. So, about the Fairies . . ."

"That's right, where was I?" She continued, plunging the sliced bread into the toaster. "Oh, okay, so one morning Bonnie came racing into the house all out of breath. 'They're here', she said, and dragged me out back and into the shrubs. Sure enough, there they were, dancing and singing their little hearts out."

"I gotta ask" I said, "you seem to take all this in stride. Why?"

She removed a crock of butter from the fridge and carefully opened it on the counter as she waited patiently for the toaster to pop. I could tell she was giving her answer serious consideration. After a moment she turned and faced me.

"I have known I was gay since I was a little girl. I had no interest in the dresses or dolls that my very traditional family forced upon me throughout my childhood, and my first crush was on the girl who sat next to me in primary school." She grabbed the steaming bread as the brown slices appeared above the toaster top and slapped some butter on them.

"I didn't come out of the closet until I was in my forties." She walked her plate of toast over to the table and sat down across from me. "So, I know what it is like to live with a secret."

That toast looked really good. She smiled and offered me the top slice, which I happily took. It was as tasty as it looked.

"When I met Bonnie, I knew right away that she was the love of my life." She washed down a bite of toast with some cappuccino. I could see she was lost in the memory.

"The first night we were together," she continued, "I promised her that no matter how strange or bad they seemed, there would never be any secrets between us. Life is just too short."

She looked across the table and suddenly burst out laughing. "But to tell you the truth, I never saw the Fairies coming!"

At that we both erupted into laughter and I almost launched my cappuccino out of my nose. We were so caught up in the moment, we did not see Bonnie quietly enter the room. She stood there silently for a moment before T spotted her.

"I'm sorry honey, did we wake you?" She asked.

Bonnie looked over at me, her sadness tangible. "Jimmy, you have to go home. Claire just reached out to me."

# CHAPTER SEVEN
# (RETURNING STATESIDE)

The entire trip to Heathrow passed quickly. T chauffeured the three of us, with Bonnie and me sitting quietly in the back seat of T's 2020 Jaguar I-PACE. The car's electric motor only added to the sounds of silence. I did not want Bonnie to walk me inside the terminal, so I hugged her quickly when we pulled up at the departure area and slipped out, standing in the doorway so she could not follow me.

"I'll see you soon," I said, leaning in and giving Bonnie a peck on the cheek. T blew me a kiss from the front seat. "Take care of each other until I get back," I said, as T popped the trunk, and I closed the car door and retrieved my suitcase.

Bonnie lowered her back window. "It's going to be a long trip brother. Make sure it's two-way. No heroics."

T honked the horn for three short bursts and then disappeared into traffic, putting her car through its paces. I could see Bonnie watching me through the back window until they were lost in the sea of departing traffic.

A few hours later, I sat silently in the first-class seat on my Virgin American flight staring out the window and replaying the morning events, as I tried to wrap my head around what was waiting for me back in Berthoud. The seat beside me was empty, so I had the luxury of nine hours of uninterrupted self-reflection.

Once Bonnie announced that Claire had somehow reached across the pond and entered her thoughts when she got up from bed to get a drink of water, another part of my ever-changing reality suffered a further seismic shift. Claire explained to Bonnie that she needed to reach me and could not wait for morning, Colorado time, to talk Gina through everything and have her risk discussing the subject matter on an open telephone line. My evolution through the system had taught me that Big Brother is always listening. Given the way the NSA had been tapping into the conversations of American citizens pre-Snowden, and how the Obama administration had further relaxed the government's standards for invading privacy for political purposes, I had kept all telephone communications with Bonnie when I first reached out to her, limited to basic family endearments, and promises of more details when I saw her. Claire was there for most of those calls. One finds wisdom in the most unusual places.

Claire's own prodigious gifts had obviously gotten a steroidal bump from that mental entanglement with the others that violent night of the new moon. When her own internal alarm was triggered by the recent messages she picked up from Everett and Michelle, she started scanning further and further until she located my thoughts and, knowing I was limited in my gifts to human standards, went searching for the closest receiver she could find. Bonnie's mind lit up like a beacon on a dark night.

Claire had told Bonnie that the messages had first come to her from a powerful, outside source in the form of numeric code. She sensed that it was meant for Everett and Michelle, since they were the only ones in the area that conversed in that language, so she believed that she was eavesdropping and let it go. But when Claire felt the responsive, heightened anxiety emanating across the road from her favorite extraterrestrials, she tuned back into the conversation.

Everett and Michelle were now reaching out telepathically to Claire and Bobbi Angelini, our new family witch, just to catch up, since they all had come together to save my ass when my former mafia associates paid their final call. It was no surprise that during those communications they often switched back and forth between numbers and English with the verbal dexterity of a New York street merchant switching between basic English and his home tongue. They had gotten so comfortable thinking in *"Pig-Martian"* as they liked to call it, that they often slipped into it during conversations among the gifted, especially if it concerned emotional issues, where English gave it a little more dramatic depth. Evidently this was one of those times.

Claire told Bonnie that Everett had been summoned back to his home planet, to answer for his actions that night, including breaching the "Prime Directive."

Everett and I never spoke about what he did for me that night. Nor did the others, not even Gina. It seemed that the seven of us had shoved all our emotional baggage into the SUV with all of those dead bodies and laid it to rest in the bottom of Crater lake. *Let the dead keep our secrets as their penance.*

I did not need to be told. I knew who had reached across the veil and brought me back. The others were talented in their own right, just like Bonnie, and could even communicate with me once I was on the other side, as they could with my dead brothers, but it was their alien technology that repaired my heart and forced my life force back into this body. I even knew how he did it. His little pocket gizmo. I had seen him work that magic on other things.

When I spoke with Gina by phone before I boarded the plane, I told her to speak with Claire and that she should contact all of the others, including Lenny and the Oracle Crew, and especially Everett and Michelle, and have them all come by for lunch tomorrow. As worried as she sounded, she avoided any compromising follow-up questions and said she would pick me up at Denver International.

I reviewed the handwritten sheet of the twelve lines of numbers and wondered if they were connected to what Claire had received.

I hated math. My entire education was an artful attempt to do the bare minimum to get by in all math related classes while excelling instead in any subject that relied solely on the verbal or written word. Hell, my lowest law school grade was in tax.

When I started working for Valachi, I was forced to regularly engage my mental nemesis, and reluctantly became proficient in mid-level accounting. However, it was watching Valachi's nephew, Dan Pearsall, move money around that finally changed my perspective. To Dan, numbers were a game, like chess, and he knew that if he could make the right moves at the right times with the vast amount of illegal money Valachi controlled, including overseas, Dan won. And if Dan won, Valachi won. So, I watched Dan and I learned how to make and hide my money, and how to love numbers. I was now secretly and comfortably wealthy as a result.

Despite all of the bad shit that went down that night, I knew that if Dan had not killed me, we might still be friends. Before I left for England, I had a cashier's check for a hundred thousand dollars delivered to his son, Douglas, anonymously. The kid had kept his promise to me all those years ago and never entered the family business. He deserved a break.

I took another glance at the numbers and thought to myself, what would DP do? I could hear him in my head: *"Use your tools. Crack the code."*

I pulled out my iPhone and, after tapping into Virgin Air's WIFI system, began searching for a binary code conversion website. I finally settled on one called "unit-conversion.info."

I saw that their examples had the numbers grouped into sets of eight, so I started carefully typing the numbers from my paper into the input data box. Given the substantial number of digits, I expected it to take me forever to finish, but I was pleasantly surprised by a newfound dexterity in my thumbs, which appeared to automatically input the numbers with incredible speed. What was most surprising is that I realized that I was not taking the numbers from the sheet of paper before me but typing them out of memory.

Thirty seconds and eight hundred and forty-five entries later, with one more keystroke to start the converter, the following message appeared on my screen:

"Everett must return at once and answer to the Council for his breach of the Prime Directive."

# CHAPTER EIGHT
# (SOMETHING UNEXPECTED)

I was excited to be home but anxious over what might be waiting for me there. During the ride upstate from the airport, I gave Gina the lighter details of the Sprites and Fairies, and of Bonnie's carrying on Nana's legacy. Her response to the supernatural was readily more accepting than when I was first trying to convince her that our mule, Claire, could talk. She mentally leapt clear over the outlandishness of the conversation and went right for the magical details. I skipped telling Gina about Bonnie's parting comments, as I had not yet figured them out and did not want to worry her unnecessarily.

"Girl Power!" She exclaimed triumphantly when I complained about Bonnie landing Nana's preternatural abilities. "Sometimes normal is as good as it gets!" She continued, "and as far as I'm concerned, your normal is more exciting than most." *True dat!*

Gina told me that she had made all of the arrangements for the luncheon tomorrow and that everyone had RSVP'd except Everett and Michelle. With the stretch of Indian Summer we had been experiencing in Colorado, everything was prepped to take place in our back yard. I told her I would reach out to the wonder twins first thing in the morning.

When we arrived at the house, I was surprised to find numerous pallets of construction materials, a portable industrial generator, a thirty-yard dumpster and a port-a-potty strategically placed along my driveway.

"What the fuck –" I stammered.

"I was hoping to get at least the demo completed before you returned from England." She cut me off, "but here you are!"

"What demo?" I continued.

"The exterior of the house. They are starting on Monday." Gina replied with a tone of finality as she hit the garage door button then slipped the car into its spot. "Helen knows a guy – Whitey Fronsdahl – who has a farm nearby and is also a local contractor. He's going to cover the exterior with James Harding materials, install new windows, and rebuild our back and front decks, all before Christmas."

I knew from my real family's business that this was going to be expensive, and I did not care about the money; we had plenty. However, I had become a bit of a recluse since my arrival in Berthoud, for good reason, and the events, both murderous and supernatural, that had transpired since then certainly did not invite public scrutiny. The last thing I wanted was crews of construction workers milling about the property.

"And what about our merry band of misfits?" I asked.

"Helen and Bobbi swear this guy is the soul of discretion. Bobbi said she read him, and he's got his own secrets that go as far back as the Norse wolf god, Fenrir, I think they said. So, he's not going to be saying anything."

"What about Claire?" I pressed.

"I've already spoken with Claire about keeping her own counsel during the hours there are workmen about." Gina said, watching in the rearview for the garage door to close. "She's in, but only after I promised her that he would fix up her Lair – I left her list on your desk." Gina slid out of the car and headed towards the interior door. "We can go over everything with the others at tomorrow's luncheon."

Gina opened the door and Blue came flying directly at me like a large furry black missile. I turned quickly to avoid the crotch shot that was coming and was almost knocked onto the front hood of the car by the impact.

"You see, she missed her daddy!" Gina said, before turning and entering the house. "C'mon Blue!"

With that, Blue ended her tongue bath and receded into the bowels of the house in search of our master. I grabbed my bag from the trunk of the SUV and followed her in, hoping that Gina's latest project did not further complicate the reason for the luncheon, dealing with Everett's issues.

# CHAPTER NINE
# (HOME ON THE RANGE)

The seven-hour time difference between England and Colorado did nothing to shift my circadian rhythm, so I continued to live on my six-decade, hard-wired New York time clock once I was back home in Berthoud. However, when I awoke the next morning at my usual four a.m., instead of jet lag, I felt completely energized. Not wanting to wake Gina, I slipped downstairs, grabbed a cup of coffee, and went out to the pasture to check on Claire and Mr. Rogers.

I found them both laying side by side, head-to-tail, in the back of the pasture by Geppetto's studio. Mr. Rogers' head was prone, and he was out for the count, but Claire rose to her feet when she saw me coming and met me halfway at a cantor. I threw my arms around her neck and gave her a warm hug.

"Welcome home, Jimmy." Claire said in her sultry, Lauren Bacall voice. "That Bonnie certainly has a lot of stories to share. Water Sprites and Fairies, you can't make that up!"

I released her neck, took her face in my hands, and kissed her on the nose.

"So, let me get this straight, the talking, telepathic mule can't get over the existence of the Fae?"

"Well, now that you put it that way –" She broke into that Lurch-like, deep throated laugh and I soon joined in with her. After a few moments I looked over at Mr. Rogers. With everything that had been going on before I left for England, I did not have the opportunity to talk about him with Claire.

"How's he settling in?" I asked.

"He's loving it here." She said, following my gaze, and then her voice sounded a little concerned. "But he's old, and he's had a tough life. So, he needs a lot of rest." She studied her sleeping beau for a few moments in silence. I wondered if she was watching his dreams.

"Now, can he –" I started to say.

"Just with me," Claire responded, without breaking her gaze. "We mules can share thoughts, but I have to fill him in on what the others may be thinking."

"Can he understand spoken human words?" I asked.

"Jimmy," Claire said turning back to me, "even the birds, rabbits and snakes can understand human English. It's just not that hard." She started to laugh again. "Especially since you guys just love to hear yourselves talk."

I made a mental note to call out politely to the snakes the next time I needed to walk the high grass out in the fields. Better to be thought mad than to accidently step on one and get bitten.

"So, do you have anything else on Everett's situation?" I asked, getting to the matter at hand.

"Nothing." She responded. "He went silent once he realized that I was listening in."

"Have you heard from the others?" I asked.

"Helen, Bobbi and Eddie will be here today." She responded. "So will Lenny."

"What about the girls?"

Claire's face suddenly assumed the closest thing to a smile I have ever seen on her.

"Yes, they'll both be here." She turned in the direction of Mr. Rogers. "He's waking up," she called over her withers. "Gotta go." And with that she headed back towards her partner.

I turned back towards the house and saw Gina standing on the back deck, illuminated by the blue light of the big screen television coming through the glass sliding doors. She was wrapped in a fluffy bathrobe and holding a steaming cup of coffee staring into the darkness in our direction. Blue was standing beside her. I removed my iPhone and flashed the flashlight towards her, and she smiled and waved back. For the first time in forever, I broke into a jog and was surprised after a few yards that my lungs were not aching. I was in the house before I knew it.

Gina met me with a fresh cup of coffee as I arrived.

"You don't need to go out this morning if you're not feeling up to it." She said, referring to her morning run and my much slower but steady walk we had been doing since we arrived in Berthoud.

I was actually feeling pretty good, so I said, "No, we can go. Just let me finish this coffee."

At the first light of the Blue Hour, Gina and Blue were out in the driveway ready to get started with their daily five-mile run. I came out a moment later with my large bag of chopped veggies and dog scoobies that I carried during my deliberate pace far behind my woman and her dog. Gina trotted over to me and gave me a quick peck, then took off, with Blue right beside her.

Today, for the first time, neither one of us was carrying our S&W MP Shield handguns. The very real threat that had mandated such protection, had been fully neutralized the month before, during that night of the new moon. Gina did not think twice about leaving her weapon behind. I was a bit less ready to lose my security blanket. Nonetheless, there I was, walking at my comfortable pace down my street towards the route that would take me to the edge of the foothills to the West, there and back again. I watched Gina and Blue disappear around the first turn a quarter mile away.

I was happy to be reuniting with the numerous horses, alpacas, goats, and other herd animals I had befriended, who all waited patiently at their respective fence lines for my approach. Claire had put the word out that I had returned from across the pond. They enjoyed the many handfuls of carrot medallions I would toss likes seeds onto the fields among them so that they would not be pushing to get to the front of the line. There was always plenty for everyone.

The same was true for the many dogs that patrolled the properties along the route. They all waited patiently sitting along their fence lines, but once the first one along the route spotted me, his bark would then be shared like a word in a game of telephone, letting all others know their scoobies were on their way. My final stop was at Pam Ervin's property, with its pristine paddock for the beautiful Arabian named Tique, who always waited at the eastern fence of the property so she could spot my approach and whinny loudly. It always made me smile.

As I headed away from Tique's corral, my eyes turned eastward for my return loop home. Behind me were the foothills and to the north, hundreds of acres of open plains with tall grass that danced in unison with the ubiquitous breeze that flowed off the mountains from the west. The slow movement of the grass was almost hypnotic. I called this the meditation stretch.

But this morning something was different. I could see streams of furrows, about a dozen of them, moving rapidly through the high grass in my direction. I started walking more rapidly, scanning for a spot I could retreat to. When I heard the first howl of the lead coyote, followed in rapid succession by yelps from the lesser members of the pack, I instinctively reached for my absent gun, hoping I could fire in the air to at least scare them, and then cursed my luck.

By now the coyotes were halfway across the field and closing fast. I started to run; the adrenaline powering legs that had not been pressed into this kind of service for decades. I could hear the intensity and pitch of their howling amplify as they closed in and I willed my body to pick up its pace, and then something unexplainable happened.

One moment I was running along the empty, unpaved gravel road with a determined pack of coyotes nearing striking distance. The next moment, I was seemingly transported a half mile away, standing on County Road 23, gasping for breath. I could not tell you how I got there. And as with all of my moments of survival since I moved to Berthoud, Colorado, I did not care. I got my bearings by finding the Three Witches mountains along the western horizon and using them as my compass, turned towards home.

# CHAPTER TEN
# (A REUNION OF SORTS)

Helen, Bobbi, and Eddie were the first to arrive that morning in Helen's red Mercedes. Helen gave me a big hug as she walked through the front door while Eddie carried large baskets of food past us and placed it on the kitchen counter. Gina entered the kitchen through the dining room from the side deck, wiping her hands on her apron, and gave Eddie a quick hug before helping him unpack the Greek goodies. Bobbi sauntered in last, stopping for a moment in front of Jack the Spruce to nod respectfully, before turning to give me a quick peck on the cheek. By then, Helen was lifting Gina off the floor and shaking her in a manic embrace.

"Even the briefest separation is too long!" Helen exclaimed as she released Gina.

"Tell me about the British Fairies and Water Sprites," Bobbi chimed in, grabbing a piece of Greek pastry from one of the plates as she passed, just barely avoiding her brother's hand slapping at her own.

"There'll be plenty of time to catch up with Jimmy after lunch." Helen said, as she lifted the platter with the pastries and turned to Gina, "where do you want these?"

Gina led Helen through the dining room and out through the side door. Eddie followed, calling out, "I'm going out to see Claire, mind if I groom her?"

"You're spoiling her," I replied with a laugh, "but go ahead, knock yourself out. She's out with Mr. Rogers by the pond. Lucian is back there by the barn, prepping their hay bags and cleaning their troughs."

"Wait," Bobbi called as she hustled after her brother, "I'll come too, Claire just told me she'd fill me in on the Fae, and I'd like to hear it from the horse's mouth."

"That's mule!" I called after her.

"Plus, I'm dying to know how she reached across the ocean like that." Bobbi continued as she exited the door. "That's serious witch shit."

I shook my head. Last year I was knee deep in hungry alligators, because I allowed myself to become immersed in a world of gangsters and hit men. Now my world lay over the rainbow, where animals talked, witches roamed, and the sky was no longer the limit. And, oh yeah, I also came back from the dead.

Blue came flying in through the side door and lifted her chest up onto a windowsill so she could peer anxiously towards the end of the driveway. A moment later, a large black SUV took the turn into the driveway fast enough to kick some of the gravel out onto the street behind it. It continued rapidly down the driveway, coming to a sliding stop, just behind the Mercedes, which stirred up a large cloud of dust.

The driver door opened and Maeve, a powerful, large white American Staffordshire, leapt over the driver and out onto the driveway, bounding towards our front door. As I got the door opened Blue came from behind me and collided with Maeve driving them both back off the front porch. Rolling together like a black and white cookie, they slammed into the trunk of Jack the Spruce.

"Out of the way, cowboy, I gotta piss." Lenny commanded as he blew past me into the house and down the hallway towards the first-floor bathroom. I could hear him sighing happily at the release, given that he did not even bother to close the door behind him.

I almost had my knees taken out from under me as Blue and Maeve flew in through the front door, passed through the kitchen and dining room and out the side door towards the back yard. Blue was the rabbit.

"Welcome one and all!" I called out to no one as I slammed the front door closed.

"Now that my tank is empty, do you have any coffee?" Lenny asked as he reappeared in the kitchen a moment later with a look of relief on his face.

I pointed towards the Keurig and Lenny grabbed a large mug from the cabinet and filled it.

"I do love your coffee," he said as he took a quick sip black, before foraging in the fridge for some half-and-half. "I see the gang from Hygiene is here."

"All out back." I responded. "Still waiting on the girls and the wonder twins."

"Okay, skipper, so what's this catered confab all about?" Lenny said, after testing his now mocha colored coffee and nodding with approval. "I haven't had a chance to speak with Bobbi for the update after Gina called with the invite."

This is what I loved most about Lenny. This tall, tough-looking son-of-a-bitch was our guardian angel U.S. Marshall, who recently proved he could efficiently and permanently end a serious threat to us with barely a second thought. But compared to the rest of the crew, he was fairly ordinary. We shared the human limitation of having to receive our information the old-fashioned way, by hearing, seeing, or reading it. Others in our group just lifted the information out of my head like pickpockets and then shared it among themselves through their ever-strengthening psychic connections.

"Not sure myself," I started to respond. "Got recalled stateside by Claire just a day into my trip to see Bonnie."

"How is your sister doing?" Lenny asked.

"She seems great," I said, trying to stay focused on the matter at hand, "but that's another story for another time."

"Okay," he said, "where were we?"

I decided to cut right to the chase. I removed my transcribed notes of my binary dream and handed them to Lenny. He read it to himself and whistled softly.

"That can't be good," he said. "Have you spoken with Everett?"

"Haven't had the chance," I said. "Hoping we can all address that today, which is why we're here."

"Well, he doesn't have to go, does he?" Lenny posited anxiously.

"Maybe not, but I'm not really sure how all that works with them." I responded, trying to sound reassuring, while burying the guilt I felt as an unwitting participant in Everett's troubles."

Our attention was drawn beyond the kitchen window to the driveway, where the others, including Claire, had all assembled expectantly just outside the open paddock gate. Just then, a late model black Jeep Wrangler materialized at the end of the driveway and pulled in beside the red Mercedes. Two beautiful, blonde young women in their early twenties leapt out of the front seats and ran towards the welcoming committee, hugging Claire and then the others, before the group all retreated back through the paddock gate. I would never forget Claire's story of how the older girl, the precocious Scarlett, her younger sister Savanna in tow, had taught the mule how to speak when they were all just toddlers. Lucian, the youngest of our crew, and a witness to Claire's first annunciation to me, pulled the gate closed behind them. They were now all part of my ever-expanding family of misfits, and I knew in my heart as I watched them pass before me that I would gladly die again for any one of them.

"Well that just leaves the guests of honor," Lenny said, finishing his coffee and placing the mug in the sink. "Are you sure they're coming?"

"Claire sent them the mental invite before they went silent." I recalled. "I guess we'll know soon enough.

# CHAPTER ELEVEN
# (THE AYES HAVE IT)

Lenny and I joined the others in the back yard, and after we completed our rounds of multiple hugs and kisses, Gina directed everyone to their seats at the large farmhouse table we had set up earlier that morning. During my trip overseas, Gina had found the table at a wonderful family-owned curiosity shop in Berthoud called Mr. Thrift. Both table and chairs had been salvaged from an estate sale and sat twelve comfortably. Gina assured me it could be stored out back in Geppetto's workshop when we were not using it. There was certainly enough room for it back there, and even if there was not, Gina would have bought it anyway.

We all took our seats, with Gina and my seat closest to the house so we could easily move the food from the basement kitchen to the table. Always the restauranteur, Helen started circling the table and filling everyone's glasses with their respective beverage of choice, wine for most of us, a coke for Lucian, and some Macallan scotch for Lenny. Claire stood by the open twelfth space next to Bobbi and sipped cold water silently from a large silver bowl Gina had placed there. Mr. Rogers stood off a few yards from the table sampling some hay from the rack Lucian had left for him. Maeve and Blue were sleeping comfortably on the deck above us.

Gina pointed to the two empty chairs and said to the gifted, "well, are they coming?"

Bobbi and Claire closed their eyes. Bobbi reached over and placed her hand against Claire's face. They both opened their eyes simultaneously, but before either could speak, a sudden gust of wind circled the table, lifting some of the napkins into the air, as Michelle appeared, carrying a struggling Everett over her shoulder. He was apoplectic, and you could see she was ignoring his silent entreaties for his release. Finally, he shouted in English.

"Put me down woman!"

"Only if you stop acting like a human child." She warned, without looking at him.

He looked around the table. When his eyes settled on Lucian, the young boy burst out laughing.

Everett's face softened. Lucian and he had become close friends since the day the three of us saved Claire from the mountain man at Mrs. Reynold's farm. The gift of childhood allowed Lucian to quickly acclimate to this special group of friends. While we never told him that he could not share what he saw at our home with his family, Everett assured us that this kid could keep our secrets.

"Okay, okay. I'll be good," Everett affirmed with a wink at Lucian.

Michelle gently placed her mate softly on the ground before her.

"No matter where in the universe you come from, men are such babies." Michelle affirmed.

"Well, sit your asses down so we can all eat!" Lenny shouted, banging his empty scotch glass on the table before him. "We have lots to discuss, but not on an empty belly."

With that, Everett and Michelle took their seats, and the plates of food made their rounds from one set of hands to another as everyone filled their plates with the delicious salads, rolls, and cold cuts Gina had spent the morning preparing. Glasses were refilled by whomever was standing at the moment, and for fun, Michelle once covered the beverage circuit before anyone noticed she had left her chair, literally leaping over Claire as she passed.

As I engaged the members of the group in closest proximity with various bits of light conversation, I could see that the others around the table were all doing the same. I could also see from Everett's face that despite his best efforts he was struggling to hide his apprehension.

"Tell everyone about the British Fairies and Water Sprites!" Bobbi called out as Helen and Gina exchanged the dinner plates with dessert and coffee settings.

Eddie appeared from the basement's sliding doors carrying the tray of Greek pastries which he placed at the center of the table.

For the next hour I employed my professional oratory skills to dramatically recount the wonders of my trip to England, including describing in detail my sister's death-defying driving skills along with her other more esoteric and relevant gifts. With each new detail of wings, levitation, waltzing, and lost time, I could see the eyes of the two young women widening, despite the fact that they had been the ones to first discover Claire's gift of speech. Lucian, in contrast, seemed unaffected by it all.

When the dessert dishes were finally cleared, and the coffee replaced with more wine and liquor, the group's brief bit of contemplative silence was shattered by Lenny again using his scotch glass as a gavel, and his booming voice demanding, "Everett! What's this I hear about you having to return to the mothership?"

At that, everyone at the table turned to face Everett and Michelle. Before he could respond, Michelle said, "he's been called back to Proxima-b by the members of the Council, a group of our planet's ruling class, to answer for our breach –"

"My breach." Everett corrected her.

"Our breach," Michelle insisted, "of our Prime Directive. I made you do it." She said, gazing anxiously at him.

"What's the Prime Directive?" Lucian asked.

"We are not allowed to do anything on our own volition that could change the future in any meaningful way." Everett replied. "We are here to observe, report and in my case, follow the instructions from the Council."

Michelle pointed at Claire. "Our Centaurian forefathers had no problem breaching the Prime Directive when they created the Centaurs of earth's myth and legend!" She slammed her hand down hard on the table, which noisily lifted every plate and cup a few centimeters. Looking instantly contrite, she appeared beside Claire and gave her a hug. "No offense, sweetie!"

"None taken," Claire replied as Michelle reappeared beside her mate.

"So, what did you do that was so bad?" Lucian asked, with the innocence of youth.

You could see Michelle and Everett silently communicating with each other, while Bobbi and Claire closed their eyes to listen in. Finally, Claire said, "Everett brought Jimmy back from the dead."

Now it was Lucian's eyes that became as wide as saucers. He looked over at me with newfound interest.

I reflexively reached under my shirt to touch my scar talisman, and my fingertips struggled for a few unexpected moments to find it.

"Wwwwoooooowwww," Lucian exclaimed, lost in his imagination as to what that entailed. "How ccccooooooooooooollllll."

"Well, you just have to tell the Grand Poobah up there that you're just not coming." Lenny said, his own worry for his friend now evident in his voice.

"It's not that simple," Everett said softly, a defeated tone in his voice. Michelle reached comfortingly around his shoulders and pulled him close to her.

Michelle continued, "it's not a request. We have to go back and defend our actions."

"We're not going anywhere," Everett countered. "The order commands only my appearance."

"I'm not letting you go alone," Michelle said.

"This sounds like a trial," Gina injected, her third glass of wine lubricating her sharply focused powers of deduction.

"That's a simple way to describe it," Michelle said, "but it's close."

"Well then," Gina said, "you're in luck."

"What are you talking about?" I whispered quietly in her ear, afraid of where this was heading.

"Michelle, you don't have to go back to Proxima-b with Everett." Gina proclaimed, now standing for emphasis while she finished the last of her wine. "Jimmy will go with him!"

"Oh no!" Everett exclaimed.

"We can't let him do that." Michelle pleaded.

"Let's put it to a vote." Lenny countered, the Macallan bringing its own clarity of thought.

"I vote yes." Savanna chirped, almost surprised by the sound of her own voice.

"Me too!" Scarlett seconded. "Claire says he's the best lawyer she's ever met."

"Can I vote?" Lucian begged.

The two girls nodded.

"Your brothers vote 'yes' as well," Bobbi cheered. *Just like them to continue breaking my balls from the other side of the veil.*

"Raise your hands if you agree that Jimmy should go and defend Everett on Proxima-b." Claire said, lifting her own front right hoof in the air for effect, and giving it a little wiggle.

Everyone raised their hands in unison, except, Michelle, Everett, and me.

The aliens locked their eyes on me.

"You don't have to do this." Everett whispered.

"It's asking way too much." Michelle followed.

I stared around at the other expectant faces now looking to me for a response. My newly clenched gut was telling me that this was a big mistake. But this same crew had materialized out of the ether to help me in my greatest time of need, and I would not have been there to think it over had Everett not hit me with that golden beam and brought me back from the other side of the veil. I slowly raised my hand.

"Why the fuck, not." I said abjectly. Gina leaned over and gave me an excited hug.

"The Ayes have it!" Lenny shouted as he gaveled his glass one last time. He stared at his empty glass with faux astonishment. "Who's a guy gotta shoot to get a refill here!"

Michelle appeared beside him and handed him a fresh glass with three fingers of Macallan. She kissed his cheek for good measure before reappearing next to me and almost crushing my ribs with one squeeze.

"Thank you, Jimmy." She whispered.

*Leap and the net will appear.* My sister's cribbed saying echoed through my mind.

# CHAPTER TWELVE
# (WHAT TO WEAR IN OUTER SPACE)

By the time everyone left the party and Claire and Mr. Rogers retired to the barn for the night, the adults, both human and extraterrestrial, were pretty lit, but before our meeting was adjourned, it was decided that Everett and I should leave as soon as possible for Proxima-b. Dutch courage.

We agreed that Monday, the shittiest day of any week, would be the perfect time to leave. I knew that if I gave myself too much time to prepare, I would find a way to get myself out of this obligation. Forty-eight hours was enough time to pack everything I needed. But what exactly was that?

My circadian rhythm was now entirely FUBAR. I lay in bed for an hour staring up at the ceiling while Blue and Gina traded snores like super heavyweight boxers traded blows, slowly and powerfully. I went downstairs and made myself some coffee and pulled up a bar stool so I could prop my feet on the kitchen windowsill and stare out into the night. I tried for a while to imagine which of the stars in the sky was the sun we called Proxima. They all looked extremely far away. Then I recalled the night when Everett and Michelle "came out" to me and Michelle lamented that you could not see it from the Northern Hemisphere. I also remembered Michelle telling me that they really did not sleep as we know it and looked over the treetops in the direction of their home, wondering if they were awake now.

Then I heard the pounding of hoof on the concrete patio below.

I ran down the interior stairs and saw the huge silhouette of Claire in the starlight standing at my sliding glass door, I could see from the large condensation cloud on the glass before her face that she was breathing heavier than usual, like she had been running. As I slid open the glass, she poked her head though the doorway and bellowed, "Michelle said 'get over there now, Everett's leaving!'"

Dressed only in my pajamas, slippers, and a bathrobe, I slid past Claire and ran up around the outside of the house. I do not really remember the effort, but I know I cleared the side gate without opening it and was in front of Everett and Michelle's property in seconds. I could see a faint glow coming from the back of their property. Again, without consciously initiating the effort, I found myself standing in the large field behind Everett's man-cave.

There was Michelle, tears on her face, standing before a spacecraft the size of an average RV. It was the expanded version of the one I first saw months before, resting in its recessed place of honor on the wall in Everett's man cave. In the darkness it now looked midnight blue, with pulsating lights emanating in different patterns and colors, and I could feel its low amplitude vibration in the pit of my stomach. It made no sound. Michelle interrupted my catatonic fascination with the words, *The entrance is on top.*

Although I do not remember her actually saying anything.

No longer controlled by conscious effort, I found myself standing on top of the spacecraft above a sealed circular portal. The wind from the west was suddenly picking up, blowing my bathrobe with such force that I shook it loose from my body. Before I could worry about my next move the portal opened. It was dark inside.

*Get in*, I could sense Michelle's command.

As I stepped through the portal my body was embraced head to toe by a force that felt like the dense heat from a sauna and slowly carried me downward until my feet touched a hard surface. There was a swooshing sound above as the portal closed. Then the interior came to life with a soft yellow glow that emanated from the walls and floor in my immediate vicinity, rather than any specific fixtures. I could see a long hallway opening before me, way too long for the RV sized spacecraft I had just entered.

As I stepped forward, I could feel the craft start to gently lift, and while I started to lose my balance with the movement, that same warm embrace that carried me through the portal, righted me and drove me forward, with the interior lights following my movements down the hallway. I could see that there was a solid barrier at its end, but the force carried me toward it without abatement. I readied for impact, half squinting and clenching my muscles, as the barrier dissolved just enough for my passage and I was ushered into a large chamber the size of my atrium living room. The entire atrium glowed with the same yellow light and at the far end, facing what I guessed was the front of the craft, stood a being, taller than I, with shoulder length golden hair, totally engaged with what must be a control panel before it.

"I'm looking for Everett." I said, cautiously.

The sound of my voice obviously startled this creature and as I watched it spin to face me, it disappeared for a moment, then reappeared right before me. The creature's Nordic blue eyes studied me with amazement while I in turn, studied its androgenous face with an odd feeling of recognition. I knew I had seen it somewhere before. It was beautiful. And then it spoke.

"Jimmy, what the fuck are you doing here?"

# CHAPTER THIRTEEN
# (BOLDLY GOING)

Before I could answer, the craft went into a sudden roll to the right while a series of lights and electronic sounds appeared to emanate from the control panel. The lurch and centrifugal force threw me towards the platform I had been standing on where I was again cocooned by that warm field. The creature seemed unaffected by the jarring movement and reappeared in front of the control panel, where, with a few swipes of his hands through the space above, materialized holographic screens and two imprints for his hands on either side of the screens. He placed his hands in the imprints.

"F-18s, Jimmy, from Buckley Air Force Base. No going back now!" The creature called out as the craft reversed rolled and I could feel the g-forces pinning my protective field against the platform. Then the numbers flooded into my head:

> 01010000 01101100 01100001 01110011 01101101 01100001
> 00100000 01010011 01101000 01101001 01100101 01101100
> 01100100 01110011 00100000 01100001 01100011 01110100
> 01101001 01110110 01100001 01110100 01100101 01100100
> 00101110

I looked at the creature, who was totally engaged with the control panel and screen as the craft reversed rolled a third time. This message was not coming from him. Then I got it: *Plasma shields activated.*

Suddenly another series of numbers materialized:

01000001 01100111 01100111 01110010 01100101 01110011
01110011 01101111 01110010 11100010 10000000 10011001
01110011 00100000 01110111 01100101 01100001 01110000
01101111 01101110 01110011 00100000 01101100 01101111
01100011 01101011 01100101 01100100 00100000 01101111
01101110 00101110

Followed by my mind's translation: *Aggressor's weapons locked on.*

No sooner had my mind seized the message then the creature drew his arms back like chicken wings and the craft shifted instantaneously into a ninety-degree, vertical angle. But this time, I no longer felt the centrifugal force or acceleration and was able to stand, despite facing directly upwards. Without any further adjustments by the creature, within a moment my perception self-corrected like a gyroscope, so that I felt like I was standing upright on level ground. The shifting motion gave me a mild feeling of vertigo, but it was gone as quickly as it arrived.

The creature stood studying the screen for a moment more before turning back to me and clapping his hands. The screen and hand controls disappeared from the panel.

"Lost them at 37,000 feet. That'll definitely give MUFON something to write about this month!" The creature shouted in a voice I finally recognized, Everett. But this creature was Everett 5.0.

He now stood directly before me assessing my pajamas and slippers and shook his head. I did the same of him. He was clearly over six-foot two and showed the build of an Olympic swimmer underneath a black, form fitting outfit with metallic silver shoes. His face was androgenous, almost pretty, and he had no facial hair. His pale skin was translucent.

"Look at you. PJs with bucking broncos on them. I just can't take you anywhere, can I?" He said, with a laugh.

I reached towards him, grabbing his shoulders, surprising both of us with my speed and strength.

"You rat bastard!" I shouted, moving forward. "It's bad enough I didn't want to come with you in the first place, but to try and leave without me –"

Everett disappeared from in front of me and I almost lost my footing, but I recovered in an instant just as he reappeared about ten feet away to my right.

"Whoa, Jimmy." Everett cautioned.

"I knew right there at the table that Gina and the others trapped you into going," he said, his voice sincere. He disappeared and reappeared on my left. "That's why I left early."

Hearing it said out loud made me feel guilty and embarrassed. My skin flushed and I felt physically drained. I looked around the room for a place to sit. Everett made a motion with his hand and a holographic chair appeared before me. I dropped into it.

"You deserve better." I finally said. "After all you have done for me."

"Well, you are here now," Everett said. "How'd did you get in here anyway?" He closed his eyes for a moment, and I could feel him probing my mind.

"That's really weird." He said, opening his eyes. "Michelle swears it was not her. Yet Jayney welcomed you right in."

"Jayney?" I asked.

"Yeah," he continued, opening his arms wide to address the ship, "I named her shortly after we arrived on earth. I liked the way you human males named your cars after pretty woman. Seemed to have something to do with the headlights. I picked Jayne Mansfield. She was quite a looker at the time."

I tried to recall exactly what she looked like and then remembered a stock, tabloid photo of her and her then husband, Mickey Hargitay. Remarkable headlights. She was beautiful and had died tragically, and ironically, in a car wreck.

"Yeah, that's her." Everett said, tuning in.

He gazed back at my pajamas. "Got to get you out of those," he said, with a smile.

"Stand up and put your arms out like this," he said assuming a mock, Vitruvian Man pose. I slowly stood and mimicked him, waving my arms up and down for the full Davinci effect.

Everett removed the Hadron Distributor from a pocket that just appeared at his hip, which still looked like a metallic, butane cigarette lighter. The last time I saw it, he was using it to shrink SUVs with dead mobster passengers down to the size of a Hot Wheels car. He had used it earlier that same night to bring me back to life. I was not sure how I felt, having him point it at me again, but before I could say anything I was engulfed, head-to-toe, in a pale blue light. It tickled for the few seconds it lasted. When my sight cleared the PJs were gone, and I was now dressed in an outfit similar to Everett's. Only my shoes were black. Its material was form fitting but not like the spandex you see on the weekend warrior bicyclists who love to slow traffic throughout Colorado in the name of health and Mother Earth. This felt cooler, more comfortable, like a thicker version of the wonderful material used in Warrior XII products back on earth. And while I did not see any openings to the fabric, when I anxiously reached towards my chest, it opened to allow my hand access to my skin. The bullet scar talisman over my heart had faded from a thick keloid disk to a small, thin, smooth circle among the forest of hair on my chest.

Everett looked me over appreciatively. "Gina must have you on a diet." I looked down and saw that I had trimmed down substantially from the night I died. My arms and chest were more defined, and I had no problem seeing my feet. My crotch looked a little too flat.

I reached down into the front of my pants and was happy to find my package right where I had left it just in case I had to pee. *So, aliens flew commando.*

"I can set up a urinal for you, when you feel the need." Everett said, following my thoughts and pointing to a wall where a holographic urinal appeared, no pipes or handles.

"What if I need to shit?" I asked, sarcastically.

The hologram changed to a high-end bathroom stall. All it needed was a nice circular lock on the door. Then one appeared and I could hear its bolt slide.

"Now that's weird." Everett said.

"You gotta have a lock." I countered.

"Yeah," Everett replied, looking intrigued. "But I did not put one there. Jayney must be tapping your thoughts."

"Can she read human minds as well?" I asked.

"Don't know," Everett said, "you are the first human passenger she's ever had." He stroked his chin pensively for a moment more and then turned back towards the control panel. "Oh well, must be beginner's luck." He materialized directly before the panel and raised the hologram controls and screen, calling out over his shoulder, "C'mon, Jimmy, let's take this baby for a spin!"

# CHAPTER FOURTEEN
# (IT'S NOT THE DESTINATION)

I was not sure how I got there but I found myself standing next to Everett 5.0 before he had finished his sentence.

"Let me just set the autopilot," he said, moving his fingers like a pianist. "Voila."

He turned and studied my face for a moment, then turned and swiped his hands through the air and a holographic screen appeared with a line of binary numbers streaming across it:

01001111 01111000 01111001 01100111 01100101 01101110
00100000 01110011 01100001 01110100 01110101 01110010
01100001 01110100 01101001 01101111 01101110 00100000
01101100 01100101 01110110 01100101 01101100 01110011
00100000

My mind instantly interpreted it: *Oxygen saturation levels*. It felt like that moment back in high school where I first dreamed in French.

01101110 01101001 01101110 01100101 01110100 01111001
00100000 01100110 01101111 01110101 01110010 00100000

01110000 01100101 01110010 01100011 01100101 01101110
01110100

*ninety four percent*

"You are about a point low on your 02-saturation count, Jimmy," He waved his hands and a small object appeared. It was a tiny silver cylinder, a half inch long, with a clear, "u" shaped cannula. This was beginning to feel like a full blown, Caesar's Palace magic show. He plucked it from the air and leaned over and attached it directly beneath my nose. I could not even feel it hanging there, but my lungs started to feel more relaxed and my head a little clearer.

"That's better." Everett said. "Now we can sit back and enjoy the trip."

With that, two holographic captain's chairs appeared, and Everett gave me first choice, settling himself into the remaining one. I was staring over at Everett's control panel, wishing the screen were larger so I could get a better view of space as we traveled through it. Suddenly, the entire exterior skin of the ship vanished, like a virtual Disney ride, and the two of us just hung there in our chairs, hurtling through space.

There is no proper way to describe the vastness of space. While I knew, intellectually, that this is how it should look, given the estimated distances between the celestial bodies, I still stubbornly expected to find stars and planets just a few blocks away from each other. Hell, I was expecting each star to have five points as well.

"The next star is outside your solar system." He said, reading my thoughts.

"How far away is Proxima-b?" I asked verbally.

"4.24 light years, give or take, as the crow flies." Everett said.

"How fast are we going?"

"About half the speed of light, at least until we clear this solar system."

I was impressed that we could travel so fast without feeling it.

"The earth travels 67,000 miles per hour through space and you don't feel that either." He stated, again reading my thoughts. I tried to force my mind blank.

"Are we there yet?" I could not help myself.

Everett smiled. He was beginning to appreciate my sense of humor.

"No, really," I said, as my chair fully opened up like a business class seat. "At this rate, not even you can live long enough to make that trip."

I could see him thinking about the best way to break it down so my human mind could grasp it.

"I know a shortcut!" Came his response. "I won't bore you with the applicable theories in quantum mechanics. Let's just say, that you folks almost have it all figured out. You are right on the edge of harnessing nuclear fusion for your engines so that takes care of your fuel storage issues. Homer Ellis and K.A. Bronnikov were onto something back in 1969 when it comes to wormholes, but my money is on a young lady named Caroline Mallary to take NASA to the promise land. It's all in the mastering of Dark Energy."

I really did not give a shit about the scientific details, as long as I got from A to B, and back again, in one piece.

A round planet in the distance grew larger as we approached. It looked red. Speaking of red, I could have sworn I spotted a rag top, cherry red Tesla sportscar sailing beyond the planet in the distance. I must have imagined it.

"You folks will be colonizing this planet pretty soon." Everett said, pointing. "Assuming, all things go as planned."

"Is that Mars?" I asked, leaning up on my right arm to get a better look as it passed to our right.

I did not know how long we had been traveling, but we could not have covered forty-million miles. I had not even needed a piss break. Space was really weird.

I did not know what to expect, but I could see clouds in Mars atmosphere and what looked like huge land masses and craters on the planet's surface. It even looked like it had vast areas of ice at its poles. I struggled unsuccessfully to see if I could spot any of the Mars rovers.

"That will be the human's final test." Everett said with the tone of a college professor. "If you guys can colonize Mars and make it a fully habitable planet without killing each other, then we will provide the necessary technology you'll need, and the rest of the universe will allow you to come out and play."

I felt good about the odds of humanity as a whole making it through the next decade, when our estimated colonization of Mars was to begin. However, given that I was into my sixth decade, I was not sure if I would make it to the finish line. *Well, maybe Gina would.*

Just as we passed Mars, the ship seemed to veer to the right and swing around to the far side of the planet.

"Okay," Everett said, sitting up straight in his chair. "We should be coming upon it any minute now."

All I saw was the blackness of space as tinted by the red glow emanating from Mars. Everett stood on what looked like open space and the control panel appeared before him. He placed his hands in the two hand templates and wiggled his fingers in a repeated pattern and then, superimposed on the open space before us, where the walls of the ship once stood, appeared florescent red hatch lines. It looked like a topographical map with unexpected curvature on the flat plane of the space before us.

Everett studied the map carefully, his finger working as a pointer on the hatch marks.

"There!" He said excitedly, pointing to a small round black space in the hatching that looked like the size of a tennis ball. The hatch marks seemed to be all bending counterclockwise around its perimeter. As I stared at it, its center looked blacker than the space around it. Even the red luminescence of Mars seemed not to shine in it.

Everett made some adjustments with his fingertips on the control panel and the ship appeared to shift its point of direction precisely at the hole in the hatch marks. Suddenly the exterior of the ship reappeared, my chair inclined, and I found myself beside Everett, directly before the control panel. Everett sat in his chair and the control panel lowered to meet his new position. I could still see the hatch marks and circular hole on the screen before us. It was growing larger and larger as we approached, and I could now make out a thin circle of faint light along its perimeter. The light appeared to be moving counterclockwise. I suddenly began to feel very strange.

"Better strap in, Jimmy." Everett said, as a four-point harness appeared to bind me into the seat, and I could feel that palpable warm embrace like a cocoon. "This is going to be a little bumpy."

# CHAPTER FIFTEEN
# (CAMEL THROUGH THE EYE OF A NEEDLE)

I noticed that two metallic bands now secured Everett's wrists, pinning his hands in their impressions on the console, while his seat appeared to evolve into something more substantial than the comfortable recliners we were just enjoying. A reddish glow transitioned into a palpable physical field around him. I could tell by watching his screen that our speed was increasing as we approached the hole in the hatch marks. Jayney was talking to me:

> 01010011 01110101 01110000 01100101 01110010 01101100
> 01110101 01101101 01101001 01101110 01100001 01101100
> *Superluminal*

I watched Everett's fingers dancing in their groves, like a court stenographer's, as we drew closer to the ring of light just inside the hatch marks. It seemed to expand as we approached, spinning counterclockwise. Jayney reached out again, my mind matching the speed of the communication:

> 01000010 01110010 01100101 01100001 01100011 01101000
> 01101001 01101110 01100111 00100000 01100101 01110110
> 01100101 01101110 01110100 00100000 01101000 01101111
> 01110010 01101001 01111010 01101111 01101110
> *Breaching event horizon*

Despite the embrace of my energy cocoon, my body began feeling an increasing gravitational force. The silver nose piece expanded like liquid mercury until it entered and formed a lining to the lower opening of my nostrils and slipped past my lips and between my teeth before expanding into a malleable mouthpiece. It did not feel metallic and adhered to my teeth like a dental mold. I could feel increased pressure as it began pumping more and more oxygen into my body.

Everett remained focused on the screen and as we passed the ring of light, he flicked his fingers, and the ship began to slowly spiral counterclockwise matching the speed of the ring. The exterior of the ship again disappeared, and I felt like I was floating in absolute darkness. I could no longer move my head and my eyes could no longer see the red glow from Everett's field. As the pressure on my chest increased, I could hear my heart pounding, pumping blood to my brain. I felt my muscles and ligaments stretching then contracting, and my bones popping as they struggled not to dislocate. I managed to slide my right hand into my shirt and felt my middle finger reach the tiny circle of flesh over my heart. I was dying all over again, and my thoughts focused on how I left without saying goodbye to Gina. Then I passed out.

When I awoke, Everett was standing over me, as I lay prone on my chair, which had converted into its fully reclined position.

"For what it's worth, you just broke the world record for the greatest gravitational force ever withstood by a human. Fifty Gs. Really impressive." He said as he ran an orange beam from his Hadron Distributor over the length of my body. "Seems like everything is still working, which is good, because I didn't want to have to resurrect you again. That would really piss off the Council."

"Did we make it?" I asked, still a little groggy.

"Oh yeah," he answered. "But you are lucky we are your closest neighbors, I'm not sure you would have survived a jump to a totally different galaxy. We would have needed to traverse a black hole for that."

My mouth felt dry. The magic cannula had reduced back to its tiny cylinder under my nose. I extended my tongue to lick my lips. *Hair!*

I reached up to my face and found it now covered with a thick beard and moustache. Back in my teens I had driven my parents crazy by growing my facial hair after my junior year of high school and I could tell by running my hand over my face that I now sported months' worth of effort. I could grab a full handful of hair extending off my chin. I pursed my lips outward and stared down my nose, expecting to see an Irish grey stash, but to my amazement, it was the same deep brown of my youth. I could not understand why hair was covering my ears, but when I reached up, the handful I brushed away, extended down from my head. I ran my hand up over my forehead and my fingers entangled in a thick, long, loose curl of hair dangling across its front. When my other hand joined the exploration, I found that I was sporting the same full, shoulder length hair style I had not worn since the seventies. Moreover, my nails on both hands extended an inch beyond my fingertips.

I bolted up in my captain's chair.

"What the fuck?"

I looked around for something reflective and a holographic mirror appeared before me.

"Jayney really likes you," Everett quipped. "Must be your new Mountain Man look. Very macho."

I could not believe the face I saw staring back at me from the reflection. Not only was it sporting what I used to call my 'Lion Mane look,' the face I saw did not reflect the man who had lived through my past sixty-four years. If the eyes are the windows of the soul, mine just got brand new glazing and trim. I looked twenty-years younger.

"I wish I could grow facial hair in my natural state." Everett mused, his own mirror appearing before his face. "That's why I do so in my earthling form. No one has facial or body hair on Proxima-b."

I looked over at his face, and realized that even in my latest youthful version, I was only a five on their beauty scale.

"That's also what I like about earth," he continued, as he studied his features in his mirror, "there's such variety among your form. All different colors, textures, shapes, sizes. At home, we all, with minor exceptions, look like me."

"How did this happen?" I asked, my gaze returning to my own visage in the mirror. "How long have I been out?" I reflexively scooped my extended locks into a ponytail; I guess everything is like riding a bicycle, once committed to muscle memory, it comes back to you naturally. A black hair tie appeared on the fingers of my right hand, and I tied it off. A silver nail clipper appeared and sheared my talons back to their normal length, then disappeared without dropping a nail clipping. *Thank you, Jayney.*

"To answer your first question," Everett said, waving away his mirror, "Not sure," – performing air quotes – "although I'm guessing it has something to do with your human DNA. Never took one of you through a wormhole before. Hell, I never took one of you, period; we leave that to the Greys."

He returned to his captain's chair, now without the bells and whistles, and placed his hands into their templates on the control panel.

"And as for the second question," he said, moving his fingers like a virtuoso pianist, "it depends on how one defines 'time.'"

I felt like I was listening to the charismatic American theoretical physicist, Dr. Michio Kaku. I loved watching him explain 'physics light' to us common people on his many programs on the more educational cable channels, and, half the time, was almost able to follow along. But inevitably he broached topics that were out of my depth. This was one of those moments. I could feel my brain shutting down any conscious effort to try to understand.

"You see, Jimmy, wormholes are not only bridges between points in space," Everett continued, "they are also bridges between points in time."

He turned away from his screen for a moment and must have seen my eyes glaze over. I could feel his mind rifling through my mental file cabinets before slamming the last drawer closed and continuing in English. He looked intrigued.

"We have just covered about four light years' worth of space in the Milky Way Galaxy by passing through a relatively short worm hole." He appeared directly before me and studied my face. He reached up and ran his fingers through my beard along my jaw line.

"I'm guessing that this dermatological phenomenon," he curved his hands around my hair and beard and then wiggled his fingertips to emphasize his own shiny nails, "probably reflects about six-months of human time."

"But I just boarded this ship this morning." I stammered.

"What I can't figure out," Everett said, continuing his assessment and using my beard as a handle to shift my face to the left and right, "is the reversal, no, resetting of your body's cellular aging process."

I knocked his hands clear of my beard and ran my own fingers along my jawline. He was right, my skin seemed tighter and there were no jowls hidden beneath my beard. I reached into my shirt to find my talismanic scar over my heart. It had disappeared along with my jowls, replaced by the thick chest hair that covered the rest of my torso. And despite being twisted and stretched to the point of unconsciousness during my trip down Alice's rabbit hole, I never felt better.

Everett returned to his seat at the panel and played a rapid tempo of silent notes on the template before calling over his shoulder, "we can get you checked out on Proxima-b, I'm sure the scientist there will have some answers. We have specialists who have studied you guys for eons."

With that, the exterior of the ship again disappeared, and I could see as our direction shifted towards a bright red dot far in the distance.

# CHAPTER SIXTEEN
# (THE FINAL STRETCH)

Visually, it looked like we were making good time by the increasing size of the red dot before us. Everett put the ship on autopilot and our two chairs moved on their own to the middle of the large room, facing each other.

Jayney must have sensed that I needed sustenance, even though I did not feel hungry. A holographic table appeared before us with two settings and glasses filled with clear liquid. The plates were filled with what appeared to be a mixture of red, yellow, and green squash.

> 01010110 01100101 01100111 01100101 01110100 01100001
> 01100010 01101100 01100101 01110011
> *Vegetables*

I pointed to the glasses.

> 01010111 01100001 01110100 01100101 01110010
> *Water*

"Thank you, Jayney," I said out loud.

Everett studied me for a moment. "You're spoiled. She doesn't do this for everybody. As a matter of fact, I'm not quite sure how she's doing it for you."

I pulled my chair up to my place setting and began shoveling in the food. I could not believe how famished I was and barely chewed the soft warm vegetables before swallowing. They were steamed in a buttery garlic sauce, just the way I liked them. I emptied my plate before even stopping to take a drink. The empty plate was replaced by another full serving.

"Wormholes will certainly give you an appetite." Everett said, sampling his own food at a much more respectable pace. "It is like putting your body in a blender, passing it through a straw and pouring it into an identical mold on the other side. Literally drains any stored energy from you in the process."

I looked at my new and improved body and said, "they must have used the wrong mold this time, but I'll take it." I dug into my second helping.

"That is a mystery," Everett pondered, looking me over carefully. "I'm sure they will be able to explain it once we get home."

I could see Everett's face become pensive. "Although I'm not sure this is home anymore."

I finished about half of the second serving and then sat back in my chair.

"You need to walk me through this process, so we can get prepared for what's coming." I said, putting on my attorney hat.

"I'm really not sure," Everett said, finishing his latest bite. There was still a large portion on his plate. He waved his hands and the table and contents disappeared.

"I've never seen one live," he said. "It's really something that was quickly taught to us all in the academy before we were given our assignments. The Prime Directive is simple. We must do nothing that can cause a material change in the evolution of the planet or people who inhabit it."

"And?" I pushed.

"And the first and last example that they used in the academy to underscore how one violates the Prime Directive is to bring one of the planet's inhabitants back to life."

"I don't understand."

He thought for a moment on how to explain it to me.

"You people have a term you call 'The Butterfly Effect'." He explained. "Let's say, now that I've brought you back to life, you drive drunk one night and have a fatal collision with the future mother of the person who was to develop the fusion propulsion system that will take your people to the heavens."

I thought about that for a moment and realized how much shit Everett was in for crossing the line that night he brought me back to life. This was not going to be a slap on the wrist, there were serious consequences if things went south. I kicked my attorney brain into high gear and silently vowed to quit drinking if we survived this, just in case.

"Well take me through it then and let's figure this out." I stated in a lawyer's cadence.

Everett collected his thoughts for a few moments before proceeding. I thought of how I would usually conduct my first interview with a client back home without any papers or pens visible, because seeing that someone is writing something down often distracts the person talking, and they sometimes hold back things without even realizing it. As a result, I had become adept at retaining most of the important facts from an interview without the need to write it down. I let them tell me their story and just listened. I gave Everett all of my attention.

"'Centauri,' which is the word we use for our planet," Everett began, "is governed by a central committee, made up of some of the most intelligent citizens on our planet. They run Centauri."

"Are there countries like on earth?"

"No," he said, "we are all one people, one planet."

"Are these council members elected by your citizens?" I asked.

"Our history tells us that the very first council was elected. Nine members, elected for life." Everett said. "But that was many millenniums ago."

"What happens now?" I persisted.

"Well, a member sits on the council until they pass, and since we live so long, most of us over five of earth's centuries, it was decided that we would trust the Council to fill their vacancies by a vote of five of their remaining members."

"What if there's a deadlock?"

"Then there is another vote by the citizens to appoint the successor." Everett said. "But that has never happened, as the remaining members always seem to come to a consensus about who should sit on the Council."

I thought about how, with all the incredible things I had experienced through my contacts with Everett and Michelle, that the idea of people coming to a peaceful consensus on any major issue was probably the most extraordinary. That is why we humans maintain vast armies.

"Does this Council have a leader?" I asked.

"Yes," Everett responded, "a beautiful female named," he thought for a moment, "the closest sounding word in your language would be 'Petrichor'."

I was distracted by the translation lesson. "Is 'Everett' the closest sounding word in English to your real name at home?"

He nodded. "'Michelle' too."

"Okay, so tell me more about Petrichor."

"She was appointed just before we left for earth, eighty of your years ago." He continued. "Because of her strong reputation of wisdom and fairness she held among the other Centaurians for someone so young – she had only reached the minimum age to vote, twenty years on Centauri – she was selected to replace the head of the Council who had passed. That post usually goes to the next senior council member still sitting on the Council."

I tried to follow his math but it was useless.

"How old are you and Michelle?" I had to ask.

"We are both fifty Centauri years." He responded.

That put them close to the same point in their lifespan as I was in mine. Definitely in the golden years. Given how perfect he still looked, I could not help but envy him. That led to my next question.

"How do you guys procreate?" I asked, feeling just a bit awkward.

"We seek to maintain a set number of citizens on our planet, about seven billion." He revealed. "When a certain number of our citizens pass, approximately one hundred thousand, a lottery is held to allow citizens to procreate."

"So, couples have to put their names in a hat?" I asked, fascinated.

"No, just the females, although we're all in the Centauri-wide AI system." He lamented. "Our males don't get a say in the matter. So, when the lottery is held, the system selects a set number of healthy individual females of breeding age and offers them the opportunity to procreate. If they decide to do so, they are provided with a fertility enzyme that allows pregnancy to occur."

"But they still need a male, don't they?" I asked, almost dreading the response.

"Of course," Everett said, laughing. "Centaurians fuck like rabbits."

I joined in the laughter, knowing that life on earth, and hopefully his exposure to me, had made Everett a little rough around the edges. After a few moments I pushed on with my interview, knowing that I had to know as much about these people as I could learn before arriving. The red spot on the horizon continued to expand.

"Did you and Michelle ever procreate?"

"No," he said, his smile disappearing. "We left for earth before the last lottery occurred."

"I'm sorry," I said, knowing from my own experience what a void that had left in Gina and my lives.

"It's all right," he said, "we've seen amazing things and had a remarkable life on earth, one I could never have foreseen. We have found our joy in each other and do love the sex. And now we have our Berthoud family to enjoy as well."

As part of that family, I certainly could empathize with his feelings. I felt a little homesick. I suddenly remembered I had not said goodbye to Gina and that we had been gone for months of earth time. "Can you get Michelle a message to let them know we're okay?"

He looked down, obviously troubled. "I told Michelle to block any messages coming from space, even mine. For her protection." He looked up at me with a pained expression. "I'm sorry, I didn't realize you would be coming with me."

"Why would you have her block your messages?" I asked, worried about the total loss of communication.

"Because" he said, "if things don't go well for me before the Council, I didn't want them to be recalling her as well. They could force me to reach out to her."

"But we have your craft," I lamented.

"There's a back-up craft stashed in the storage area behind my man cave." He responded. "Just in case my craft was shot down by your military during one of my forays. Michelle knows how to fly the craft. Truth is she's better at it than I am." I detected the hint of pride in Everett's voice.

Then it dawned on me. "But if the Council doesn't let you return to earth, how do I get back?"

Everett's eyes returned to the floor. "You don't."

# CHAPTER SEVENTEEN
# (THE WELCOMING PARTY)

Everett's last answer hit home. Where I came from, no matter how bad a trial went, the lawyer always gets to leave the Courthouse when it is all over, unless he pisses in the Judge's pocket. The competitor in me has always compelled me to pull out all of the stops and leave everything I have to give in the courtroom. But now, by deciding to stow away on this craft, my own future became part of the ante in this high-stake card game. Everett and I were '*All in*.' Nothing like a little pressure.

That pressure immediately mounted when I saw a set of twenty pulsating lights appear as points in a giant circle between us and the bright red sun that had evolved on the horizon, just as I spotted another blue planet in the distance off to the lower right. It reminded me of the photos I have seen of earth. I did not see the circle of lights arrive; it was as if God had thrown a switch.

> 01001001  01101110  01110100  01100101  01110010  01100011
> 01100101  01110000  01110100  01101111  01110010  01110011
> *Interceptors*

Everett returned to his control panel and assumed control of the craft. I watched how, as we approached, the circle of lights began to rotate and constrict around us until I could see that they looked like more modern, sleeker versions of

Jayney. They remained at a cautious distance from us but converted into a globe formation around us. Their exteriors were not transparent, and as they drew closer Jayney's exterior followed suit.

"Shit!" Everett uttered softly under his breath.

01010011 01101000 01101111 01110101 01101100 01100100
00100000 01001001 00100000 01100101 01110110 01100001
01100100 01100101 00100000 01110100 01101000 01100101
01101101 00111111

*Should I evade them?*

"Evade who?" I shouted.

Everett spun around like he had been pinched on his ass.

"How are you doing that?" He demanded, clearly agitated by the conflation of whatever was happening outside the ship, with what was happening inside.

"I'm not doing anything," I responded, "just hearing shit in my head. I think it's Jayney."

Everett was abruptly distracted by messages I was not hearing and turned back towards the control panel. The light from the hand imprints went dark. A moment later the control panel disappeared.

01000011 01101111 01101110 01110100 01110010 01101111
01101100 00100000 01101111 01100110 00100000 01110100
01101000 01100101 00100000 01100011 01110010 01100001
01100110 01110100 00100000 01100110 01110101 01101100
01101100 01111001 00100000 01110010 01100101 01101100
01101001 01101110 01110001 01110101 01101001 01110011
01101000 01100101 01100100 00101110

*Control of the craft fully relinquished.*

"Please tell me that this is your normal welcoming reception?" I pleaded, feeling a sudden urge to use the bathroom.

He looked over at me and said nothing. Slowly he shook his head no.

"Keep your mouth shut and let me do the talking," I said, while my mind tried to get out in front of what was happening. Then I realized that I was the deaf-mute in this show and that I needed a way to make them deal with me alone. I thought about the radio silence Michelle was maintaining back home.

"Can you block their telepathic communication?"

Everett thought hard for a moment and then nodded yes.

"Do it, and don't open it up unless I tell you to in plain old English."

He nodded again and then I could see him really concentrating.

"They are not going to like this." He said softly, returning to his seat in the captain's chair.

"They are the ones that changed the game with the welcoming party." I observed. "We need them to compete on my playing field going forward. Don't give them anything unless I tell you to, and only in English. Even when we're separated; especially when we're separated." I stood and began to pace in circles, my usual practice when preparing for a hearing. It helps to get my blood pumping. "Do they all speak English?"

"If the animals on earth can figure it out, what do you think?" he snapped, a bit too bitchy for my liking. I was sure at this moment he wished he had never met me. Once you realize that it is your ass in the wringer, there is always 'buyer's remorse.'

I came to a stop just before his captain chair. I reached down and took his chin in my fingers and forced him to look up at me. I could feel some initial resistance give way to my insistent grip.

"Listen to me carefully, Everett." I said, trying to inspire a lot more confidence from him than I was feeling myself, "I'm sorry I got you into this mess. I really am. But now I am going to prove to you that it was all worth it. You just need to believe in me. Just do everything I tell you to do."

And then I saw it. There is a moment when every lawyer makes that connection with his client. A moment when they surrender their fate to your hands. They turn over the reins of their problem and let you take the lead. It is a truly scary moment for both of you, but you must bury your fear to alleviate theirs. I saw it like a spark at the center of Everett's Nordic blue eyes. I released his chin and gave him a gentle slap on the cheek. Then I saw him stiffen uncomfortably, and then I blacked out.

# CHAPTER EIGHTEEN
# (ANOTHER GIANT LEAP)

I knew it was a dream. I was racing around the house in Berthoud, searching frantically for my car keys. They were not on the key rack where I always hung them by the front door. I checked all of the drawers in the storage areas in the kitchen and dining room and slammed them shut harder at each resulting failure. I called out for Gina but there was no response. I looked up at the large clock in the dining room and saw both hands spinning rapidly widdershins.

"Check your pockets, Jimmy." I heard that familiar smokey sounding female voice.

I looked over at the dining room window and there was Claire, the sun creating an angelic halo around her. She gestured with her nose toward my front pocket. I patted the front of my jeans and to my surprise, felt a hard object in my right, front pocket. I reached in and withdrew my car keys, holding them up proudly for Claire to see.

She laughed that strange deep laugh of hers, then said, "You got this, Jimmy."

Then everything went black.

01010111 01100001 01101011 01100101 00100000 01110101
01110000 00101110
*Wake up.*

I ignored the voice in my head. This was not Jayney.

01001010 01100001 01101101 01100101 01110011 00100000
01001101 01100011 01000011 01100001 01110010 01110100
01101000 01111001 00101100 00100000 01110111 01100001
01101011 01100101 00100000 01110101 01110000 00101110

*James McCarthy, wake up.*

I had not heard my real name in voice or thought for over an earth year, so this caught the attention of my subconscious like a hard slap in the face. I felt like I was at the bottom of a deep black hole, struggling to climb towards the circle of light at the top. I was wondering if I was dead.

01001110 01101111 00101100 00100000 01111001 01101111
01110101 00100000 01100001 01110010 01100101 00100000
01100001 01101100 01101001 01110110 01100101 00101110

*No, you are alive.*

I felt a cool breeze on the exposed skin of my face and willed my eyes to open, for just a moment before the brightness of my surroundings forced them tightly shut again. I raised my hands to shade my eyes and made another attempt.

01010010 01100101 01100100 01110101 01100011 01100101
00100000 01110100 01101000 01100101 00100000 01101100
01101001 01100111 01101000 01110100 01101001 01101110
01100111 00101110

*Reduce the lighting.*

I was lying in a bed with a soft and thin material covering me. I could tell I was naked beneath the sheet and my head was resting on a foam-like pillow, only this foam appeared to actively respond to the movement of my head, filling in any depression and never reducing its support for my weight. I felt my upper body start to incline as if I was sitting up on my own power. The sheet slipped down to my waist, exposing my hairy torso. My left hand instinctively lifted it back up to the center of my chest, as my eyes tried to focus on the area around me.

01001000 01101111 01110111 00100000 01100001 01110010
01100101 00100000 01111001 01101111 01110101 00100000
01100110 01100101 01100101 01101100 01101001 01101110
01100111 00111111

*How are you feeling?*

"Speak to me," I said, my throat feeling the raspy post-operative way it did after my hernia operation when I was a teenager. It was dry and sore to swallow. "Out loud. In English."

My eyes came into focus and there beside my bed stood three humanoids. They all shared Everett's general features, shoulder-length, golden hair, translucent skin, and Nordic blue eyes. They were all within a few inches in height of each other. The smallest, who was standing out in front and closest to me, appeared by the rounded curve of her breasts, to be a female. She was also a few inches shorter than the two males. But all three cleared six feet in height. They were each dressed in a floor-length gown of flowing pastel-colored material and they each had a small cylindrical object in one of their hands.

The female turned to the others and I could see by the exchange of their glances that they were communicating telepathically. The two males nodded.

"You know, it's rude to whisper in front of guests." I quipped.

The female turned back to me and spoke. Her voice reminded me of Michelle's.

"I am Nim." She began carefully, "I am the chief scientist in charge of –" she turned back to the men and exchanged another set of nervous looks. She turned back to me, "I believe the closest word in your language is 'genetics.'"

"Okay," I said. "Nice to meet you Dr. Nim, my name is Jimmy Moran." I offered her my free hand.

The three of them stared at my outstretched hand like I was giving them the finger. The two men exchanged nervous looks and I could feel Nim peeking through my memories. Satisfied that I meant her no harm, she smiled and then reached out and took my hand. Her flesh was cool, like Everett's and her grip strong, like Michelle's. I gave her hand a gentle shake and then released it.

"So, you are not James McCarthy?" One of the men challenged from over Nim's shoulder. His voice was as close to that of a sibling's to Everett's in tone and depth, but it lacked the emotion that eighty years on earth had given my friend.

"It's a long story," I responded, "but no, James McCarthy is dead."

This led to another round of telepathic telephone among the three of them.

I took this opportunity to get a better sense of my surroundings. The room was windowless, with the same soft, artificial light emanating from the walls, ceiling, and floor as it did in Jayney. The bed looked stark, and I could not make out its framework, which appeared to blend into the floor and wall. There was no other furniture in the room. I did not see a doorway.

I finally interrupted them. "Where is Everett?"

Now it was the other male's chance to practice his monotonic elocution lessons. "He is being held at the Central Ministry Building awaiting his hearing before the Council."

I pulled the sheet around me and swung my legs off the bed. The three of them literally transported across the room in apprehension. As I stood, the bed, which was holographic, disappeared from behind me. Unfortunately for me, the sheet disappeared as well. I was again, commando.

Back on earth, men my age are not inclined to shed their clothes in public, for good reason. The body that warranted engaging in the ubiquitous fad of "streaking" back in the early 1970s, had long ago faded into myth and memory. Now I would only subject my poor wife, Gina, to that exposure in a darkened room or hot tub, and then only after we both had our beer goggles on.

But I have to say, that at that moment I did not feel shy at all. I was nowhere near as beautiful as these beings, but on this side of the wormhole, I showed definable remnants of what was once a streaker-worthy body; its curly black chest and pubic hair covering a muscular, middle-aged triathlete. Since they controlled the hologram, it was their move. Dr. Nim was the last to look away.

One of the males pointed the object in their hand at me and I was encased in a pale blue light. Within moments I was back in a similar body suit to the one I had worn during the trip, but this one was a fluorescent white. Elvis would have been jealous.

I gave myself the once over and, satisfied, looked at the others and declared with a new sense of bravado, "Okay, now I would like to see my client."

# CHAPTER NINETEEN
## (PLAY THE CARDS YOU ARE DEALT)

The Dr. Nim Trio disappeared right before my eyes, leaving me all alone in an empty room. A moment later I felt a strange electrical charge building throughout my skin, like you experience when sitting outdoors during an approaching thunderstorm. I could feel the hair on my body rise, as if galvanized, and then kaleidoscopic, colored lights obscured my vision. On my next exhale, my breathing froze, and it all went black for a one-Mississippi count.

When my eyes cleared and breathing resumed, I was sitting in a completely different room at a large holographic table. A moment later, Everett appeared with a quick flash of light in a chair directly beside me. When he acclimated, his face displayed both relief and concern, and he leaned over and hugged me.

"Say nothing, they are listening." He whispered.

"Fuck them, I've got nothing to hide." I whispered back before we broke.

By the time I sat fully back in my seat, another flash brought another Centaurian to a seat on the opposite side of the table directly across from our position. He looked remarkably like Everett, more so than the Dr. Nim Trio, with the exception that he wore the kind of outfit that a lawyer in my world would describe as "a ten-thousand-dollar suit." Everett immediately recognized him.

"Aldor!" he exclaimed.

The other Centaurian gazed quietly across the table at Everett, his face stoic. He began to speak in the same monotone English displayed by the two males in the Dr. Nim Trio.

"So, it's true," Aldor began, "you have blocked all capacity to communicate in our natural state."

With reflexes I did not expect, I reached over and placed my hand over Everett's mouth before he could respond.

"With all due respect, Mr. Aldor," I said, "he did so on advice of his counsel."

I could feel Aldor rifling through my brain like a sale bin at *Rock Bottoms*. It did not seem to take him too long, which made me feel a bit inadequate. I really wished I had brought along a tinfoil hat.

"Well," Aldor continued, obviously feeling more comfortable with the spoken word, "it seems I can learn most of what I need from your memories, Mr. Moran."

"And what exactly is it that you 'need' Mr. Aldor?" I responded, as coolly as I could.

"Oh, I'm sorry," he said. "I should have explained, I will be prosecuting the charges against Everett on behalf of Centauri."

"Wait a second," I said, suddenly indignant over the fact that I unwittingly allowed this blonde bimbo, Aldor, to literally pick my brain. "Where the fuck do you get off pulling a stunt like that? Back where I come from, that crap would get your professional ticket punched. And probably your nose as well."

Aldor watched my emotional outburst with open amusement, which for him was a Mona Lisa smile. Everett placed his hand firmly on my arm to keep me from reaching across the table.

"There was one earthling line I plucked from your memory that seems deliciously applicable to this moment Mr. Moran," Aldor said aurally, his apparent joy belied by his slightly less robotic, Stephen Hawking monotone, "never bring a knife to a gun fight."

He disappeared before I followed my hardy "fuck" with "you."

"I'm sorry," Everett said, "I should have blocked your mind from his reach. I was just so surprised to see him after all these years that I dropped my guard."

"Wait," I said, "you can do that?"

"Yes," he replied, "unless the Council orders me not to."

"Then do it, now," I said, "we can cross the Council bridge if we come to it. It is bad enough he has already taken his trip down my memory lane. I just don't want Aldor getting a preview of my game plan for the hearing."

"He's changed so much," Everett said, not really listening to me.

"What do you mean?"

"We all came through the Academy together." Everett explained. "The choice was between me and Aldor to see who would get the second spot for the earth deployment. Michelle was the first selected."

Again, I spotted that fleeting moment of pride in his eyes.

"We were all such close friends," Everett continued. "I barely recognize him now."

"Wait, weren't you and Michelle already married?" I asked.

"No," Everett said, "we don't have your concept of 'marriage' on Centauri."

I could not believe what I was hearing. I watched Everett and Michelle interact for almost a year, and I was sure there was a no more committed couple anywhere in the universe.

I could feel Everett listening in on my thoughts. I guess I should have been clearer and told him to block himself as well.

"Of course, I love Michelle," Everett said softly, "in the same way you love Gina. But that didn't happen until long after we arrived on earth." He smiled at some passing memory. "But it is forever, I guess you sentimental earthlings wore off on us."

I let him revel in his memories a bit longer and then brought our conversation back to the matters at hand.

"So, when does this hearing take place?" I queried.

"Converting it to earth time," he said, "twenty-four hours."

"Then we better get started." I said, hoping Everett was not picking up that I was feeling like a one-legged man in an ass-kicking contest.

# CHAPTER TWENTY
# (BAFFLE THEM WITH BULLSHIT)

There's an old canon among trial lawyers that goes something like this: "If you have the law on your side, argue the law; if not, but the facts are on your side, argue the facts. But if neither the law nor the facts are on your side, then baffle them with bullshit." I was leading with the third option.

In American jurisprudence, a defendant, civil or criminal, is tried before a jury of their peers. Sometimes, that was it. You won at trial and went home. If you lost at trial, you could take the case up to an appellate court to argue before a panel of judges, no peers, that the court below, or those peers, got it wrong. Depending on a number of factors, like how strong your case was, or how much money your client had, or just how stubborn you were, you could repeat the appellate process through a couple of levels, and sometimes you got lucky and won above what you lost below. Once in a career, a lawyer may find that unicorn of a case that you can ride all the way to the Supreme Court of the United States. I never got that golden ticket working for the Valachi crime family. Criminal enterprises and death were more pedestrian than one would think.

Proceeding to argue this matter before the Centaurian Council seemed, from what I could derive from Everett, to be more like a hybrid of both trial and appellate proceedings. The citizens on the Council were your peers, with no apparent specialized training, just a set of simple rules to follow and the ability to read your mind. Transgressing a rule was a rare event, Everett reminded me, having explained to me on the night of our first meeting back on earth that Centaurians lived a strife free life. But when it did occur, Council members were also the final arbiters, so there would be no appeal.

Notwithstanding that I was at a telepathic disadvantage, given that the Council was the supreme law of the planet, I had finally found my unicorn, and I only had to travel 4.2 million light years to get there. One way or the other, this was going to be my last hurrah, the big show, so I was going to give it everything I got.

We worked like dogs for the next twenty-four hours, stopping only long enough to eat, and in my case, to relieve myself, but then only once. I took Everett through every day of his time on earth, covering every successful mission he accomplished on behalf of the Centaurians. I hammered home the strategy that he was to tell the Council how much he had sacrificed to carry out their mission. He had moved trillions of miles from home, away from his people, to live among an arguably violent and hostile race, and to frustrate their technological endeavors at great risk to his personal safety. He had to live as a human, which given what he had experienced on Centauri, was quite a step down on every level, even his physical appearance. He had forfeited his chances to rise through the ranks of the Centauri, and maybe even lost an opportunity to sit on the Council. There was no arguing that he did not violate the Prime Directive, I was exhibit A, so I was going for the sympathy vote.

I was used to not working with notes because most of my legal knowledge seemed to be uploaded into this weird mental cloud storage, where it lay dormant until a certain issue required its application, in which case it was quickly located and downloaded, and appeared instantly at the tip of my tongue. I had once described it as like playing the television version of "Who Wants to Be A Millionaire" with Clarence Darrow as my lifeline. It had basically carried me through my legal career on earth, so I was happy to see that it had made the trip with me.

But given that this was so fact intensive, at the hearing before the Council, I really only had to serve as a living cue to the relevant sections of the story of Everett's life, which had indeed been incredible.

I was about to take Everett through it all again, one final time, when he suddenly stiffened in his seat. Instantly, the galvanization returned to my body and the kaleidoscope colors appeared before my eyes. Then blackness.

# CHAPTER TWENTY-ONE
# (HUMAN IN THE ARENA)

This time, as my eyes cleared, I sucked in air like I had just completed an underwater, hundred-yard swim. My lungs were burning. My gasp was audible and echoed throughout the room.

I was sitting at a holographic table of clear material, with matching chair, in a huge, rectangular room with thirty-foot ceilings. My table and chair sat directly in the middle of the room, which had to be one hundred feet long by fifty feet wide. Rising up on either side, starting above fifteen-foot walls, were ascending stands with rows of far more luxurious, blood-red seating than you would find at most sports venues. Behind me was an additional section of equally ostentatious seating. The walls, floor and ceiling gave off the ubiquitous yellowish glow that provided enough light to see clearly. There were no obvious portals.

On the wall before me were what appeared to be nine separate balconies, one large one in the center with the eight others encircling it like identical, equidistant points on an octagon. They each had a single, magenta colored *cátedra* that could have passed for a decent throne.

I was completely alone. I stood and took a better look around the room. It had the feel of those combo gym-theatre rooms you could find in some universities on earth. As I stared at the surrounding walls, I could feel a palpable energy that appeared to be responding to my growing attention to it. It felt like Jayney, on steroids.

01010111 01100101 01101100 01100011 01101111 01101101
01100101 00101110
*Welcome.*

Then the numeric whispers started.

01010100 01101000 01100001 01110100 00100111 01110011
00100000 01101000 01101001 01101101 00101100 00100000
01110100 01101000 01100101 00100000 01100101 01100001
01110010 01110100 01101000 01101100 01101001 01101110
01100111 00101110
*That's him, the earthling.*

01001000 01100101 00100111 01110011 00100000 01110011
01101111 00100000 01100100 01100001 01110010 01101011
00101110
*He's so dark.*

01010100 01101000 01100101 01111001 00100000 01110011
01100001 01111001 00100000 01101000 01100101 00100000
01101000 01100001 01110011 00100000 01101000 01100001
01101001 01110010 00100000 01100001 01101100 01101100
00100000 01101111 01110110 01100101 01110010 00100000
01101000 01101001 01110011 00100000 01100010 01101111
01100100 01111001 00101110
*They say he has hair all over his body.*

These and similar comments started to flood my brain to the point where it became like white noise in the background.

A movement drew my attention upwards, and suddenly the stands were completely filled with Centaurians of both sexes, though uniform in beauty, fitness, and size. Some were dressed in the long robes of The Nim Trio and others wore various colored outfits similar to my own. They all gazed back at me *en masse* in aural silence, like I was the main attraction at the circus. Given I could hear their thoughts, and apparently that of the room, Everett's invisible tinfoil hat must have been limited to blocking just Aldor's mental eavesdropping.

"Welcome and thank you for coming." I shouted as I raised my right hand above me in a salute and slowly rotated to face the entire crowd. If this was going to be Ringling Brothers, I was intent on being the Ring Master, not the clown.

The sound of my voice must have been as palpable to the Centaurians as the energy of the room was to me, because the entire audience sat back in their chairs in one motion as if trying to avoid a wave of water at the killer whale exhibit in Sea World.

Then the white noise in my head intensified as they turned back and forth to each other with silent expressions of excitement on their faces. I was the talking monkey.

My brain suddenly quieted, as the audience all stood in unison and faced the front of the room. There, in each of the eight octagon points, stood one Centaurian, each facing the center balcony, which remained empty. There was an equal number of males and females, and while I could not be sure from this distance, they each looked older than the general population in the stands, their hair a shade whiter than the golden blonde manes of the others. Their outfits were also more comparable in obvious splendor to that of Aldor's, than to the others, or mine for that matter.

I could have heard a pin drop in my head as they all stood waiting.

01010111 01100101 01101100 01100011 01101111 01101101
01100101 00100000 01010000 01100101 01110100 01110010
01101001 01100011 01101000 01101111 01110010 00101110
*Welcome Petrichor.*

I could not tell if that thought came from the room or the crowd.

A bright white flash heralded the materialization of another Centaurian in the center balcony.

Given my human limitations, I could not trust my perception of this being. In this world, where even the men were more beautiful than most women on earth, this woman that appeared was the pick of the Centaurian litter. She was well over six feet tall, with thick, golden tresses that cascaded over her bare shoulders and came to rest on the upper edges of her ample, yet firm breasts. Her body was clothed in an off the shoulder, full-length gown that shimmered with its own luminescence, but did not hide her slender waist and full, curvaceous hips. The gown had a thigh-high slit up one side, which from just above the balcony wall, displayed the top of her pale, perfectly formed, leg.

Her divine face embodied the Greek golden ratio of beauty, *Phi*. It was perfectly symmetrical, slightly longer than its width, and her almond shaped, Nordic blue eyes, slightly upturned nose and full lips could not have been improved by the most talented plastic surgeon. She wore no makeup, yet her skin glittered in the ambient light. Matching thin dark blonde eyebrows completed the mesmerizing effect.

Unlike all of the other Centaurians I had met, there was nothing androgenous about her. She looked as though she had just descended from Mount Olympus. I could not take my eyes off her.

Petrichor extended her arms in a welcoming fashion to the crowd and then the others in the surrounding balconies. I could tell by the increase in the melded numerical white noise in my head that the crowd was reciprocating. Then she sat in her seat and all others did as well. I continued to stand by my table and chair, hypnotically gazing up at the balcony, hoping my mind did not reflect my mental tongue hanging to my chin. I was almost startled by the aural sound of a voice.

"Our citizen Everett has requested that his friend, Jimmy Moran, represent him in this matter before the Council." Aldor said from a chair and table that, like him, was not present on the floor a moment ago. "Everett also requests that we conduct this hearing in spoken English, so as to not put his representative at any more of a disadvantage. I have no objection to this request"

Petrichor turned to face each of the other members of the council, communicating as a group in silence. The numbers they exchanged were too fast for me to decipher.

Petrichor turned to face me and nodded her head. "At first, the Council voted to deny Citizen Everett's request, as your presence was neither summoned by the Council, nor have we ever allowed for anyone but the accused to present their arguments before us. Indeed, your patent limitations will unduly delay the resolution of this hearing."

"I understand, but –" I started to say.

"However," she continued, holding up her hand to silence me, "this is an unusually grave matter, and given the possible repercussions, it is – what is the human word I'm looking for – oh yes, fair, that we indulge Citizen Everett's request for your limited representation."

Her euphonious voice and beauty did little to take the sting out of her public and pessimistic assessment of my intellect and abilities. This was not the first time in my life that I had been publicly shit on by the Prom Queen and thankfully it snapped me right back into my adversarial mindset. Still, I felt my face flush as I stood and bowed respectfully. Game on.

# CHAPTER TWENTY-TWO
# (A ONCE RIGHTEOUS MAN)

I saw a flash to my right in my peripheral vision and, before I could turn, Everett appeared, dressed in an emerald green, floor length robe that was of comparable quality to Aldor's and that of the lesser Council members. My holographic table expanded with an additional chair beside me. The white noise in my head rose another level as the audience in the stands telepathically conferred excitedly with one another. I waived Everett into the seat and leaned over to him.

"Why am I hearing everyone's thoughts?" I whispered.

"What?" Everett responded, looking surprised.

"Didn't you block them from accessing my head?"

"I did, they can't," he replied.

"But I'm hearing them." I whispered.

"That's impossible." Everett said dismissively.

01001010 01101001 01101101 01101101 01111001 00100111
01110011 00100000 01101100 01101111 01110011 01101001
01101110 01100111 00100000 01101001 01110100 00101110
*Jimmy's losing it.*

I reached over and pulled him close enough that my mouth was right by his ear.

"I'll show you who's losing it, you prick. I'm now hearing you. What the fuck's happening to me?"

Everett turned to me and focused. I could feel him entering and rifling through my mind. He paused for a moment, his eyes reflecting his astonishment.

"I can't explain it," he whispered, "my shield is still in place, so they can't read your mind, but you did, you can, read our thoughts."

"How does it work?" I asked him, hoping that it may come in handy. He just stared at me.

01001010 01110101 01110011 01110100 00100000 01100110
01101111 01100011 01110101 01110011 00100000 01101111
01101110 00100000 01110100 01101000 01100101 00100000
01110000 01100101 01110010 01110011 01101111 01101110
00100000 01101111 01110010 00100000 01100111 01110010
01101111 01110101 01110000 00100000 01111001 01101111
01110101 00100000 01110111 01100001 01101110 01110100
00100000 01110100 01101111 00100000 01101100 01101001
01110011 01110100 01100101 01101110 00100000 01110100
01101111 00101110

*Just focus on the person or group you want to listen to.*

01000011 01100001 01101110 00100000 01110100 01101000
01100101 01111001 00100000 01100010 01101100 01101111
01100011 01101011 00100000 01101101 01100101 00111111

*Can they block me?*

01001111 01101110 01101100 01111001 00100000 01101001
01100110 00100000 01110100 01101000 01100101 01111001
00100000 01110010 01100101 01100001 01101100 01101001
01111010 01100101 00100000 01110111 01101000 01100001
01110100 00100000 01111001 01101111 01110101 00100000
01100001 01110010 01100101 00100000 01100100 01101111
01101001 01101110 01100111 00101110

*Only if they realize what you are doing.*

I nodded and winked at him.

"Members of the Council," Aldor interrupted our silent parley. "Jimmy Moran is something of a counselor back on earth. So, I ask your indulgence and allow us to follow his antiquated procedure as we proceed. Having chosen his champion from a lesser race, Citizen Everett needs every advantage we can give him."

I could hear the binary interactions between Aldor and the Council as he displayed a summary of my legal career from what he mined from my mind during our first meeting. It was moving way too fast to catch it all, but I was able to capture the gist of it.

"So, Members of the Council, let me begin by stating why we are here today," Aldor said, doing his poor man's best to work some emotion into his voice. "Citizen Everett has been brought before this Council to answer to the charges that, during an incident that occurred not more than two Centaurian months ago, when he was voluntarily and openly interacting with humans, and other creatures, back on earth, Citizen Everett violated the Centauri Prime Directive, when using our technology, he did resuscitate and revive the dead body of a human."

Aldor turned from the Council and pointed directly at me.

"Jimmy Moran is that human!"

Suddenly, the walls of the room came alive like a 3-D Jumbotron and I again witnessed the final events the night that Dan Pearsall, the last standing member of the Valachi hit squad sent to find me, shot and killed me in front of my home in Berthoud, Colorado. However, these memories were not from my point of view, as I was able to witness what had occurred when I had passed to the far side of the veil. I turned to Everett who was staring, apologetically.

01001001 00100000 01101000 01100001 01100100 00100000
01110100 01101111 00100000 01110000 01110010 01100101
01110011 01100101 01101110 01110100 00100000 01110100
01101000 01100101 01101101 00100000 01110111 01101001
01110100 01101000 00100000 01101101 01111001 00100000
01101101 01100101 01101110 01110100 01100001 01101100
00100000 01110010 01100101 01100011 01101111 01101100
01101100 01100101 01100011 01110100 01101001 01101111
01101110 00100000 01101111 01100110 00100000 01110100
01101000 01100101 00100000 01100101 01110110 01100101
01101110 01110100 01110011 00100000 01110101 01110000

01101111 01101110 00100000 01101101 01111001 00100000
01100001 01110010 01110010 01101001 01110110 01100001
01101100 00101100 00100000 01101001 01110100 00100000
01110111 01100001 01110011 00100000 01100010 01100101
01100110 01101111 01110010 01100101 00100000 01111001
01101111 01110101 00100000 01101001 01101110 01110011
01110100 01110010 01110101 01100011 01110100 01100101
01100100 00100000 01101101 01100101 00100000 01110100
01101111 00100000 01100010 01101100 01101111 01100011
01101011 00100000 01110100 01101000 01100101 01101101
00101110

*I had to present them with my mental recollection of the events upon my arrival, it was before you instructed me to block them.*

My fingers instinctively reached for the now missing scar above my heart. I felt someone's stare and looked up to see Petrichor gazing at me. I attempted to look behind her mental curtain but could not sense anything. It was a vault. But she continued to study me.

01000010 01110101 01110100 00100000 01001001 00100000
01100100 01101001 01100100 01101110 00100111 01110100
00100000 01110100 01100101 01101100 01101100 00100000
01110100 01101000 01100101 01101101 00100000 01100001
01100010 01101111 01110101 01110100 00100000 01000011
01101100 01100001 01101001 01110010 01100101 00101110

*But I didn't tell them about Claire.*

The mental noise in my head from the stands suddenly reached a deafening crescendo as the crowd absorbed and shared what might have been the first murder anyone on this planet had witnessed visually. I had to force myself not to wince from its strain on my brain.

01000011 01100001 01101110 00100000 01111001 01101111
01110101 00100000 01100010 01101100 01101111 01100011

01101011 00100000 01110100 01101000 01100101 00100000
01100011 01110010 01101111 01110111 01100100 00100000
01100011 01101111 01101101 01101101 01100101 01101110
01110100 01100001 01110010 01111001 00111111

*Can you block the crowd commentary?*

Everett did not look over at me, but just imperceptibly nodded. The crowd sounds disappeared like he had turned off a radio.

One of the older men on the counsel slowly raised his hand, and Petrichor nodded in acknowledgment. He spoke haltingly, like there was a lot of rust on his voice box.

"Does Citizen Everett deny breaching the Prime Directive in this manner?"

Everett rose to respond but I reached over and stopped him. I stood instead.

"Esteemed Members of the Centauri Council," I began, pushing my chair back and stepping out from behind the table, "there is no denying that Ev, er Citizen Everett did, in fact, bring me back from the dead, using his Hadron Distributor." My well-practiced courtroom voice made all others sound like they came from an old Victrola Vinyl Record player.

This time one of the women on the Council spoke, with an ease that led me to believe she may have secretly been talking out loud to herself when she showered, assuming they did shower. "Then what is there left to decide, except for the punishment?"

I looked over and saw that Aldor was preening before the crowd in the stands, and without needing to look into his head, could tell he thought this game was over.

"Well, Madam Council member," I said with a deferential nod in her direction, "back on earth, even when there is proof that a crime has been committed, the defendant is allowed to present his interpretation of the facts in order to establish that there were mitigating circumstances that would impact both the judgment, and if warranted, the punishment."

I peeked into her head and knew that she not only understood my position, but that she was fascinated by this change in the hearing process, like the first time a modern earth child, weaned on an iPhone, gets to play with an antique Underwood typewriter.

She nodded back, "proceed, Jimmy Moran."

I leaned over Everett's chair from behind, placing my two hands on either side of his shoulders, and whispered. "It's showtime."

Just like we practiced, Everett began to roll out his visual memories from the moment he left the academy, to his flight with Michelle to earth, then through each mission he carried out on behalf of the Centauri people in the skies and space around earth for the past eighty earth years. At first, the visual stream was moving at their natural speed of thought, which for me played like a blur on the Jumbotron walls but did not seem to negatively impact the attention given by the citizens in the stands or the Members of the Council. Everyone in the room had their eyes closed as they tuned in directly to the mental presentation on their own mind's screens. Everyone in the room, that is, except me and Petrichor. Our gazes locked.

01010111 01101000 01100001 01110100 00100000 01101101
01100001 01101110 01101110 01100101 01110010 00100000
01101111 01100110 00100000 01101000 01110101 01101101
01100001 01101110 00100000 01100001 01110010 01100101
00100000 01111001 01101111 01110101 00100000 01110100
01101000 01100001 01110100 00100000 01111001 01101111
01110101 00100000 01100011 01100001 01101110 00100000
01110010 01100101 01100001 01100100 00100000 01101111
01110101 01110010 00100000 01110100 01101000 01101111
01110101 01100111 01101000 01110100 01110011 00111111

*What manner of human are you that you can read our thoughts?*

I looked away and waited for his show to end where we had planned, when he took the last of his assigned satellites out of commission. I leaned back over and whispered to Everett.

"You sure Petrichor can't tune in on my thoughts?"

Everett thought about it for a moment then whispered back, "not unless there's been some form of evolutionary leap in my absence."

01010111 01101000 01100001 01110100 00100000 01110100
01101000 01100101 00100000 01100110 01110101 01100011
01101011 00100000 01100001 01110010 01100101 00100000

01111001 01101111 01110101 00100000 01110100 01100001
01101100 01101011 01101001 01101110 01100111 00100000
01100001 01100010 01101111 01110101 01110100 00111111

*What the fuck are you talking about?*


01001001 01110100 00100000 01101000 01100001 01110011
01101110 00100111 01110100 00100000 01101000 01100001
01110000 01110000 01100101 01101110 01100101 01100100
00100000 01100110 01101111 01110010 00100000 01110100
01100101 01101110 00100000 01110100 01101000 01101111
01110101 01110011 01100001 01101110 01100100 00100000
01111001 01100101 01100001 01110010 01110011 00101110

*It hasn't happened for ten thousand years.*


With Everett's show-and-tell about his exemplary foreign service to the citizens of Centauri and by extension, the other inhabitants of the galaxy now concluded, I again addressed the Council.

"As you have witnessed, with all due respect, no one among you has made the sacrifices Everett has had to endure for all this time, and still follow every assignment he has received from home." I turned to the audience in the back of the hall. "In the end, as part of those same duties to carefully shepherd my people of earth towards their ordained future place among the more enlightened members of the galactic family, and as a representative of the good people of Centauri, as clearly presented by Citizen Aldor, Everett acted in the heat of a moment, to render aid to another, less fortunate, being. If there was ever to be an exception to the strict adherence to the Prime Directive, this is it."

One of the other men on the Council now raised his hand and, with Petrichor's indulgence, asked in an annoyingly high-pitched voice, like he had been sucking helium, "what of Citizen Michelle? Did we not just witness that she demanded that Citizen Everett breach the Prime Directive?"


01000100 01101111 01101110 00100111 01110100 00100000
01101100 01100101 01110100 00100000 01110100 01101000
01100101 01101101 00100000 01100010 01110010 01101001
01101110 01100111 00100000 01001101 01101001 01100011

01101000 01100101 01101100 01101100 01100101 00100000
01101001 01101110 01110100 01101111 00100000 01110100
01101000 01101001 01110011 00101110 00100000 00100000
01001001 00100000 01101101 01100001 01100100 01100101
00100000 01110100 01101000 01100101 00100000 01100110
01101001 01101110 01100001 01101100 00100000 01100100
01100101 01100011 01101001 01110011 01101001 01101111
01101110 00101110

*Don't let them bring Michelle into this. I made the final decision.*

"Citizen Michelle has not been recalled on this matter," I said, doing my best to tap dance around the logic of his enquiry, "and it is Citizen Everett who has appeared before the Council to accept full responsibility for this conduct, which was concededly carried out on his own volition."

I could see from his thoughts that Councilman Squeaky had bought my bullshit.

"Honorable Members of the Council," Aldor's voiced now interjected, "even if you were to accept Jimmy Moran's argument that Citizen Everett's past foreign service to our populace warranted some dispensation for what he purports was life-giving aid to another worthy member of our galaxy, which I do not, the evidence does not support his position."

Aldor turned and stared directly at me.

"I put it to the Council," Aldor slowly continued, pointing in my direction, "there is nothing 'worthy' about Jimmy Moran."

It all happened so fast, I barely remember crossing the space between us, or the blow I landed on Aldor's cute little nose, and I did not even notice the galvanization or see the speckled colors that immediately followed. It all just went black.

# CHAPTER TWENTY-THREE
## (A PAIR OF COOL NEW GENES)

I awoke back in the doorless chamber I first found myself in, again in my holographic bed, commando under my holographic sheets. But this time I could not move. I was wrapped in one of those energy cocoons that would not even allow me to turn my head. I was able to move my mouth, so I stuck out my tongue and licked my lips. The beard still felt strange to me.

01010100 01101000 01100001 01110100 00100000 01110111
01100001 01110011 00100000 01110001 01110101 01101001
01110100 01100101 00100000 01100001 00100000 01110000
01100101 01110010 01100110 01101111 01110010 01101101
01100001 01101110 01100011 01100101 00100000 01111001
01101111 01110101 00100000 01110000 01110101 01110100
00100000 01101111 01101110 00100000 01100010 01100101
01100110 01101111 01110010 01100101 00100000 01110100
01101000 01100101 00100000 01000011 01101111 01110101
01101110 01100011 01101001 01101100 00101110 00100000
01001001 01110100 00100000 01110100 01101111 01101111
01101011 00100000 01110011 01100101 01110010 01101001
01101111 01110101 01110011 00100000 01100101 01100110
01100110 01101111 01110010 01110100 01110011 00100000

01100010 01111001 00100000 01110011 01101111 01101101
01100101 00100000 01101111 01100110 00100000 01101111
01110101 01110010 00100000 01100010 01100101 01110011
01110100 00100000 01110011 01100011 01101001 01100101
01101110 01110100 01101001 01110011 01110100 01110011
00100000 01110100 01101111 00100000 01110010 01100101
01100010 01110101 01101001 01101100 01100100 00100000
01000011 01101001 01110100 01101001 01111010 01100101
01101110 00100000 01000001 01101100 01100100 01101111
00100111 01110011 00100000 01101110 01101111 01110011
01100101 00101110

*That was quite a performance you put on before the Council. It took serious efforts by some of our best scientists to rebuild Citizen Aldor's nose.*

I strained my eyes to the left and saw Dr. Nim, flying solo, standing there with a look of disapproval I had not seen since Sister Anna Cleta caught me kissing Elaine Staltare behind the St. Margaret's rectory.

01000100 01101111 01101110 00100111 01110100 00100000
01110000 01101100 01100001 01111001 00100000 01100100
01110101 01101101 01100010 00101110 00100000 00100000
01001001 00100000 01101011 01101110 01101111 01110111
00100000 01111001 01101111 01110101 00100000 01100011
01100001 01101110 00100000 01101000 01100101 01100001
01110010 00100000 01101101 01111001 00100000 01100010
01101001 01101110 01100001 01110010 01111001 00100000
01110100 01101000 01101111 01110101 01100111 01101000
01110100 01110011 00101110

*Don't play dumb. I know you can hear my binary thoughts.*

I looked back at Nim with as blank a stare as I could muster. "How long have I been here?"

01000101 01101001 01100111 01101000 01110100 00100000
01100101 01100001 01110010 01110100 01101000 00100000
01101000 01101111 01110101 01110010 01110011 00101110

*Eight earth hours.*

I did not react.

"Okay," Nim said out loud, "have it your way, but genetics don't lie."

"What are you talking about?" I asked, as innocently as possible.

"I've run your genome against our historical database for your species, *Homo Sapiens.*" Nim continued aurally. "Humans have 22 pairs of distinct, active autosomal chromosomes, plus two chromosomes more to determine your sex."

Nim manifested a floating holographic workstation which she engaged telepathically at a speed I could not follow. Then it all slowed down to my speed.

01000011 01100101 01101110 01110100 01100001 01110101
01110010 01101001 01100001 01101110 01110011 00100000
01101000 01100001 01110110 01100101 00100000 01110100
01110111 01100101 01101110 01110100 01111001 00101101
01100110 01101111 01110101 01110010 00100000 01110000
01100001 01101001 01110010 01110011 00100000 01101111
01100110 00100000 01100011 01101000 01110010 01101111
01101101 01101111 01110011 01101111 01101101 01100101
01110011 00101100 00100000 01110000 01101100 01110101
01110011 00100000 01110100 01101000 01100101 00100000
01110100 01110111 01101111 00100000 01110011 01100101
01111000 00100000 01100111 01100101 01101110 01100101
01110011 00101100 00100000 01110100 01110111 01100101
01101110 01110100 01111001 00101101 01110100 01110111
01101111 00100000 01101111 01100110 00100000 01110111
01101000 01101001 01100011 01101000 00100000 01110111
01100101 00100000 01110011 01101000 01100001 01110010
01100101 00100000 01110111 01101001 01110100 01101000
00100000 01101000 01110101 01101101 01100001 01101110
01110011

*Centaurians have twenty-four pairs of chromosomes, plus the two sex genes, twenty-two of which we share with humans.*

"Would you like to guess how many chromosome pairs you have?" She said out loud, waving away the workstation and returning to my bedside.

"The same as the rest of us evolved, hairy earth monkeys," I said, still ignoring her attempt to trap me and refusing to consider where she was taking this, "and I would like to be freed from this wrapper, I really need to piss."

"You're not going to hit me in the nose, are you?" She teased, the curl of the smile rising in her cheeks.

"I may," I quipped, as lightly as I could manage, "if you don't release me before I piss myself."

Suddenly, the energy cocoon disappeared. I quickly stretched my neck and limbs, wrapped the sheet around me, stood and looked around the room. I focused on the wall closest to the bed and a holographic urinal appeared, *circa* 1964, St. Margaret's school. It even had a metallic handle. I had not fully expunged the ghost of Sister Anna Cleta from my memory.

"Thank you," I said as I went about my business.

```
01010100 01101000 01100001 01110100 00100000 01110111
01100001 01110011 01101110 00100111 01110100 00100000
01101101 01100101 00101100 00100000 01110100 01101000
01101111 01110101 01100111 01101000 00100000 01101110
01101001 01100011 01100101 01101100 01111001 00100000
01100100 01101111 01101110 01100101 00101110
```
*That wasn't me, though nicely done.*


My penis has gotten me into trouble a few times in my youth, but this took it to a whole new and totally unexpected level, without any of the benefits. I took a few extra seconds giving it a shake while I figured out my next move.

```
01010111 01101000 01101111 00100000 01100101 01101100
01110011 01100101 00100000 01101011 01101110 01101111
01110111 01110011 00111111
```
*Who else knows?*


"Now you're just showing off." Nim said out loud. "Even if a bit slow, that was pretty impressive."

I turned back to face her. The urinal disappeared.

01001010 01110101 01110011 01110100 00100000 01101101
01100101 00100000 01100001 01101110 01100100 00100000
01010000 01100101 01110100 01110010 01101001 01100011
01101000 01101111 01110010 00101110

*Just me and Petrichor.*

"She is the one who ordered the tests after she saw the way you moved through the Council Hall," Nim continued aurally, "Everyone who was there is talking about it."

I thought I detected some excitement in Nim's voice.

"I guess I'm finished representing Everett," I said.

"Well, the men on the Council were very upset, as they are all friends with Aldor, and wanted you barred from the remainder of the proceedings," Nim said, a little conspiratorially, "but the female members of the Council argued that it would not be fair to Citizen Everett to bar you at this point of the hearing, since you have also become a central issue in this matter. So, they overruled the men five to four."

"Exactly, how much does Petrichor know?" I asked.

"She was reviewing your files as fast as I uploaded them."

"And those files told her, just what exactly?"

"While you are not a perfect match, given that humans still have some of those dormant genes that we do not have, you now match us to our twenty-four pairs, plus the two fun genes. And that is just since you arrived. Pairs twenty-three and twenty-four just came on-line. In short, you're evolving."

"How?" I asked, incredulous.

"Not sure. Still working on that. Could be something happened to your body when Everett zapped you with the Hadron Distributor. Could be your trip through the wormhole. Could be a combination of both."

She held up a tiny clear vial of milky colored fluid between her thumb and middle finger and gave it a little shake, as if trying to wake something up, then slipped it into her pocket. "I will have to run some more tests." She paused to give me the once over. "Either way, you are one of us now."

With that, the hologram bed and sheet disappeared, and I stood naked before Nim for a one-Mississippi count before my clothes again covered me. I could not help but smile when she winked, and then disappeared.

Then the hair and goosebumps on my body rose and the colored speckles flooded my vision. This time I sucked in a deep breath before passing out.

# CHAPTER TWENTY-FOUR
# (FOOL FOR A CLIENT)

When I recovered my senses, I was again sitting at the large clear table in the Council Hall. This time, I was the last to the party. I looked around the stands and saw that the seats were gone, and it was now standing room only. The ubiquitous blue eyes all devoured me with the same anticipation you see in the faces of Bronx zoo visitors as they wait for the gorilla to throw itself against the thick, plexiglass enclosure. Thank God Everett had tuned them out of my head.

01000001 01110010 01100101 00100000 01111001 01101111
01110101 00100000 01101111 01101011 01100001 01111001
00111111

*Are you okay?*

I turned and saw Everett in his seat beside me. He looked concerned. I gestured towards Aldor, sitting quietly in his chair, avoiding my gaze. They did a hell of a job on his nose. His eyes were not even blackened.

01001001 00100000 01101000 01100101 01100001 01110010
00100000 01001001 00100000 01100100 01101001 01100100
00100000 01100010 01100101 01110100 01110100 01100101
01110010 00100000 01110100 01101000 01100001 01101110

00100000 01100110 01110101 01100011 01101011 00101101
01100110 01100001 01100011 01100101 00100000 01101111
01110110 01100101 01110010 00100000 01110100 01101000
01100101 01110010 01100101 00101110

*I hear I did better than fuck-face over there.*

Everett laughed for the first time since we left earth. The crowd became animated in response.

"Are you ready to proceed, Citizen Aldor?" Came Petrichor's beautiful, but unemotional voice.

Aldor nodded respectfully.

"And you, Jimmy Moran, are you ready to proceed?" She asked me in turn.

01001110 01101111 00100000 01101101 01101111 01110010
01100101 00100000 01110110 01101001 01101111 01101100
01100101 01101110 01100011 01100101 00101110

*No more violence.*

I stood and nodded respectfully to each of the Council Members, Petrichor last.

"I apologize to the Council for my misconduct," I said, before turning towards Aldor, "and I especially apologize to Citizen Aldor, I hope I did not cause him any permanent damage."

Aldor looked away.

"If I had my way, you would be permanently energy locked." He spat out in response.

I could tell from the snippets I could pull from the minds of the members of the Council that I had lost the men completely and that the women were on the fence. This was going to be an uphill battle.

"We are a passionate race," I continued. "But that is no excuse for my actions. I should not have taken offense at Citizen Aldor's poor choice of words. After all, English is not his native tongue."

I stared over at Aldor, who continued to avoid my gaze.

"Proceed, Citizen Aldor." Petrichor said.

Aldor stood and addressed the Council. "As previously stated, even if Citizen Everett could be excused for transgressing the Prime Directive, his returning Jimmy Moran to life by the use of our sacred technology was completely unwarranted. Because, as the human demonstrated during our last hearing, and as I will now demonstrate in more detail, the earth, indeed our galaxy, was better off with Jimmy Moran dead."

Again, the 3-D Jumbotron walls came to life, and a series of memories poached by Aldor from my mind upon my arrival began to play for the crowd and the Members of the Council.

The first memory that played was so old, at first, I did not remember it. There were a bunch of teenagers sitting around a fire in the woods. It was clearly summer because the teens were all dressed in shorts and t-shirts. I could see cars and motorcycles parked in the surrounding woods, just outside the light from the fire. Bottles and cans of beer at different levels of consumption were passing among the teens. One of the teens, who I recognized now as my childhood friend, Mark Wallen, could be seen polishing off a half-pint of vodka, before tossing the empty bottle into the fire. He was clearly drunk, by the way he staggered towards the only person I could not see, but who I now realized was me, sitting on a log by the fire.

"C'mon Jimmy," Mark said, his words slurring. "Let's get the fuck out of here."

"Can't you wait a bit?" I could hear my young voice ask him. "I'm kinda working on something here."

My eyes went from Mark to a pretty young brunette whose name now escaped me.

"C'mon Jimmy," Mark insisted. "She'll keep, won't you darling." He said, nodding appreciatively at my companion. "I'm too drunk to ride the bike home."

"Jimmy," the teenage girl said with enough feigned innocence to suggest seduction, while reaching over and placing her hand reassuringly on my thigh, "you said you were going to drive me home tonight."

I looked up at Mark who had been witnessing the exchange. "Just give me an hour," I pleaded. "I'll come back for you and take you home then. We can come back and retrieve your bike tomorrow."

Mark smiled and gave me a wink. He grabbed the half-finished beer from my hand, chugged the rest of it, then tossed the empty glass bottle into the fire.

"Sure thing, Jimmy," Mark called over his shoulder as he staggered out into the woods. "I'm just going to take a piss and a nap. I'll be waiting for you when you get back."

The walls all faded to black.

The next memory consisted of shaded silhouettes of glistening arms, legs, and more tantalizing body parts maneuvering in close proximity in the reclined front seat of a 1969 Dodge Dart, softly back lit by a faded streetlight through the condensation on its front windshield. The soundtrack of moans and slapping moist flesh seemed to agitate the crowd in the stands as much as it embarrassed me. I looked up at the Council members but only Petrichor returned my gaze. Her mind was silent, but her face was flushed.

The event triggered; I knew what was coming next.

The interior of St. Margaret's church appeared, and I could see through tear-distorted vision that the seats were filled with every friend and family from my Riverdale neighborhood. Everyone was weeping as I slowly passed them down the center aisle to the mournful sounding organ music coming from somewhere above me. I could see the white-haired, tonsured rearview of the head of Father Murphy, slowly leading a procession of altar boys carrying a large cross and incense thurible a few feet ahead. I glanced to my immediate left and saw the front corner of the silver casket resting on my left shoulder. The walls faded to black.

A beautiful headstone appeared before us. It was a warm sunny day in what I recognized was Gate of Heaven Cemetery in Westchester County, New York. The inscription in the smooth marble read Mark F. Wallen, May 1, 1956 to May 23, 1974. I could hear my younger voice talking through the weeping, "I'm sorry Mark, I did come back, but you were gone. I should have driven you home when you asked." The walls faded to black. I felt Everett's hand on my shoulder in an attempt to console me. He did not need to say anything, aurally or telepathically.

"Members of the Council," Aldor's voice shattered the memory before the darkness could take it completely, "the people on earth form special bonds with others, sometimes from their earliest years. Some relationships are more important than others. Some less."

He turned to the crowd in the stands. "Personally, I don't understand it, but so be it." Aldor waved his hands dramatically as he continued to pace. He engaged as many eyes in the crowd as he could while allowing his punctuated silence to build the drama. Something about him reminded me of a certain New York City douchebag Assistant District Attorney named Sam Douglas I had crossed swords with on a number of occasions. If Aldor had ever managed to fully incorporate the use of human inflection, he could have been a stellar member of any legal bar on earth.

"What you have just witnessed was one of the special bonds Jimmy Moran had with another young human named Mark Wallen. I think the term the humans use is 'best friend.'"

Aldor let that settle in a moment.

"Indeed, I put it to you that Citizen Everett has formed just such a bond with Jimmy Moran," Aldor said. "And he would have the Council believe that the bond was so strong that he had no choice but to save his friend from death."

"But you can see, on the night in question, Jimmy refused the request of his obviously disabled 'best friend' for assistance returning home. Jimmy instead chose to copulate with the young female earthling." Aldor let that last part seep in before continuing. I thought I saw some of the women on the Council squirm in their seats.

"And as a result of Jimmy Moran's selfishness, that young friend died when he tried to make it home on his own. There was no one around to bring Mark Wallen back."

Aldor stopped for a moment and raised his finger in the air to emphasize his point, "nor should there have been. Humans in general do not deserve to receive the ultimate benefit of recaptured reanimation through the use of our technology. Indeed, it is something that is sparingly used among our own people here on Centauri. But as I will continue to show you, Jimmy Moran, specifically, did not deserve to be brought back to life."

The darkened walls came to life with my memory of the night Uncle Ty Valachi made the decision to kill Joey and Phil Santiago, two ambitious, but low-level drug dealers who tried to encroach on Valachi's territory in the Inwood neighborhood of upper Manhattan. We were sitting around a table in the back room of one of Valachi's automobile chop shops, close to the Broadway Bridge on 225th Street. Dan Pearsall was finishing off the last of the Chinese take-out from one of the many containers littering the tabletop. Valachi was firing up his after-dinner Cohiba, its thick smoke clinging over the table like LA smog. I was making some final notes on some foolscap relevant to a movie deal Valachi had been discussing that he wanted to close the following week. My eyes were straining under the fluorescent lighting which hung directly over the table. The pungent cigar smoke only exacerbated the irritation in my eyes.

Three of Valachi's street soldiers entered the room and stood by the doorway until Dan put down his chop sticks, acknowledged them and waved them over. The largest one, whom everyone called Tiny, remained at the doorway while the two relatively more intelligent looking men approached the table, one falling back a few feet away while the smallest one, who I knew as Franco, walked over and handed Dan an envelope. Franco looked more nervous than I had seen in the past. Dan opened the envelope and quickly reviewed its contents.

"Little light this week, Franco." Dan said as he handed me the envelope, which I then initialed and placed in my leather briefcase; besides the other stack of envelopes we had collected throughout the evening.

"I'm sorry Mr. Valachi," Franco stammered, his voice tightening with the stress. "It's the goddam spics from Washington Heights. They've been selling their cheap shit over by Fort Tryon Park. That's where all the white boys from Kingsbridge come South to score. Prime real estate!"

"Do these young Latinos have names?" Dan asked.

"They're two brothers," Franco said. He turned to the soldier a few feet away. "Dino, what's their names?"

"The older one is Joey, the younger one is Phil. I think their last name is Santiago." Dino responded.

"They gotta go." Valachi grunted, barely audibly, as he removed the Cohiba and examined it under the fluorescent lighting.

Dan looked over at Franco. "Ten g's for both brothers, package deal." He then pointed to me. "Payment on delivery, see Jimmy for details."

My next memory appearing on the 3-D Jumbotron was Franco standing in my office a few weeks later showing me a photograph from his iPhone of two contorted teenage Latinos, uncomfortably dead, in the bottom of a dumpster. If not for the severely bruised and swollen faces and the blood-splattered centered bullet hole marking each of their foreheads, they looked like a couple of sleeping kids. I removed the pair of thin leather driving gloves I kept in my upper left drawer of my desk and then stood and opened a wall safe, while Franco averted his gaze. I retrieved a vacuumed sealed bundle of twenties that I could barely get my hand around and handed them to Franco, who placed it in a small satchel.

"Thank you, Jimmy." Franco said.

"Have a nice day." I replied. Then the screen went dark.

I scanned the male members of the Council who, while visually stoic, were silently communicating in binary among themselves so quickly that I could not keep up. I tried the women, whose minds confirmed what their more expressive faces suggested, that they were horrified by the images of the dead boys, as well as my involvement.

01000010 01100001 01110010 01100010 01100001 01110010
01101001 01100011

*Barbaric*

I met Petrichor's gaze and allowed her to peek into the memory I recalled that immediately followed the last one on the Jumbotron. It was my bird's eye view of me vomiting into the waste receptacle by my desk as I recalled the recently viewed images of the two dead brothers. Then I shut her down before she could go any further.

Staying with his theme of dead siblings, Aldor next presented memories of my separate and group interactions with each of my three brothers. There were snippets from our childhood and then graduations and weddings and the birth of their children, all showing the best of what human families have to offer.

Then the screen switched to my view of the holding cell in the belly of the Metropolitan Corrections Center in lower Manhattan. It was the night I, along with all of Valachi's crew, including Dan Pearsall, had been rounded up by the Feds over the Santiago murders.

The screen transitioned to images of later that same night, after I decided to flip on the others, while I was waiting for word on the safety of my wife, Gina.

I watched along with the others as the Assistant U.S. Attorney, Mark Lafayette, walked into the room, looking sick to his stomach, and then I heard my voice.

"Did you find Gina?"

Mark Lafayette nodded, and whispered, "She's okay. We have her."

"Then what's the fucking problem?"

"Your brothers are dead."

The walls went black. But it did not matter because I had not been watching those screens. I had been watching every one of the presented memories, just like the Centaurians, in my mind's eye.

"Members of the Council," Aldor bellowed, "I put to you that Jimmy Moran's three human 'brothers,' all dead, were killed because of the contemptible choices that Jimmy Moran has made in his human life. Indeed, it was Jimmy Moran's involvement with the earlier deaths of the other young men that you have witnessed that directly led to the murders of his brothers. While Jimmy Moran, who sits before you today, walked away, unscathed."

I could literally feel the mental energy rising from the crowd, and it was brutally negative.

"But honored Council members," Aldor barked, channeling Stephen Hawking at a carnival sideshow, "death has not only followed Jimmy Moran throughout his human life, but he has also actually forfeited the life of others with his own hands."

With that, the walls again came alive with the memory of my night-time visual of the front of my home in Berthoud. I was watching the street end of my driveway from behind what I had dubbed "Gnome Island," a long rise of earth about four feet high that ran across the front of my property.

My memory displayed the approach of three men moving stealthily down the driveway toward my house. You could barely make out the weapons in their hands in the darkness. I knew that the one to my left was Dan Pearsall. I could see my Smith & Wesson handgun rise over the dirt mound and fire off a single round, then watched as the man in the middle of the group fell down dead. My eyes followed the gun's barrel as it chased the man from the group who sprinted off to my right, with the muted sounds of the rounds firing until that figure also fell forward, sliding across the grass and coming to rest against a stump, dead. Then my thoughts went black.

Every eye in the room was upon me. Aldor, ostensibly pleased with himself, glanced over at me with what appeared to be the slightest smile on his face.

"As they like to say on earth, the prosecution rests."

I considered racing across the room and breaking his nose again, but before I could execute, Petrichor stood and addressed the room.

"The Council will take a short adjournment to consider what Citizen Aldor has presented to us."

"If I may," I shouted, now on my feet, "I request the opportunity to offer a rebuttal to Citizen Aldor's clearly one-sided presentation."

Aldor looked perturbed and I could see the Council members silently but actively communicating amongst themselves. I could tell from the snippets of the binary code that the men were clearly against it. Petrichor turned to address the hall.

"We will provide Jimmy Moran with one human day to prepare this rebuttal he seeks. We will return here in 24 earth hours."

Before I could thank the Council, my skin and hair galvanized, the colors returned, and I blacked out.

# CHAPTER TWENTY-FIVE
## (WHERE THE DAY TAKES YOU)

This was beginning to feel like Ground Hog Day. I woke up back in my spartan room in my holographic bed, commando under the sheets. But this time, instead of the cute and inquisitive Dr. Nim staring at my sleeping form, I was met with the penetrating gaze of the stunningly beautiful Petrichor, who had exchanged her floor length ensemble for something that looked a bit like a golden toga.

I diverted my eyes and settled on the nicest pair of legs I had ever seen that had not been forced into shape by a pair of long stilettos. When I caught myself transfixed by her form, I hastily shifted my gaze upwards, only having to force myself to bypass her breasts, or risk focusing on her very perky nipples that were fighting against the confinement of her gown. I guess underclothes are just not a thing on Centauri. My gaze now safely above her exposed collar bones; her hair, pulled back away from her face, exposed her long and elegant neck. Every patch of visible skin was flawless. When my eyes finally returned to her face, I could see the remnants of a smile.

01000011 01101001 01110100 01101001 01111010 01100101
01101110 00100000 01000001 01101100 01100100 01101111
01110010 00100000 01101000 01100001 01110011 00100000
01100100 01101111 01101110 01100101 00100000 01100001
00100000 01110110 01100101 01110010 01111001 00100000

01101001 01101101 01110000 01110010 01100101 01110011
01110011 01101001 01110110 01100101 00100000 01101010
01101111 01100010 00100000 01100010 01100101 01100110
01101111 01110010 01100101 00100000 01110100 01101000
01100101 00100000 01000011 01101111 01110101 01101110
01100011 01101001 01101100 00101110

*Citizen Aldor has done a very impressive job before the Council.*

I had to give credit where credit was due, so I took some.

01011001 01100101 01110011 00101100 00100000 01001001
00100000 01110100 01101000 01101001 01101110 01101011
00100000 01110100 01101000 01100001 01110100 00100000
01100010 01110010 01101111 01101011 01100101 01101110
00100000 01101110 01101111 01110011 01100101 00100000
01110100 01101111 01101111 01101011 00100000 01101000
01101001 01101101 00100000 01110100 01101111 00100000
01100001 00100000 01110111 01101000 01101111 01101100
01100101 00100000 01101110 01100101 01110111 00100000
01101100 01100101 01110110 01100101 01101100 00101110

*Yes, I think that broken nose took him to a whole new level.*

She actually laughed, and it was intoxicating. She finally recovered and I felt her engaging my mind again.

"Can we do this aurally?" I asked, almost giggling at the unintended double entendre. "Keeping up with your binary transmissions is exhausting."

She thought it over and then said, "All right, we'll do it your way. Besides, you have a very pleasant-sounding voice."

"So, to what do I owe the honor of your visit?" I asked, fashioning the sheet into my own form of toga, and sitting up on the side of the bed.

She pointed to the now open end of the bed. "May I sit down?"

I scooted up a little towards the head of the bed to give her plenty of room. Then I patted the open area with my hand. "It's all yours."

I did not see her move, she just appeared beside me on the bed. As feminine and graceful as she looked, she was still an imposing figure, being at least two inches taller than I was, even in my new body. Her Nordic blue eyes emitted a sensation of gravity, and I fought the overpowering urge to draw closer to her.

"The hearing is not going very well for you or Citizen Everett." She said, earnestly.

I welcomed this distraction from the attraction I was feeling. She was right, Aldor had drawn first blood, and capitalized on the worst of my memories.

"The men on the Council are totally concurring with Citizen Aldor but the women are undecided." Petrichor continued. "You could very well lose."

I had been so busy playing catch-up since I arrived, I never had the time to consider the possibility of losing what had turned into an inquisition.

"Would the Centauri really keep Everett here, forever?" I asked.

She nodded.

"Away from Michelle?"

She nodded again. "As part of his punishment, she could never return to Centauri."

Like doctors, lawyers should never become emotionally engaged with their clients, because no matter how talented you are, you just cannot win them all. While, in some cases, like this one, the client can lose everything dear to them. Engaging in the pain of that potential outcome can paralyze you, which does not help your client. But here, I had skin in the game.

"And I guess I don't get to go home either," I said.

Petrichor stared at me for a moment with a look of disbelief, and I could not help but feel embarrassed over my self-indulgence.

"You really don't know?" She asked.

"Know what?" I responded.

"What happens to you if the Council votes against Everett."

"Everett told me I don't get to go back to earth."

Petrichor stared down at her hands, which she had anxiously clasped in her lap. A tiny tear formed at the corner of one eye. Without intending, I reached into her head.

01010111 01101000 01100001 01110100 00100000 01100001
01110010 01100101 00100000 01111001 01101111 01110101

00100000 01101110 01101111 01110100 00100000 01110100
01100101 01101100 01101100 01101001 01101110 01100111
00100000 01101101 01100101 00111111

*What are you not telling me?*

01010100 01101000 01100101 00100000 01000011 01101111
01110101 01101110 01100011 01101001 01101100 00100000
01110111 01101001 01101100 01101100 00100000 01100110
01101111 01110010 01100011 01100101 00100000 01000011
01101001 01110100 01101001 01111010 01100101 01101110
00100000 01000101 01110110 01100101 01110010 01100101
01110100 01110100 00100000 01110100 01101111 00100000
01110010 01100101 01110110 01100101 01110010 01110011
01100101 00100000 01110100 01101000 01100101 00100000
01110010 01100101 01100001 01101110 01101001 01101101
01100001 01110100 01101001 01101111 01101110 00100000
01110000 01110010 01101111 01100011 01100101 01110011
01110011 00101110

*The Council will force Citizen Everett to reverse the reanimation process.*

# CHAPTER TWENTY-SIX
# (FORBIDDEN FRUIT EXTRACT)

Your awareness of your own mortality is not blunted by the fact that you have briefly vacationed on the other side of the veil and have decided that it might be the perfect place to move once you retire from this mortal coil. I thought back to how I impulsively left on this intergalactic adventure without even saying goodbye to Gina, and unlike the first time I died, I may now never get that chance. And that is what really sucks about the possibility of dying, the residual pain you leave behind for your love ones to deal with. As much as I missed my dead brothers, I did not want to have to spend the foreseeable future like they are, passing messages from whatever version of heaven I deserved to Gina through my menagerie of psychically gifted meta-humans and animals back in Berthoud. Dying on Centauri was just not an option.

Petrichor was obviously still in my head.

00100000 01010111 01101000 01100001 01110100 00100000
01101001 01100110 00100000 01001001 00100000 01100011
01101111 01110101 01101100 01100100 00100000 01100111
01110101 01100001 01110010 01100001 01101110 01110100
01111001 00100000 01110100 01101000 01100001 01110100
00100000 01111001 01101111 01110101 00100000 01110111
01101111 01110101 01101100 01100100 00100000 01101110

01101111 01110100 00100000 01101100 01101111 01110011
01100101 00111111

*What if I could guaranty that you would not lose?*

Any lawyer who tells you that he would not, in an instant, enter a Faustian contract to win an otherwise unwinnable case deserves whatever other quiet desperation life has to offer, because that lawyer does not belong in a courtroom. However, the last time I made a deal with the devil, or at least with his incarnate version, the mafioso, Tiberius Valachi, I received all the success and riches he had promised me. In the end, that deal not only cost me my life, but also the lives of my three brothers. Its other unintended consequences landed me and Everett in the present shit storm. It is like getting in too deep with a bookie, you are always just paying off the vig. You are always in the hole.

But as in every negotiation, there was no harm in listening to the offer on the table.

01010000 01101100 01100001 01111001 00100000 01110100
01101000 01101001 01110011 00100000 01101111 01110101
01110100 00100000 01100110 01101111 01110010 00100000
01101101 01100101 00101110

*Play this out for me.*

01000010 01110101 01110100 00100000 01100100 01101111
00100000 01101001 01110100 00100000 01100001 01110101
01110010 01100001 01101100 01101100 01111001 00101100
00100000 01001001 00100000 01110111 01100001 01101110
01110100 00100000 01110100 01101111 00100000 01110101
01101110 01100100 01100101 01110010 01110011 01110100
01100001 01101110 01100100 00100000 01110111 01101000
01100001 01110100 00100000 01110100 01101000 01100101
00100000 01100100 01100101 01100001 01101100 00100000
01101001 01110011 00101110

*But do it aurally, I want to understand what the deal is.*

Petrichor smiled. I was beginning to think she was more human than I was.

"As I told you, the men on the Council are firmly behind Citizen Aldor. You have lost any chance for their votes." She watched my expressions to make sure I was following her.

"That means I need the votes of all four women," I said, "and yours."

"I am willing to offer you that," Petrichor said, "the women will vote as I ask them to. You and Citizen Everett can return back to earth, free of any further obligations to Centauri or its citizens."

Everything has its price, and I was about to find out what this beautiful devil in a gold dress wanted for my weary and well-worn soul.

"What's it going to cost me?"

"Very little," she replied.

"That's a relative term," I stated, surprisingly enjoying this negotiation.

Petrichor's face flushed as she considered her next sentence.

"Centauri is a very non-confrontational world. We all live by the same set of rules, and society and technology provide for all of our needs. We all get along and have been doing so for eons. We all live full and rewarding lives and at some point, after hundreds of years, some of us pass into another plane of existence." I realized at that moment that I would happily sit and listen to Petrichor read James Joyce's Ulysses just to hear the sound of her voice. She continued.

"When a sufficient number of Centaurians pass, the AI that provides for our daily needs of existence, selects an equal number of our women to reproduce and maintain our population's equilibrium."

"One hundred thousand." I interjected, remembering Everett's lecture on the subject.

Petrichor smiled, and I felt my heart flutter. Now I was blushing.

"That's right," she said, again with the smile. "And in this last series, I was offered the opportunity to procreate."

"Everett did mention something about the process," I said, thinking back to his comment about *fucking like rabbits.*

A look of confusion crossed Petrichor's face and I knew she was still in my head. I provided a vivid, mental vision that placed it in context. Her eyes sparkled.

"Which brings me to my offer," she whispered. "I want to procreate with you."

I cannot lie, unless paid well to do so, so I will not strain your credulity and tell you that I did not slightly suspect the possibility of something like this, given the direction of the conversation. But given that I was, even in my present, refitted, human form, at best a 'five' out of the consistent 'ten' that every male Centaurian I had seen since my arrival manifested without effort, I could not comprehend it. Moreover, given that I had never slept with another woman since I married Gina forty years before, I knew I could not do it now, just to save my sorry ass one more time. I was not sure Petrichor would understand that antiquated concept of human emotional loyalty, that I had seen Aldor freely trample on during the hearing. In the abstract, I could rationalize that by engaging in a meaningless biological act, I could make all my problems go away. But that was just it. My erudite rationalizations throughout my life, had landed me right where I was, and I just could not allow my resourceful intellect to bail me out one more time. But I hoped that I could still use it to explain why it was such a bad idea.

"Petrichor," I said, "you honor me with your request, but there are at least a million, possibly millions of more deserving Centaurian men who would gladly sacrifice their testicles, just to breed with you."

She began to respond but I held up my hand to cut her off.

"In addition," I continued, "you would be trading down to breed with me. I mean, just look at me, I let the top of the sheet fall into my lap. Everett, as old as he is, looks like a god compared to me."

I looked down at my recently muscled chest and flat stomach, then looked up at Petrichor, who was doing the same. I quickly raised the sheet back up to my chest.

"And finally," I said, with my best lawyer's summation, "you don't even know if we can breed. I mean, Gina and I could not conceive back on earth. I am probably shooting blanks. And I wouldn't want you to squander this important opportunity."

The last comment was true. Gina and I stopped using condoms once we were married. We left it to God. When nothing happened, we decided that we did not want to figure out where the physical blame lay, because we were afraid it could lead to some form of resentment over time. So, we let it go. We had each other and that was more than enough.

I could tell by Petrichor's face that she was not buying any of it.

"Yes," she said, "you are right, there are actually five-hundred-million eligible Centaurian males who have expressed, through AI, their desire to procreate with me. And yes, objectively speaking, they are all in many ways, physically superior to you."

I would be lying if I said that her ready acceptance of my aesthetic arguments did not sting a little.

"But what none of those Centaurians possess is the innate passion that you have revealed during the hearing. I have witnessed it first-hand from your presented memories and those of Citizen Everett. Indeed, your ability to resort to violence is just another reflection of that passion, and that, I am afraid, is what is totally lacking from the genetic core of even the most perfect Centaurian." Petrichor's face was now flushed, and her Nordic eyes were flashing. Again, I was feeling the sexual gravity, and wanted to embrace her.

"And there is nothing wrong with you physically that would prevent procreation, at least not now. Dr. Nim has confirmed it."

She was leaning in towards me in a very seductive manner. I guess mating rituals transcend the heavens. I leaned away from her, distracted by her last comment concerning my fertility. *Maybe the Hadron Distributor brought my family jewels back to life as well.* Petrichor continued to lean in, closing the gap. I could feel and smell her breath. It was ambrosia.

"But what about our genetic differences?" I pleaded, tilting my face away from hers with faltering hope.

"I have thoroughly examined Dr. Nim's files on you. I know we are genetically close enough to conceive a healthy child."

I had exhausted all rational arguments, and my mind retreated to over forty years of memories of my love for Gina, where I had never violated our own Prime Directive. I also knew that she would forgive me if to do so now brought me home safe to her, but I also knew I could not take the easy way out one more time.

Petrichor remained in my mind throughout this last exchange and when I looked into her eyes, I could see the tears welling up.

"I'm so sorry, I just can't." I whispered, defeated.

This time there were no tell-tale warnings, I just blacked out.

# CHAPTER TWENTY-SEVEN
# (CHANGE OF PERSPECTIVE)

I have never been a real fan of the self-help movement. I believe that most of the purveyors are well meaning characters, and I cannot say their bromides do not help millions of their disciples. It is just not my thing. However, I do recall catching one man, Dr. Wayne Dyer, on PBS while channel surfing one night. I am not sure whether I identified with his baldness, enjoyed his self-deprecating demeanor, or just liked the sound of his voice, but there was something about him that made me put down the remote. The one thing that really stuck with me that night was a concept he kept returning to: *"If you change the way you look at things, the things you look at change."* Over the years since, I had pulled that principle out of my mental quiver whenever I became stuck on a problem, with decent success. I wondered how it would play on Centauri.

When I regained consciousness, I was in a completely new room, sitting across a holographic table from Everett, who looked less than thrilled to see me.

```
01001001 00100000 01110100 01110010 01101001 01100101
01100100 00100000 01110010 01100101 01100001 01100011
01101000 01101001 01101110 01100111 00100000 01101111
01110101 01110100 00100000 01110100 01101111 00100000
01001101 01101001 01100011 01101000 01100101 01101100
01101100 01100101 00100000 01100010 01110101 01110100
```

00100000 01100011 01101111 01110101 01101100 01100100
00100000 01101110 01101111 01110100 00100000 01100111
01100101 01110100 00100000 01110000 01100001 01110011
01110100 00100000 01101000 01100101 01110010 00100000
01101101 01100101 01101110 01110100 01100001 01101100
00100000 01110011 01101000 01101001 01100101 01101100
01100100 00101110

*I tried reaching out to Michelle but could not get past her mental shield.*

01010111 01100101 01101100 01101100 00101100 00100000
01110111 01100001 01110011 01101110 00100111 01110100
00100000 01110100 01101000 01100001 01110100 00100000
01110100 01101000 01100101 00100000 01110000 01101100
01100001 01101110 00111111

*Well, wasn't that the plan?*

01011001 01100101 01110011 00101100 00100000 01111001
01100101 01110011 00100000 01101111 01100110 00100000
01100011 01101111 01110101 01110010 01110011 01100101
00101100 00100000 01100010 01110101 01110100 00100000
01100111 01101001 01110110 01100101 01101110 00100000
01101000 01101111 01110111 00100000 01100010 01100001
01100100 00100000 01110100 01101000 01101001 01101110
01100111 01110011 00100000 01100001 01110010 01100101
00100000 01100111 01101111 01101001 01101110 01100111
00101100 00100000 01001001 00100000 01110111 01100001
01101110 01110100 01100101 01100100 00100000 01110100
01101111 00100000 01100111 01101001 01110110 01100101
00100000 01101000 01100101 01110010 00100000 01100001
01101110 00100000 01110101 01110000 01100100 01100001
01110100 01100101 00101110 00100000 00100000 01001001
00100000 01110111 01100001 01101110 01110100 01100101
01100100 00100000 01110100 01101111 00100000 01110000
01110010 01100101 01110000 01100001 01110010 01100101
00100000 01101000 01100101 01110010 00100000 01100110

01101111 01110010 00100000 01110100 01101000 01100101
00100000 01110111 01101111 01110010 01110011 01110100
00101110

*Yes, yes of course, but given how bad things are going, I wanted to give her an update. I wanted to prepare her for the worst.*

The last thing my ego needed right then was Everett throwing in the towel before the final bell had rung. I needed to focus my energy on coming up with a counter argument to Aldor's highly effective "Jimmy Moran is a worthless scumbag" approach, which, according to Petrichor, seemed to be working.

01001110 01101111 01110100 00100000 01110100 01101111
00100000 01100011 01110101 01110100 00100000 01111001
01101111 01110101 00100000 01101111 01100110 01100110
00101100 00100000 01100010 01110101 01110100 00100000
01001001 00100111 01110110 01100101 00100000 01100111
01101111 01110100 00100000 01101101 01101111 01110010
01100101 00100000 01101001 01101101 01101101 01100101
01100100 01101001 01100001 01110100 01100101 00100000
01110000 01110010 01101111 01100010 01101100 01100101
01101101 01110011 00100000 01110100 01101000 01100001
01101110 00100000 01110111 01101111 01110010 01110010
01111001 01101001 01101110 01100111 00100000 01100001
01100010 01101111 01110101 01110100 00100000 01110100
01101000 01100101 00100000 01101000 01100101 01100001
01100100 01101100 01101001 01101110 01100101 01110011
00100000 01100010 01100001 01100011 01101011 00100000
01101000 01101111 01101101 01100101 00100000 01101001
01100110 00100000 01110111 01100101 00100000 01101100
01101111 01110011 01100101 00101110

*Not to cut you off, but I've got more immediate problems than worrying about the headlines back home if we lose.*

It was a shame that my new-found fluidity with the binary code could be all for naught if I ended up having my "reanimation" reversed. I was getting quite good at it. I wondered if I could teach it to my brothers on the other side. I'm guessing they would tell me to fuck right off!

```
01000010 01110101 01110100 00100000 01111001 01101111
01110101 00100111 01110010 01100101 00100000 01101110
01101111 01110100 00100000 01101100 01101001 01110011
01110100 01100101 01101110 01101001 01101110 01100111
00101110 00100000 01001001 00100000 01100110 01101001
01101110 01100001 01101100 01101100 01111001 00100000
01100100 01101001 01100100 00100000 01100111 01100101
01110100 00100000 01110100 01101000 01110010 01101111
01110101 01100111 01101000 00101110
```

*But you're not listening. I finally did get through.*

"Okay, okay, let's do this in English," I said, my mind selfishly seizing on the possibility of reaching out to Gina one more time. "Start from the beginning."

"As I said, I couldn't get past Michelle's mental shield," Everett said, excitedly, "but I was able reach Claire."

This amazing creature had come into my life by fate and happenstance when the United States Federal Government had uprooted my wife and I and dumped us in rural Northern Colorado as part of its Witness Protection Program; she was the gift that kept on giving. But as with everything else about her, I was usually the last to know.

"She literally snatched my thoughts out of the ether like a vacuum. It wasn't a clear connection, but she let me know she would share what she got with Michelle before I lost contact."

"And what was that message?"

```
01001110 01101111 01110100 00100000 01100111 01101111
01101001 01101110 01100111 00100000 01110111 01100101
01101100 01101100 00101110 00100000 01000001 01101100
01101100 00100000 01101000 01101001 01101110 01100111
01100101 01110011 00100000 01101111 01101110 00100000
```

```
01001010 01101001 01101101 01101101 01111001 00100000
01110000 01110010 01101111 01110110 01101001 01101110
01100111 00100000 01101000 01101001 01110011 00100000
01101001 01101110 01101110 01100001 01110100 01100101
00100000 01110110 01100001 01101100 01110101 01100101
00100000 01110100 01101111 00100000 01110100 01101000
01100101 00100000 01000011 01101111 01110101 01101110
01100011 01101001 01101100 00101110 00100000 01001001
00100000 01101100 01101111 01110110 01100101 00100000
01111001 01101111 01110101 00101110 00100000 00100000
01001010 01101001 01101101 01101101 01111001 00100000
01110011 01100101 01101110 01100100 01110011 00100000
01101000 01101001 01110011 00100000 01101100 01101111
01110110 01100101 00100000 01110100 01101111 00100000
01000111 01101001 01101110 01100001 00101110
```

*Not going well. All hinges on Jimmy proving his innate value to the Council. I love you. Jimmy sends his love to Gina.*

"You gave Claire the message in binary?" I asked, my slender hopes dissipating rapidly.

"I was sending it to Michelle, I didn't expect Claire to intercept it." He replied, his own hopes now following mine down the intergalactic toilet. We knew from recent experience that Claire, despite her rapidly expanding psychic powers, could not understand Centaurian binary thoughts unless first translated into English.

I was back at square one. Aldor had rifled through my memories and presented the absolute worst conduct he had found. The problem was, there was nothing left in those memory files to counter such egregious behavior. Handing out dollar bills to homeless people or giving my seat on the subway to a pregnant woman did not make up for all the death that occurred at my hands. I was fucked, and then Dr. Wayne Dyer popped into my head.

I was about to share my idea with Everett when the room around us and all of its contents, including the two of us, began to vibrate like the plucked string of a guitar. I did not feel the galvanization or see the colors. I did not even black out.

# CHAPTER TWENTY-EIGHT
# (A DARK MULE)

Before I realized what was happening, Everett and I were now sitting at the table in the Council Hall. The standing room only crowd looked more compacted than ever, and every eye in the stands were focused on me. The men on the Council were in their assigned balconies and must have all gotten together before hand to practice their constipated look. Their minds were as closed as their faces. The women members of the Council looked distressed, but their minds were equally closed to my prying.

```
01001001 00100000 01100001 01100100 01101101 01101001
01110010 01100101 00100000 01111001 01101111 01110101
00100000 01001010 01101001 01101101 01101101 01111001
00100000 01001101 01101111 01110010 01100001 01101110
00101110 00100000 00100000 01011001 01101111 01110101
00100000 01100001 01110010 01100101 00100000 01100001
00100000 01101101 01100001 01101110 00100000 01101111
01100110 00100000 01110000 01110010 01101001 01101110
01100011 01101001 01110000 01101100 01100101 00101110
00100000 00100000 01010111 01100101 00100000 01110111
01101001 01101100 01101100 00100000 01101110 01101111
01110111 00100000 01110011 01100101 01100101 00100000
```

01101001 01100110 00100000 01110100 01101000 01100001
01110100 00100000 01101001 01110011 00100000 01100101
01101110 01101111 01110101 01100111 01101000 00101110

*I admire you Jimmy Moran. You are a man of principle. We will now see if that is enough.*

Petrichor's eyes burned into my own, but I refused to be the first to break the gaze. Finally, she looked away and commanded in an icy tone.

"Proceed with your rebuttal, Jimmy Moran."

I stood and walked around to the front of the holographic table, then turned and slowly panned the crowd in the stands. I wanted to make sure that they were listening carefully. If this was going to be my swan song, I wanted to make sure that everyone's eyes were on me.

I turned back towards each member of the Council, made eye contact, and nodded respectfully. Everyone but Petrichor.

"Members of the Council," I began, in my most sonorous voice, "we have all listened and watched as the honorable Citizen Aldor has presented his argument, that my life was not worth saving the night Citizen Everett used his Hadron Distributor to bring me back from the dead."

I looked over at Aldor, who was doing his best Centaurian impression of a smug look.

"Citizen Aldor has shown you a number of cases, where people that I have loved died as a result of bad decisions I have made, while people that I have hated, have died at my hand."

I could see the faces in the crowd growing more animated, as they began to communicate amongst themselves telepathically.

"And I'm not going to stand here and deny that any of those things happened, or that they were not my fault."

I could see that the men on the Council were all now leaning forward just a bit in their chairs as if waiting for the confirmation of their preconceived notions about me. The women were fully engaged as well, although I could see that they looked more inquisitive, unsure of where this was heading.

01010111 01101000 01100001 01110100 00100000 01100001
01110010 01100101 00100000 01111001 01101111 01110101
00100000 01100100 01101111 01101001 01101110 01100111
00111111 00100000 00100000 01010100 01101000 01101001
01110011 00100000 01101001 01110011 00100000 01100101
01111000 01100001 01100011 01110100 01101100 01111001
00100000 01110111 01101000 01100001 01110100 00100000
01000011 01101001 01110100 01101001 01111010 01100101
01101110 00100000 01000001 01101100 01100100 01101111
00100000 01110111 01100001 01101110 01110100 01110011
00100000 01111001 01101111 01110101 00100000 01110100
01101111 00100000 01100100 01101111 00101110

*What are you doing? This is exactly what Citizen Aldor wants you to do.*

I could see unexpected worry in Petrichor's eyes. Maybe she had not completely given up on me. I winked.

"Truth is, I am a bad man. I have done bad things in my life because they were expedient, because they made my life better." I continued. "What you saw were only the big-ticket items. To invoke a commonly used phrase from back home on earth, 'I am a sinner.'"

I looked over at Aldor and could see his complacency start to turn to concern.

"But here's the thing." I said, letting it hang for a moment for dramatic effect. "None of that matters."

Now Aldor was on his feet, looking confusingly back and forth between me and the Council members. He felt that something was wrong but did not know how to fix it. His mouth hung open, but no sound came out.

"You see, members of the Council, you recalled Citizen Everett to Centauri to answer to the citizens for breaching the Prime Directive. Bringing a human back to life is certainly the hallmark example that your people use to show how it can be breached. But that doesn't mean that every time a Centaurian brings a human back to life, it breaches the Prime Directive, or, for that matter, that the Prime Directive should not be breached."

"This is preposterous!" Aldor shouted, pulling a ten-dollar human word out of his aural quiver.

"Members of the Council, please hear me out." I responded in equal volume, "Is it not true, that the Prime Directive provides, in words or substance, that a Centaurian must do nothing that can cause a material change in the evolution of the planet or people who inhabit it?"

I could see the council members conferring silently among themselves. Petrichor then responded, "that is a fair definition of the Prime Directive, Jimmy Moran."

I hung their ears on my most pregnant pause before proceeding.

"But isn't that exactly what the Centaurians have been doing to the humans since before we walked upright?"

For the first time I could hear individuals in the stands start to verbalize their excitement with ooohhhsss and aaaahhhhssss. They did not know what was coming because my mind was locked, but they could feel it.

"Isn't it also true, members of the Council, that your ancestors have been tinkering with our DNA at every evolutionary stage of our development? Each time you decided we were ready, it was a genetic tweak here, and a genetic tweak there, and on and on and on as you dragged us up the evolutionary ladder!"

"And this is how you repay our beneficence?" Shouted the oldest male member of the Council. "We should have left your kind swinging in the treetops."

I could see the women on the Council all turning *en masse* to face down the speaker, their expressions displaying their disapproval. I guess even earth monkeys matter.

"Ah," I said, holding up my right index finger. "But you didn't leave us up in those treetops. You played God and slowly fashioned us into your own image. Thus, I put it to the Council, the Centaurians as a race, have so consistently broken their Prime Directive that they have rendered it a nullity."

"Humans were a unique, controlled experiment." Shouted another man on the Council. "There was great planning, direction, supervision, and a slow and prescribed evolution. Great care was taken to make sure only your species evolved according to our plans."

I was about to reply when Everett leapt to his feet and addressed the Council directly.

"With all due respect, Members of the Council," he began, before shutting his eyes tightly.

The 3-D Jumbotron flickered as if it was powering up and then, for all to see, stood a lifelike hologram of Claire, in full glory.

"Jimmy," she shouted with excitement, "lost a little weight! Have you been working out?"

At that, the crowd of Centaurians transmitted in groups down from the stands and out onto the main floor of the hall, all inching forward to get a better look at my mule.

"What's the matter fella," Claire said to Aldor, who stood mutely staring at her, "cat got your tongue?"

She turned back to me, "which one of them is Petrichor?" Claire asked, then turned and scanned the balconies. "Hold on, I got her." She gazed directly up at Petrichor, whose eyes were so wide open, they lost their almond shape. Her mouth was agape.

"Listen, sweetie," Claire began, "I have to make this quick, because I don't know how long Michelle and Bobbi back on earth are going to be able to hold this channel, or whatever it is, open."

She nodded towards Everett. "Not for nothing Everett, but you look marvelous." She laughed in that Lurch fashion.

Claire turned back to the Council. "Everett made his choice to bring Jimmy back from the dead, not because of who Jimmy was in the past, but because of who Everett is now. Whatever qualities Jimmy has brought out in Everett, including his compassion, are in all of you, you have just forgotten it. So, all the bad stuff that I now see playing in Everett's head, that Blondie over there has been saying about Jimmy, doesn't matter. It's all about Everett, who knew about Jimmy's past and yet made the decision that he was worth saving."

Claire rested a moment to let this sink in, then proceeded. "And don't give me that bullshit that was not his call to make. I'm sure no one filed any requests back home when they decided to see if they could make my ancestors talk, or think, or do any of the other fun stuff I can now do. I'm sure that particular Centaurian meant well, but, as we say back on earth, shit happens."

Suddenly, Claire's signal started to fade and with that, her image.

"Jimmy, I gotta go!" Claire shouted anxiously, and her voice started to break up, "Gina says to say she loves you."

And with that, Claire was gone, and Everett's eyes opened up. I strode over at human speed and hugged him. "Would have loved to know you were carrying that around in your back pocket," I whispered.

"Honestly, I did not see it coming." He whispered back. "It was all Michelle; she must have reviewed the binary code message in Claire's head. Seems her and Bobbi came up with a plan. I just answered the call and got out of the way." He played it all over in his memory and then smiled. "I'm impressed, that was quite a trick."

I could hear the crowd behind me all aurally whispering amongst themselves, with the name 'Claire' popping up regularly. The members of the Council were communicating silently, with some of the men's facial expressions giving away that they were not liking what they were hearing from the others.

Aldor tried to recover his momentum.

"Nothing in Jimmy Moran's sideshow makes any difference!" He shouted. "Everett broke the Prime Directive."

"But you can't punish Everett for doing something that your people have been doing for millennia." I countered. "From what I have witnessed, your real Prime Directive is fairness. Everett saw a bad situation and made the call."

"Unlike our ancestors," Aldor interjected, "all Everett did was bring a bad human back to life."

"That's not true," Petrichor interrupted him. "I have seen into this man's mind and he is not a bad human."

Suddenly, Dr. Nim appeared on the balcony beside her.

"In fact," Petrichor continued, "Jimmy Moran is not a human."

The entire crowd went silent, including Citizen Aldor. Petrichor nodded towards the doctor.

Dr. Nim spoke. "Jimmy Moran's genetic profile proves, beyond challenge, that he is now Centaurian."

"If this is all true," said the eldest woman on the Council, "then we cannot hold Citizen Everett liable for breaching a Prime Directive that no longer has any relevance."

"I call for a vote of the Council," said another of the women.

Petrichor looked over at each member and nodded as they exchanged communications. The oldest male on the Council disappeared immediately after his exchange.

"By an eight-to-one margin," Petrichor stated, "the Council votes that citizen Everett transgressed no laws of Centauri when he reanimated Jimmy Moran."

Now it was Everett's turn to appear in my space and nearly crush the life out of me with a hug. The crowd seemed to dematerialize as a group as he held me tight. One by one the remaining members of the Council disappeared from their respective balconies, all except Petrichor and Dr. Nim. As Everett released me, I met Petrichor's gaze, her cheeks were flushed, her eyes, luminous.

01010100 01101000 01100001 01101110 01101011 00100000
01111001 01101111 01110101 00101110

*Thank you.*

01011001 01101111 01110101 00100000 01100001 01110010
01100101 00100000 01110111 01100101 01101100 01100011
01101111 01101101 01100101 00101110 00100000 00100000
01011001 01101111 01110101 00100000 01100001 01101110
01100100 00100000 01000101 01110110 01100101 01110010
01100101 01110100 01110100 00100000 01100001 01110010
01100101 00100000 01100110 01110010 01100101 01100101
00100000 01110100 01101111 00100000 01110010 01100101
01110100 01110101 01110010 01101110 00100000 01101000
01101111 01101101 01100101 00101110

*You are welcome. You and Everett are free to return home.*

As I turned back to Everett, I glanced back over my shoulder at the center balcony one last time, just to sear Petrichor's image into my memory, but she was gone. Dr. Nim gave one final wink and disappeared.

I looked over at Aldor, who was staring daggers at me.

01000010 01100101 01110111 01100001 01110010 01100101
00100000 01110100 01101000 01100101 00100000 01101100
01100001 01110111 00100000 01101111 01100110 00100000

01110101 01101110 01101001 01101110 01110100 01100101
01101110 01100100 01100101 01100100 00100000 01100011
01101111 01101110 01110011 01100101 01110001 01110101
01100101 01101110 01100011 01100101 01110011 00101100
00100000 01001010 01101001 01101101 01101101 01111001
00100000 01001101 01101111 01110010 01100001 01101110
00101110 00100000 00100000 01010100 01101000 01101001
01110011 00100000 01101001 01110011 00100000 01101110
01101111 01110100 00100000 01101111 01110110 01100101
01110010 00100000 01100110 01101111 01110010 00100000
01111001 01101111 01110101 00101110

*Beware the law of unintended consequences, Jimmy Moran. This is not over for you.*

A moment later, the molecular guitar strings were plucked again and, in less than a blink of an eye, Everett and I found ourselves back safely on Jayney.

01010111 01101000 01100101 01101110 00100000 01111001
01101111 01110101 00100000 01100011 01101000 01100001
01101110 01100111 01100101 00100000 01110100 01101000
01100101 00100000 01110111 01100001 01111001 00100000
01111001 01101111 01110101 00100000 01101100 01101111
01101111 01101011 00100000 01100001 01110100 00100000
01110100 01101000 01101001 01101110 01100111 01110011
00101100 00100000 01110100 01101000 01100101 00100000
01110100 01101000 01101001 01101110 01100111 01110011
00100000 01111001 01101111 01110101 00100000 01101100
01101111 01101111 01101011 00100000 01100001 01110100
00100000 01100011 01101000 01100001 01101110 01100111
01100101 00101110

*When you change the way you look at things, the things you look at change.*

# CHAPTER TWENTY-NINE
# (GOODBYE YELLOW BRICK ROAD)

Since I really did not get to see Proxima-b during our arrival due to my being rendered unconscious by the welcoming committee, I really wanted to catch a good look at this planet on the way out. Everett assumed his position at the control panel and was busy doing whatever it took to get us started. I figured I would use the time to take a shot at exercising some of my newly acquired abilities.

```
01001111  01101011  01100001  01111001  00100000  01001010
01100001  01111001  01101110  01100101  01111001  00101100
00100000  01100011  01100001  01101110  00100000  01111001
01101111  01110101  00100000  01110011  01101000  01101111
01110111  00100000  01101101  01100101  00100000  01110111
01101000  01100001  01110100  00100111  01110011  00100000
01101111  01110101  01110100  01110011  01101001  01100100
01100101  00111111
```

*Okay Jayney, can you show me what's outside?*

I almost squealed when the walls of the ship disappeared, and then again when I could not see anything. It was pitch black. Everett looked up from the control panel, obviously amused.

"We're still underground, hold on," he said. A moment later the yellow ambient light outlined a long perfect tunnel appeared before us. I could see that it curved upward and out of view about a half mile ahead of us. A captain's seat appeared beside me and once I sat down, moved me up beside Everett at the control panel.

01001101 01100001 01101011 01100101 00100000 01111001
01101111 01110101 01110010 01110011 01100101 01101100
01100110 00100000 01100011 01101111 01101101 01100110
01101111 01110010 01110100 01100001 01100010 01101100
01100101 00101100 00100000 01001010 01101001 01101101
01101101 01111001 00101110

*Make yourself comfortable, Jimmy.*

"Thank you, Jayney." I said out loud.

"You're welcome." Responded a voice like Stephen Hawking. Everett laughed.

"Oh, that will never do," he said, as he materialized a small holograph panel in the air before him and flipped a few levers.

"Let's try that again, Jayney."

"You're welcome, Jimmy." This time it sounded just like Petrichor. Everett winked at me. Despite my rising flush, I could not help but smile.

"We can change it back when we get back to earth," he said, laughing. "But seriously, we dodged a bullet back there on so many levels."

He placed his hands in the imprints on the control panel and the ship was suddenly encased in what had to be the plasma shield, which emanated its own golden counterglow to the yellow from the tunnel. Everett took his seat in the chair that appeared behind him as the ship slowly moved forward. After a few feet, the ship began to rapidly accelerate so that by the time we reached the upward turn, I could feel the pressure from the G forces compressing me into the captain's chair.

A small reddish circle of light which marked the end of the tunnel quickly expanded as we approached. When we passed through it, I heard a swoosh as the ship was expelled like a spitball hurtling through the air.

"Hang on, Jimmy!" Everett shouted gleefully while he guided the ship into a clockwise rotation as we exited the tunnel. "That never gets old." When we appeared above the exterior of the planet, Everett made some fingertip adjustments and the ship changed course to fly parallel to the planet's surface.

01001010 01100001 01111001 01101110 01100101 01111001
00101100 00100000 01110100 01100001 01101011 01100101
00100000 01110100 01101000 01100101 00100000 01101000
01100101 01101100 01101101 00100000 01100110 01101111
01110010 00100000 01100001 00100000 01100010 01101001
01110100 00101110

*Jayney, take the helm for a bit.*

For what seemed like the next earth hour, Everett played tour bus conductor, pointing out various geographical formations and giving me the cook's tour of what appeared to be a very earthlike planet below us. There were vast continental land formations with majestic snow-capped mountains and fertile sweeping valleys covered in various forms of earthlike trees and shrubs, with dazzling waterfalls and pristine rivers flowing through their interiors. The continents were each larger than North America and surrounded by active blue oceans, although none of the latter looked as large as either of our Atlantic or Pacific.

"We have twelve continents," Everett stated with authority. "Earth only has seven. But then again, Centauri is almost twenty percent larger than earth."

"Which one is yours?" I asked, ignoring my urge to find fault with something below us, just to tweak his nose a bit.

"They all are," he replied proudly, "we move freely from one to another, as our needs and desires dictate."

I remembered Everett's past lecture about the Centaurians' peaceful, one-world philosophy, and while I still could not believe in its underlying altruistic foundation, given my recent experience in being secretly coveted by Petrichor, and openly despised by Aldor, I was willing to accept some of the blame for being the fly in their otherwise pristine ointment. It was best that I was getting out of there when I did, or who knows, I may have taught them the art of war. I was certain that Aldor was not about to burst into a chorus of *Kumbaya* the next time he thought of me.

Everett then resumed control of the ship and brought us closer as we passed over one expansive land mass.

"This is where I last lived before leaving for earth." He reflected.

I could see abundant fields of corn, grains, leafy vegetables, and fruit along with healthy looking orchards. I saw automated machinery moving around, tending to the plowing, and harvesting, but no humanoids. There also were no obvious artificial structures.

"Where are the people, cities and buildings?" I asked.

"Everything is subterranean, other than the crops, all spread out under each of the land masses."

"Why," I asked, "when it is so beautiful up here?"

"It has to do with our sun," he said, "it's perfect for growing every crop we could desire and provides plenty of warmth and solar energy for our planet, but because of the length of our days, it provides higher radiation levels than would be tolerable to our bodies. Our central artificial intelligence keeps the planet's magnetic field functioning at acceptable levels, but it still cannot completely protect us. Indeed, having to come to grips with radiation's long-term impact, and eliminating free radicals from our cellular systems, were what led our final eradication of all disease among the Centaurians. That, in turn, resulted in the slowing of our aging process and the extension of our life expectancy. So, many earth-millennia ago, our people built subsurface cities which are now fully controlled by our AI. In that way, we are all able to remain healthy and vibrant."

I thought about all of the doorless and windowless rooms I had been an involuntary guest of, including the Council Hall. They had all been functional and comfortable, but there was no psychological warmth to them. They all felt a little bit sterile. To tell the truth, while it was great to be able to holographically materialize anything you needed when you needed it, I felt a little bit exposed in their clutter free environment. I like my visual cues to navigate my world. I like walking down hallways.

"That is also what led us to our exploration of space." Everett continued. "We started searching for other habitable environments as potential alternatives in case we were unable to master the environment and other issues that were slowly destroying Centauri. Luckily for you earthlings, we were successful, or otherwise you would all still be monkeys. Our monkeys."

"Now you're sounding like Aldor," I said with a smirk. "And there's no one up here to fix your nose."

"I've always got this," Everett said, producing his Hadron Distributor from his invisible pocket, "It brought you back from the dead, so a nose is a piece of cake." He waved his hands and a holographic screen appeared.

"Your oxygen's stable, no need for the ventilator. I guess you really are one of us."

He slid the tiny tube back into his right side. The opening of his pocket disappeared as soon as his hand withdrew.

I slid my hand towards where my pocket should be, and the pocket appeared as expected. I wondered if that worked if anyone else reached in there.

"Now, if you look carefully," Everett continued as tour guide, "you can see locations where we can enter the interior of the planet."

Everett pointed to a tall mesa that looked quite at home among other similar surrounding geographical topography. As we watched, the top of it started to vibrate just enough to make the features blurry and then suddenly another craft launched from its core, rotating just as we did when we exited the tunnel. It was obviously in a hurry because it no sooner appeared in sight then it changed directions and then disappeared.

"You normally can only spot them just before entry or after exit," Everett said, "because that is the only time they are traveling slow enough to visually register. We exited from one just like that."

I was getting a little bored with the repetitively beautiful scenery and remembered that I had another world waiting for me across the galaxy. Everett, on the other hand, was mesmerized by the view.

01001111 01101110 01100101 00100000 01101101 01101111
01110010 01100101 00100000 01110011 01100101 01100011
01101111 01101110 01100100 00101100 00100000 01100001
01101110 01100100 00100000 01110100 01101000 01100101
01101110 00100000 01110111 01100101 00100111 01101100
01101100 00100000 01100111 01101111 00101110

*One more second, and then we'll go.*

When he finally looked away, I could see a tear in his eye. It reminded me of the story my great-uncle Barney once told me about the night he and Spaghetti left Ireland for good. They were leaving on a fishing trawler from the port of Derry in the middle of the night, and despite the danger they had faced to obtain this passage, and the troubles they were leaving behind them, Spaghetti refused to go below deck until the last of the lights on the shore had all disappeared from sight. Barney said that it was the only time he had seen his older brother cry, before or since. I could sense now that Everett was saying his own goodbyes to Centauri.

He was about to resume his position at the control panel when he stopped and gestured to it. "Would you like to take it for a spin?" Everett asked.

I felt like someone had offered me the golden ticket to Willy Wonka's Chocolate factory.

"Are you sure?"

"Absolutely." He said, as he moved out of the way and gestured me to the control panel.

I stood up and let him guide my hands to the corresponding imprints on the control panel.

"Now your right-hand controls direction," he said, "middle digit up, ring digit down, index left, pinky right."

"What does the thumb do?"

"Hover in place."

"Left hand controls the speed," he continued, "pinky to thumb increases, the reverse slows it down."

01001010 01100001 01111001 01101110 01100101 01111001
00101100 00100000 01110000 01110101 01110100 00100000
01110100 01101000 01100101 00100000 01110011 01101000
01101001 01110000 00100000 01101001 01101110 00100000
01110100 01110010 01100001 01101001 01101110 01101001
01101110 01100111 00100000 01101101 01101111 01100100
01100101 00101110

*Jayney, put the ship in training mode.*

"Okay," Everett said excitedly, "let's ease it out of orbit. Jayney is preprogrammed with the coordinates for the wormhole, so she won't let you veer too far-off course. Start by taking us upward out of our atmosphere."

My index finger applied moderate pressure and the nose of the ship turned upwards from the reddish glow from the atmosphere towards the blackness of space. While I could feel a gyroscopic transition, I never felt unsteady on the floor of the ship, even though the planet that was just below-was now fading into the distance somewhere behind me.

"Give it some speed, we need to reach the escape velocity to get free of Centauri's gravitational field," Everett said, sounding like my High School Driver's Ed teacher coaching me onto a highway for the first time. I maneuvered the left hand's digits as instructed, as if I were playing the keys on a piano.

"Okay," Everett said gently, "that's good."

I did not feel like we were traveling any faster, but I could see their red sun, Proxima Centauri, growing larger on the far right of the ship. Moments later it too started to recede in size as we passed to its far side away from Proxima b.

Everett pointed to a small ringed planet far off to my right.

"Is that Saturn?" I asked.

"No, Saturn's back in your solar system on the other side of the galaxy. That is our closest neighbor, what you call Proxima Centauri c."

"Any more of you guys on that planet?" I asked.

"No," Everett responded, "it's an ice giant. Uninhabitable. But we mine it for its rich natural resources."

I was only half listening to him because I was focusing on the craft. I was definitely having a lot more fun leaving Centauri than I did when I arrived. I ran my left hand again up the finger roll and suddenly both sun and planet were out of view.

"That's enough for now," Everett said as he gently lifted my hands off the control panel. "Jayney, take the ship out of training mode and please assume control."

Again, Petrichor's voice arrived like smooth jazz. "We breach the event horizon in one earth hour."

# CHAPTER THIRTY
# (AND BACK AGAIN)

Everett seemed lost in his own thoughts, fully reclined in his chair with his eyes closed, and I did not feel right intruding. I had never seen him sleep, and remembered Michelle telling me back on earth that Centaurians did not really need to. I guess all of those times I passed out during the many transporting transitions on Centauri were something different. It sure felt like sleep to me. And I did not feel tired.

I distracted myself by exercising my enhanced telekinetic powers interacting with Jayney. First, I had her create weird holograms of diminutive animals, like rabbits, turtles, and birds, and then advanced to smaller versions of classic cars, and finally cityscapes, like New York and Paris, which was really cool, and probably wrong, given that I did not have the clearest memories of some of their details. Then I asked Jayney to rustle up a seared Halloumi salad, with raspberry vinaigrette dressing, and it was as good as anything Gina had ever prepared back at home. The accompanying glass of Cabernet Sauvignon was spectacular. Finally, I had her whip up a six head, glass-encased shower, like my sister had back in London, and spent a good twenty minutes just letting the hot water pummel my body. I could not figure out where the steam from the shower went or where the water drained to. Once I finished drying off with a fluffy warm towel, it disappeared, and there I was, clean as a whistle and fully clothed.

I could not get my head around how Jayney could do any of these things, but I was thrilled that my binary communication with her was getting pretty damn good. I was just checking out my appearance in a holographic mirror when I heard Everett rousing from whatever it was he had been doing.

01010100 01101000 01100101 00100000 01100101 01110110
01100101 01101110 01110100 00100000 01101000 01101111
01110010 01101001 01111010 01101111 01101110 00100000
01101001 01110011 00100000 01100100 01101001 01110010
01100101 01100011 01110100 01101100 01111001 00100000
01100001 01101000 01100101 01100001 01100100 00101110

*The event horizon is directly ahead.*

The mirror disappeared and I could see Everett awake and at the control panel.

"Take a seat Jimmy, the return trip will be even more fun!" He exclaimed.

With just a thought I was back in my seat beside him. I was really liking these new skills.

01000001 01101101 00100000 01001001 00100000 01100111
01101111 01101001 01101110 01100111 00100000 01110100
01101111 00100000 01100010 01100101 00100000 01100001
01100010 01101100 01100101 00100000 01110100 01101111
00100000 01101101 01101111 01110110 01100101 00100000
01101100 01101001 01101011 01100101 00100000 01110100
01101000 01101001 01110011 00100000 01100010 01100001
01100011 01101011 00100000 01101111 01101110 00100000
01100101 01100001 01110010 01110100 01101000 00111111

*Am I going to be able to move like this back on earth?*

"Depends on how quickly you fully acclimate to your new genetics." Everett responded aurally. "There's a few more tricks Michelle and I can show you once you do."

Everett again placed his hands on the control panel and bands secured them to the imprints tightly. The console lowered so he could manipulate it from his sitting position in the beefed-up version of the captain's chair. An energy field enveloped him like an egg in a translucent protective cocoon.

There was no hatching along the exterior of the craft this time. I strained to try to locate the wormhole with my eyes alone.

"You had better lie down, Jimmy." He said, as my seat adjusted to its fully reclined position and I felt Jayney's warm embrace swaddle me in a similar energy field.

I could again see the luminescent edge of the worm hole expanding as we approached, but this time it was circling clockwise. Jayney was back.

01010011 01110101 01110000 01100101 01110010 01101100
01110101 01101101 01101001 01101110 01100001 01101100
00100000
*Superluminal*

Everett again handled the controls with expertise, totally focused. I lay back, determined to remain conscious this time through.

01000010 01110010 01100101 01100001 01100011 01101000
01101001 01101110 01100111 00100000 01100101 01110110
01100101 01101110 01110100 00100000 01101000 01101111
01110010 01101001 01111010 01101111 01101110
*Breaching event horizon*

The pressure mounted as we passed through the ring of circulating light, but where it looked like a thin rim the first time through, here I could see that it expanded along with us as we breached its edge and passed onto a spinning luminescent funnel that appeared to grow smaller as we advanced. Then I could feel Everett turning the ship in a counterclockwise motion against the movement of the wormhole just as we left the last trails of light behind us and passed into that black abyss, where I could no longer see anything on the ship, or anywhere else. I was completely blind, and I fought the panic that washed over me.

01010111 01101000 01100001 01110100 00100111 01110011
00100000 01101000 01100001 01110000 01110000 01100101
01101110 01101001 01101110 01100111 00111111
*What's happening?*

Jayney was really growing on me, and I was happily becoming dependent on her.

01001010 01110101 01110011 01110100 00100000 01110010
01100101 01101100 01100001 01111000 00101100 00100000
01001010 01101001 01101101 01101101 01111001 00101110
00100000 00100000 01001001 01110100 00100000 01110111
01101001 01101100 01101100 00100000 01100010 01100101
00100000 01101111 01110110 01100101 01110010 00100000
01110011 01101111 01101111 01101110 00101110

*Just relax, Jimmy. It will be over soon.*

And then, there it was, the memory of my death. Losing control, crossing the veil. The coldness, the fatigue. My thoughts became random. Blurred images of my extended family appeared, in no particular order, but none stayed long enough for me to focus on them. Spaghetti, Nana Burke, and my siblings all danced around the perimeter of my line of sight. Images of Gina morphing through every stage of our life together came and went. My last memory of my face in a mirror back on earth morphing into the younger, harder face I just saw in the mirror after my shower. Claire's thoughts mixed with my own. *Hang on.*

I focused on the sudden physical compression and stretching of my body that was occurring like the last time, but I would not give in to the blackness. When I did not think I could withstand any more, I saw the image of a beautiful child, with bright Nordic blue eyes and burgundy hair, suspended in the blackness directly before me. It was like it was floating in amniotic fluid. Then I heard Petrichor's voice, humming a melody, soft and comforting. It was familiar but I could not place it.

01000101 01111000 01101001 01110100 01101001 01101110
01100111 00100000 01100101 01110110 01100101 01101110
01110100 00100000 01101000 01101111 01110010 01101001
01111010 01101111 01101110 00101110

*Exiting event horizon.*

The image was lost in an explosion of plasma energy from all sides, and I could feel the pressure build from behind as the ship was literally expelled from the other end of the wormhole, as if we were being catapulted from the sea at the crest of a tsunami. It tumbled end-over-end through space, and I could see Everett straining at the console to regain control. As the rotations finally slowed, I spotted a large planet in the distance that looked like a child had painted horizontal bands on it for Easter. I focused on it to reduce the vertigo I was experiencing.

01010100 01101000 01100001 01110100 00100111 01110011
00100000 01001010 01110101 01110000 01101001 01110100
01100101 01110010 00101110

*That's Jupiter.*

As the ship righted itself, Everett leaned back as the straps released his hands. He looked tired. I looked at my hands and felt my face and head. The beard and long hair remained, and my body remained in its rejuvenated state.

"Take us home, Jayney," Everett commanded, "and no detours."

01010100 01100101 01101100 01101100 00100000 01001101
01101001 01100011 01101000 01100101 01101100 01101100
01100101 00100000 01110100 01101000 01100001 01110100
00100000 01001010 01101001 01101101 01101101 01111001
00100000 01100001 01101110 01100100 00100000 01001001
00100000 01100001 01110010 01100101 00100000 01100011
01101111 01101101 01101001 01101110 01100111 00100000
01101000 01101111 01101101 01100101 00101110

*Tell Michelle that Jimmy and I are coming home.*

That broadcast came through to me loud and clear. Everett had a huge smile on his face. Then I heard Aldor's voice in my head one more time, but it was verbal, not binary.

*"Beware the law of unintended consequences, Jimmy."*

# CHAPTER THIRTY-ONE
## (THE INCOMMUTABLE LAW)

Everett must have heard Aldor's voice in my head, because when I attempted to engage him telepathically about it, I was blocked.

"Okay," I said aurally, "what the fuck is he talking about?"

"Who?" Everett replied, his attention apparently preoccupied with the control panel.

"Jayney," I said aurally, "a little help here?"

A holographic image of Aldor appeared on the far side of the control panel. It repeated the phrase aurally. "Beware the law of unintended consequences, Jimmy."

Everett looked up at the image and then withdrew his hands from the control panel.

01010100 01100001 01101011 01100101 00100000 01101111
01110110 01100101 01110010 00100000 01100001 01100111
01100001 01101001 01101110 00101100 00100000 01001010
01100001 01111001 01101110 01100101 01111001 00101110

*Take over again, Jayney.*

01001000 01101111 01110111 00100000 01100100 01101111
00100000 01111001 01101111 01110101 00100000 01110111

01100001 01101110 01110100 00100000 01110100 01101111
00100000 01100100 01101111 00100000 01110100 01101000
01101001 01110011 00101100 00100000 01001010 01101001
01101101 01101101 01111001 00111111

*How do you want to do this, Jimmy?*

01010011 01110100 01110010 01100001 01101001 01100111
01101000 01110100 00100000 01110101 01110000 00101100
00100000 01101001 01101110 00100000 01000101 01101110
01100111 01101100 01101001 01110011 01101000 00100001

*Straight up, in English!*

The captain chairs reappeared opposite each other in the center of the room. I was secretly thrilled that I managed to reach mine before Everett reached his. Perhaps his heart was not in it.

"You remember our talk about 'The Butterfly Effect'?" he began.

"Yes."

"Well, that's just an analogy for 'The Law of Unintended Consequences'."

"Trust me," I quipped, "I have no intention of drinking and driving. I'm not going to accidentally kill the savior of our earth."

"I know," he responded, patiently, "but that's only one aspect of it."

"Everett," I argued, "I'm not going to do anything that will change the course of human history."

"You don't get it!" Everett implored, "it's not about what *you* have done or will do. It's not about the future of your earth."

Suddenly, a holographic scene appeared in the air between us. It was a cemetery plot, with the back of the marble headstone towards me. It slowly rotated until it was facing me, and I gasped out loud. On its face in beautiful calligraphy script was the carving: *'Gina Maria Moran December 30, 1956 – August 17, 2035,'* and directly below that was the inscription: *'James Paul Moran, November 14, 1956 - '.* There was no date of death for me.

"You see, Jimmy," Everett continued, his voice straining with emotion, "Gina is going to live to a ripe old age," he wrung his hands in his lap, his head hanging downward, "but it still will be a human lifetime."

With all the shit Gina and I had been through in our life together for almost four and a half decades, even when the mafia reprisal took place back in Berthoud, I never contemplated her death. She was the athlete, the gymnast, the marathoner. She still looked twenty years younger than me, at least the old me. She was going to outlive me, because I knew in my heart, I could not survive without her.

"You, Jimmy," Everett whispered softly, "are now going to live more than five times longer than that."

# CHAPTER THIRTY-TWO
# (SHORT NIGHT'S JOURNEY INTO DAY)

Spaghetti used to have a saying which I never fully understood, until now: *"You'll never be shot, if you're meant to be hung."* It sounds better when said with a brogue.

01011001 01101111 01110101 00100000 01100011 01100001
01101110 00100111 01110100 00100000 01100101 01110011
01100011 01100001 01110000 01100101 00100000 01100110
01100001 01110100 01100101 00101110
> *You can't escape fate.*

01010111 01100101 01101100 01101100 00101100 00100000
01100110 01110101 01100011 01101011 00100000 01100110
01100001 01110100 01100101 00100001
> *Well, fuck fate!*

I had been rebelling against fate since I could walk and talk. I beat the odds more times than I could count. I scraped hundreds of generations of soil out from under my family's collective fingernails and washed a few more recent generations of cement off our clothing. I went from *Carhartt* to *Brooks Brothers* in one generation. Hell, I even came back from the dead.

'Everything is negotiable' is well-established legal dogma. I spent my entire professional life negotiating deals and outcomes. Everything had a price, a trade-off. But not Gina. She was priceless; non-negotiable.

Bobbi Angelini, the most powerful psychic-witch in the northern hemisphere, and now an integral member of my Berthoud crew, assured me a while back that the future is malleable. What she saw in her discerning mind's eye at any moment was indeed the future unless you intentionally changed your course to avoid it. I was intent on changing my stars one more time. But I needed leverage.

"You need to zap Gina!" I declared.

"What?" Everett recoiled, obviously confused.

"Like you did me," I continued, "with your silver thingy."

Everett let that thought sink in for a moment. He was obviously conflicted. But I could also see that he was scared. He had just dodged a bullet back on Centauri.

I entered his thoughts, and they were all focused on Michelle. He was weighing the impact on her of his crossing that line again. When he realized I was eavesdropping, he blocked me.

"I'm sorry," he whispered, his face wincing and pained.

I barely resisted my initial urge to fly across the room and grab him by the throat. Didn't I cross the galaxy just to defend his sorry ass. Shit, I never asked him to bring me back from the dead in the first place. This was all his fault. I was furious, and I did not care if he heard every thought.

01001111 01101110 01100101 00100000 01100101 01100001
01110010 01110100 01101000 00100000 01101000 01101111
01110101 01110010 00100000 01110101 01101110 01110100
01101001 01101100 00100000 01100001 01110010 01110010
01101001 01110110 01100001 01101100 00101110

*One earth hour until arrival.*

Everett used this opportunity from Jayney to end the silent impasse and return to the control panel. He remained this way, with his mind blocked, for the rest of our journey. He never once looked over at me. The more I stewed in silence, the angrier I became.

I tried to distract myself by thinking about Gina waiting for me back on earth, but that was short lived, and quickly wound its way back to my crisis.

01001000 01101111 01110111 00100000 01101100 01101111
01101110 01100111 00100000 01101000 01100001 01110110
01100101 00100000 01110111 01100101 00100000 01100010
01100101 01100101 01101110 00100000 01100111 01101111

01101110 01100101 00100000 01100110 01110010 01101111
01101101 00100000 01100101 01100001 01110010 01110100
01101000 00100000 01101001 01101110 00100000 01100101
01100001 01110010 01110100 01101000 00100000 01110100
01101001 01101101 01100101 00101100 00100000 01001010
01100001 01101110 01100101 01111001 00111111

*How long have we been gone from earth in earth time, Jayney?*

01000101 01111000 01100001 01100011 01110100 01101100
01111001 00100000 01101111 01101110 01100101 00100000
01100101 01100001 01110010 01110100 01101000 00100000
01111001 01100101 01100001 01110010 00101110

*Exactly one earth year.*

"You better take your seat, Jimmy." Everett said without looking over at me. "We're landing at night, and if we run into any military welcoming committees, it may get bumpy."

Jayney materialized a holographic captain's chair by where I was standing, a few feet away from the console. Everett glanced over at its placement, dismissively. "Suit yourself. You need to stay telepathically silent until we land."

That was not going to be a problem for me, because after everything I had been through, I'd had it with Everett and the Centaurians in general. They could collectively shove their telepathy where their beloved Proxima did not shine.

The landing was uneventful. No fighter jets, no gyrations, no extreme maneuvers, no G-forces. But as we gently touched down in that open area directly behind Everett's man cave, we were both stunned by the obvious. There was no one to greet us.

As I leapt from the top of the craft onto the grass, my mind involuntarily expanded outward, looking for contact. Everett was also out of the craft, directing the Hadron Distributor's red beam towards it, shrinking it back to its scale model size. I could feel his thoughts now reaching out beyond me. And then I heard Claire's sultry woman's voice echoing in my head, its inherent sadness was overwhelming.

"We're all over here, Jimmy. Come home. Mr. Rogers is dead!"

# CHAPTER THIRTY-THREE
# (WHEN DEATH COMES)

I do not recall experiencing any physical movement, just an intention to be home followed by a sense of passing through space and instantaneous arrival. I was standing at the side gate of my house, staring down into the back property, looking for any movement. And then I spotted them.

A moment later, Everett appeared beside me, now back in his human form. It took me a moment to register the reappearance of his earthly *alter ego*. I pointed to the group standing out past the Bat House mound in the center of the back property, in the area I call the soccer field. They were encircling a large rectangular pit, and all were gazing into its darkness. A large pile of dirt, six feet high, sat nearby.

Claire stood at the edge of the far end of the pit, staring down. Gina was standing directly beside her, her arm around her neck, her face buried into the mule's jawline, visually sobbing. Michelle stood on Claire's other side, softly stroking her mane. I could see Michelle was trying to comfort both Claire and Gina. Helen, Eddie, Lenahan, Lucian, Scarlett, and Savana stood somberly, three abreast on opposite sides of the large pit, which I now realized was a grave. They were each holding long, lit altar tapers, which provided soft circles of light that illuminated their faces, each with the telltale signs of tears on their cheeks.

Bobbi's back was to me. She was dressed in a long, black robe, and I could see her arms extended above her out over the pit. She was casting small items into the darkness before her, while chanting rhythmically. The others seemed to sway slightly with her cadence.

I almost looked into their minds, but realized that I did not want to intrude, even on Gina. Not now. Everett tapped me on the shoulder and pointed to my clothing. I was still wearing my Centaurian garb. He removed the Hadron Distributor from his right pocket and zapped me back into a faded pair of jeans and a sweatshirt.

"Do you want me to do something about the hair and beard?"

I shook my head; I was quite comfortable with my renewed locks.

Suddenly, the most pitiful sound I had ever heard, on earth or Centauri, pierced the darkness, invoking chilling memories of Nana's Banshees. Claire had risen on her two hind legs and was circling her forelegs, boxing with God, as she cried out in her own language for her lost love. Her pain was palpable, and my heart was breaking for her. I turned to Everett, who was weeping, lost in his own feelings.

"Isn't there anything –" I started to say.

01001000 01100101 00100111 01110011 00100000 01100010
01100101 01100101 01101110 00100000 01100100 01100101
01100001 01100100 00100000 01110100 01101111 01101111
00100000 01101100 01101111 01101110 01100111 00101110

*He's been dead too long.*

I looked over and saw Michelle standing at the gate. Before she visually registered, she had crossed the distance and was embracing and comforting Everett.

"C'mon," she said to me, giving me a careful once over, "Claire's waiting for you."

Michelle took my hand and the three of us materialized at the far end of the pit, beside Claire. Gina gazed across Claire's withers for a moment before she recognized me. She tried to smile, and I could see in her mind the pain she had been carrying on her own, and I just wanted to hold her and make it all go away. But before I could, Claire suddenly collapsed on her knees and began to weep in human tones. I threw myself upon my mule, hugging her neck tightly and crying into her fur. I felt Gina's gentle touch on the far side of Claire's mane as she stroked my hand, ignoring her own anguish and trying to comfort me.

"Jjjjiiiiimmmmmmmmmmyyyyyyy," Claire wailed in her raspy feminine voice.

"Shoosh, shoosh, shoosh," I whispered softly between my sobs as I rocked her gently while on my knees beside her, "I'm so sorry, so sorry, Claire." I could feel her tears on my cheek as they soaked into my beard.

I gazed into the pit and discerned the outline of the large mule beneath a beautiful shroud, his head, closest to where we were, rested on a royal blue, satin pillow.

Bobbi and the others had gathered all around us. One by one they extinguished their candles.

"Claire," Bobbi said softly, "Mr. Rogers' is here. He wants to say goodbye."

Claire rose to her feet, literally carrying me up onto mine. She turned towards the back of the property facing where Bobbi was pointing. It was the high ground at the farthest end of the pond. She looked over at Bobbi and I could feel their connection, then Everett and Michelle did the same. I reached into Bobbi's mind and then I saw it too.

There on the hillside, stood a version of Mr. Rogers I had never witnessed before. He was young and powerfully built. His coat was full, and I could see every hair moving across his body in waves, like grain before a gentle wind. Gone were the scars from his life on earth. He was luminescent and his eyes literally sparkled. He tilted his head playfully sideways, as he always did in life when begging treats from me. Despite the tears that were now flowing freely from my eyes, I smiled and waved, and he nodded in acknowledgement. *Thank you.*

Claire made that excited whinny-bray sound and galloped over to where he stood and the two curled their necks together and began nuzzling each other like swans, as they often did in life. His glow slowly expanded to encase her and then increased in intensity until you could no longer see either of them in the brightness of the light. They were sharing that one last moment on an ethereal plane between life and death. Then there was a blinding flash, which emanated outward as an energy blast towards us, and I felt its impact as it passed through my heart, like an electric current. I heard Claire's voice in my head, *"Goodbye my love."*

When my eyes reclaimed the darkness, there stood Claire, alone on the rise, staring off into the night.

I felt a gentle touch on my shoulder from behind me and turned at my new speed. Gina grabbed me by my beard and pulled me into a passionate kiss, which I returned with the added intensity of the love I had just experienced from Claire and Mr. Rogers. When she finally broke our embrace, Gina wiped her mouth and chin with her hand. The redness of her eyes belied the playfulness of her next comment.

"I love the new look," she said with a wink, pointing to my thick mane of brown hair tumbling around my shoulders and then running her index finger seductively down my chest and along my abs, "but don't they have razors in outer space?"

The others now gathered around us and began the scrum of a group hug. I could hear their thoughts shifting between their condolences for the loss Claire has suffered to their excitement and relief over Everett and my safe return.

Lenny called out, "whatever it is that you've been drinking, I'll have a gallon please."

"I'll take a vat," Helen seconded.

Then I heard Claire's voice from outside the circle.

"Let's finish this." She said softly.

Bobbi stepped out of the scrum to Claire's side and waved in the general direction of the house towards the far western corner of the property. I heard the menacing roar of a diesel engine starting up in the darkness, followed by two intense headlights which illuminated the pit and our group. The others squinted and shielded their eyes as the Caterpillar Backhoe emerged from the shadows, the sound of its meshing gears carving through the silence of the night.

I intercepted Bobbi's voice with my mind as she telepathically issued her instructions.

*Fill the grave, Whitey.*

We all stepped back as the machine slowly rumbled towards us, except Claire, who maintained her position at the head of Mr. Rogers' grave. The bulldozer blade lowered and slowly pushed the mountain of earth into the pit, covering her lover. Claire's gaze never shifted from the bottom of the grave until the last of the earth had been brought level to the rest of the surrounding field.

When the grave had been completely covered and tamped down, the large machine retreated into the darkness, and the sound of its engine silenced.

A moment later, I saw a large figure approaching from the direction of the machine. I could sense a powerful, male energy and the silhouette's movements seemed more feral than human. The others, with the exception of a pensive Everett, seemed completely comfortable with his approach. Everett generated a soft green light from his Hadron Distributor which encircled the group and the grave, just as the man stepped into view.

He was over six-feet tall and broad shouldered and built like a football linebacker. As he entered the light, I could see that his youthful looking face belied the mane of short, thick white hair brushed back from a uniform hairline that unnaturally encroached his forehead. He did not seem to notice me and walked directly over to Claire and Bobbi. Over his shoulder, he was carrying a long post with an engraved wooden sign at its peak. In his other hand he held a yellow and black handled DeWalt twenty-pound sledgehammer, like it was a chopstick.

"Right there," Claire said as she patted a central spot at the top of the grave with her hoof.

I was the only one who seemed surprised by Claire's candor before this enigmatic being.

The man lifted the signpost off his shoulder and with one shove of his left arm, embedded it deep into the earth at the appointed spot. A single tap from the sledgehammer, finished the effort. The group parted to both sides of the grave to get a better look at the memorial. Gina led me around to the far side of the grave and we both gazed upon the words on the wooden plaque.

*Here lies Mr. Rogers in his forever home, home forever.*

# CHAPTER THIRTY-FOUR
# (IN MEMORIUM)

Helen called out to everyone. "We are having a dinner back at the house, which we invite you all to attend."

She reached over and took Bobbi's hand and proceeded back towards the house while the others, including Whitey, all fell in behind her. Gina nodded towards Claire and fell in with the rest of the group.

"You go ahead Jimmy," Claire said, "you must be starving."

"Nah," I replied, placing my arm over her withers, "I'm good."

She leaned her head onto my shoulder.

"Why didn't you tell me?" I asked, gesturing towards the grave, "I mean you made it to Centauri to save my ass, you could have said something. Maybe we could have –"

"Jimmy," she cut me off, "that was months ago. I didn't know then."

"Months ago? It couldn't have been."

"You've been gone a year." Claire continued.

The impact of that thought distracted me from the heartache I was feeling.

"No, there were no signs, it happened so suddenly," she said, "his great big loving heart just gave out."

I looked into her mind and could see her replaying those last moments on the rise beyond the pond together. She started to sob, and I embraced her tightly, again rocking gently.

*I miss him so much.*

"We all do." I said.

"Wait," Claire said, pulling back from my embrace. "You heard that?"

I nodded.

*Can you hear me now?*

*Yes.*

Claire shook her head in disbelief, distracted momentarily from her own grief. *How? When?*

*Not sure on either. Just happened.*

Claire was now fully engaged. "You hear that Mr. Rogers," she called out into the darkness, "Jimmy finally got his wings."

I could not help but laugh at her reference to *It's a Wonderful Life*.

*You do know how bizarre this is -- me explaining to a telepathic, talking mule -- that I can also communicate like this with the rest of you now.*

It was her turn to laugh in her Lurchy manner. It was great to see.

"I knew you looked different when I saw you those few moments on Centauri," she said giving me the full once over, "but I had no idea they rewired your brain to go with the new body." She nuzzled my chest muscles.

*If you don't mind me saying so, this is definitely an improvement. Must have charged you extra.*

"It gets better," I said.

*Really?*

01001001 00100000 01100011 01100001 01101110 00100000
01110011 01110000 01100101 01100001 01101011 00100000
01101001 01101110 00100000 01100010 01101001 01101110
01100001 01110010 01111001 00101110

    *I can speak in binary.*

Claire's eyes bugged out in her head. Once again, I was glad I could divert her attention from her pain.

*Numbers!*

"I can speak in binary," I repeated aurally.

"No fucking way!" Claire shouted.

"What did they do to you up there?" She asked.

"Nothing," I said. "It happened when Everett brought me back from the dead. It just took some time, and maybe a trip through the wormhole, to kick in."

"What else can you do?" She asked.

I moved with Centauri speed to five different points around her, moving again each time before her eyes could fully locate me.

*That's amazing.*

"So, are you Centaurian now, like Everett and Michelle?"

"I don't think so," I mused, "I'm close, but more of a hybrid."

She thought about that for a moment. "Just like me," Claire whispered softly.

She was right, we were both hybrids, and given the genetic tinkering the Centaurians had done on both man and equine over the millennia, we were more closely related now than ever. *Family takes all forms.*

Just then, I felt something behind us, a pulse of energy. I spun around and there before me stood the glowing hologram of Mr. Rogers. He bowed playfully.

*Claire, there's someone here to see you, again.*

As she turned, I could feel her tapping into my mind. She could now see him as well. Her eyes welled up, as she softly sighed, and they began to nuzzle. She turned back to me and said, "I don't know how you just did this, but thank you."

The two walked off, shoulder to shoulder, to their spot on the rise by the pond.

I had no idea how I did it either, or if I did it at all. Weird things just seemed to keep happening to me. But I took that as my cue to return to the house. Hopefully, the rest of the crew would have some answers.

# CHAPTER THIRTY-FIVE
## (CRYING WOLF)

I walked at an earthly pace back up towards the house, thinking about Claire and Mr. Rogers, and about their love that transcended death. As moving and inspiring as it was, I knew I could not handle dwelling on it. And now, with my physical and telepathic evolution, it was staring me right in the face. I was sure that prick Aldor was having the last laugh back on Centauri. I wondered if my ardent *"fuck you"* would make it back to him through the worm hole. *Beware the law of unintended consequences.*

When I reached the backyard, I was stunned to see the changes in the exterior of my home. Gone was the faded and worm-holed green cedar exterior, which was now replaced by beautiful new beige James Harding siding with brown window trim around brand-new windows. The small, wooden back and side decks had been blown out to three times their size in a new reinforced composite deck that extended in a fifty-foot square. The Marquis hot tub – now identified as *Skyclad* in black cursive lettering on a red background – was set in a perfectly discrete alcove tucked underneath the side deck. Various Bacchanalian Greek and roman reliefs were secured to the surrounding retaining walls. There was an oversized outdoor dining set centered below a huge, Casablanca outdoor ceiling fan mounted under the back deck. A large, carved stone fountain and a string of colored lights running along the perimeter of the under deck, completed the lower outdoor living area. I could see a complete set of beautiful teak deck chairs and love seats laid out invitingly on the upper deck through the cast iron railings that encompassed it. All of the original outdoor lighting on the house had been replaced with antique, Central Park styled sconces that cast a warm and comforting glow over all of the gathering areas. Gina had indeed kept herself busy during my absence.

As I entered into the lower level through beautiful new Marvin sliding doors, I could hear the others on the floor above laughing at some story Lenny was telling in his usual boisterous fashion. Then I heard Bobbi's voice in my head.

*C'mon up, your dinner is getting cold.*

As comfortable as I was becoming with communicating telepathically, every time someone new made a connection, it took some getting used to. However, hearing Bobbi, with her bubbly conversational manner, I realized that my mind was adding the actual sounds of their voices to the thoughts, as if I were actually hearing them. As I thought back over the evolutionary experience, I realized that it was the same back on Centauri. Even Jayney had her own voice. Indeed, she now sounded like Petrichor. With that, my mind flashed back to that image of the floating infant, but just for a moment. This time it was Claire, in her husky female voice, interrupting my thoughts.

*Would you ask Helen to send out some of her garlic vegetables?*

I took the stairs to the first floor in one leap and was met by the combination of Blue and Maeve on the first-floor landing. Blue had added some muscle since I had left and the two now looked like black and white twins, quite formidably standing guard, their hackles up. I had forgotten how dramatically my appearance changed. I could sense their thoughts, which traveled between them telepathically, but they were not in English, and I was unable to interpret canine.

"Relax girls, that's Daddy." I heard Gina call from the living room as she approached the hallway. Both dogs immediately shifted into understanding her human words and dropped their guard. More interested in pursuing their table scraps than in welcoming me home, they retreated in tandem back towards the dining area.

Gina appeared around a corner with a determined look in her eye and shoved me up against the closest wall with enough force to make the nearby hanging paintings shake. The kiss that followed electrified me, as my hybrid brain registered all of the sensations simultaneously in real time – the soft, fullness of her lips, heat of her skin, salt from her tears, and pheromones that exploded as she forced her tongue deeply within my receptive mouth. Her hardened nipples raked my chest. I had not been that instantly aroused since I was a teenager, and she pressed her body into mine with more intensity as she registered my response. Without breaking contact, she dragged me through the doorway of the closest guest bedroom and slammed the door behind us, locking it.

To say the next few minutes provided the best sex I had ever experienced would be an understatement of intergalactic proportions. Gina was always athletically gifted, but I had lost a step or two over the years. That first step had now returned at a masterful level, and we never even hit the mattress. Gina bit hard into my shoulder to keep from screaming. The pain was delightful, but she did not leave a mark. Once it was over, I was not even out of breath.

With that proper welcome out of the way, we both returned to the dining room looking a bit disheveled and aglow.

"I'd say, get a room, you two," Lenny shouted out across the table, "but it looks like you already did."

"Lenny was just explaining the difference between an Irish wake and funeral and those of most other cultures." Helen interjected, doing her best to change the subject from our post coital bliss.

"Booze and laughter!" Lenny shouted the punch line, "and the occasional fist fight at follow-up festivities."

I recalled the time my brothers and I had gone out drinking following the burial of Spaghetti's wife, Posey. It was an anniversary death, as she had passed a year to the day that Spaghetti had crossed the veil. My oldest brother kept playing an Irish song he said reminded him of her on the juke box in the bar, I believe it was *The Rose of Tralee*, and the bartender made the mistake of finally lowering the volume as my brother was energetically joining in the song's chorus for the tenth time. My older brother did not drop a note as he leapt over the bar after the bartender. The Ginger, on instinctive cue, locked the front door, and then joined the rest of us in the exploding knuckle donnybrook. There was not a glass, bottle or stick of furniture left in one piece by the time our youngest brother dragged his three older siblings out of the bar, one-by-one into his waiting van, the sound of police sirens rapidly approaching from a distance. Despite returning the next day to pay for the damages, including for the bartender's extensive dental work, we were barred for life from the establishment. A small price to pay to become a neighborhood legend. Those were the good old days. You got drunk, fought, licked your wounds, and paid the bill. It was considered un-manly to call the cops. I looked at my new hands and noticed all of the scars on my knuckles had disappeared.

Scarlett and Savannah moved their chairs over to make an opening at the table for me beside Gina, and Helen brought over a plate full of vegetarian Greek delicacies. I realized at that moment, as the steam from the marinated vegetables rose off the plate and permeated my nostrils, that as good as the food was on Centauri, it lacked the deep aromas that awakened the senses and initiated a Pavlovian response. I also observed that each individual on Centauri ate only when they were really hungry and did not socialize as part of their eating ritual, the way humans did. It was purely functional. Everett's sharing meals with me during our trip, and here, was a learned human attribute. Not all evolution is good.

"Everett has been telling us about your adventures on Centauri." Lucian said, excitedly. The boy had grown a foot since I last saw him.

"He explained why you look so different," Scarlett chimed in.

"You don't know the half of it," Gina said with a wink. Lenny and Helen laughed as they caught it.

"Love the hair!" Savanna said with approval. "Not that you weren't cute back when you were bald," she added quickly, to politely cover any unintended *faux pas*.

01000100 01101111 01101110 00100111 01110100 00100000
01110111 01101111 01110010 01110010 01111001 00101100
00100000 01001001 00100000 01101000 01100001 01110110
01100101 00100000 01101110 01101111 01110100 00100000
01101101 01100101 01101110 01110100 01101001 01101111
01101110 01100101 01100100 00100000 01010000 01100101
01110100 01110010 01101001 01100011 01101000 01101111
01110010 00101110

*Don't worry, I have not mentioned Petrichor.*

"Hey, no fair." Bobbi chided. "Everett and Jimmy are communicating in numbers."

Michelle had a suspicious look on her face. She shot Everett the stink eye.

01011001 01101111 01110101 00100000 01100011 01100001
01101110 00100000 01110100 01100101 01101100 01101100
00100000 01101101 01100101 00100000 01100001 01101100
01101100 00100000 01100001 01100010 01101111 01110101
01110100 00100000 01101001 01110100 00100000 01110111
01101000 01100101 01101110 00100000 01110111 01100101
00100000 01100111 01100101 01110100 00100000 01101000
01101111 01101101 01100101 00101100 00100000 01100100
01100001 01110010 01101100 01101001 01101110 01100111
00101110

*You can tell me all about it when we get home, darling.*

Now Michelle's stink eye was focused on me. I was praying that Everett was not tapping into my mind back on Centauri when Petrichor was propositioning me. The fact that he never mentioned it on the trip back gave me hope he would be discrete.

My attention returned to the group. I had almost forgotten our newest guest, Whitey, who was engaged in a quiet conversation with Eddie at the far side of the table. He was finishing a large, rare slice of filet mignon with enthusiasm while listening thoughtfully to Eddie's comments. I could see the pink remainder of the largest tenderloin sitting curled on a turkey-sized platter on the countertop. The chunks he was shoveling into his mouth would have choked me during my best days as a carnivore. He barely chewed them before swallowing and replacing it with another. I did not see remnants of the meat on anyone else's plate.

"Whitey certainly did a stellar job on the house," Bobbi stated, picking up on my sudden interest.

"I was just checking out some of your remarkable work," I said. "An excellent job!"

He studied me quietly, assessing my status around this table. His eyes looked almost feral, and his ears seemed to retract rearwards just the slightest bit as he contemplated me.

"Jimmy and his family come from the construction trades." Gina offered, trying to draw Whitey into the conversation.

"Whitey's done some remarkable work for me at the restaurant." Helen added. "I knew he would be perfect for Gina's projects."

"In case you hadn't already figured it out, I'm Jimmy," I said with my friendliest smile, continuing to make the effort to engage him by extending my hand across the table. He leapt effortlessly to his feet as he grasped my hand and gave it a shake with more strength than I ever possessed as a human. I had shaken a lot of tradesmen's hands during my youth, and Whitey's grip did not come from just shaping rebar or hauling hands of bricks. I thought back to the effortless way he had wielded that large sledgehammer at the grave. I tried to reach into his mind, but I must have been picking up on the dogs' thoughts, who were ecstatically sharing scraps under the table.

"Warren Fronsdahl," he said with a deep timbre to his voice. "But my friends call me 'Whitey.'"

I noticed that even the thick hair on his arms was as white as that on his head. The Irish are notorious for going grey at an early age, even silver, but Whitey's mane shone the purest of white like it was under a constant black light. And while his skin on his arms was leathery, like he had spent a lifetime out in the sun, his face was flawless, and youthful looking.

*Sorry to interrupt folks, but I have company out here, and they don't seem too friendly.*

It was Claire, and she sounded anxious.

"Go!" Bobbi commanded. Michelle and Everett were through the sliding back door before her voice had carried across the table. I followed immediately in their wake. When I materialized next to the grave site, Michelle and Everett were already standing, shoulder-to-shoulder with Claire, facing a pack of about a dozen hungry looking coyotes as they advanced slowly from the gulley area. The Alpha coyote was the largest and his bared fangs telegraphed that they meant business. I was not sure if the Prime Directive prevented my Centaurian neighbors from reigning hell down on these threatening predators, so I moved to a spot in between the coyotes and my friends. My presence, even in its athletic Centaurian form, did not slow the coyote's approach.

01010100 01100001 01101011 01100101 00100000 01000011
01101100 01100001 01101001 01110010 01100101 00100000
01100010 01100001 01100011 01101011 00100000 01110100
01101111 00100000 01110100 01101000 01100101 00100000
01111001 01100001 01110010 01100100 00101110

*Take Claire back to the yard.*

I looked back as Everett and Michelle locked their hands underneath Claire's belly and together, the two Centauri and the thousand-pound mule disappeared in a blink, leaving only Claire's surprised audible "what the fuck?" in their darkened wake.

Turning back to the coyotes, I could now see that as large as they were, they were emaciated, and their fur ravaged by mange. They were starving.

"Get out of the way!" Lenny shouted as he approached from behind me. I could hear the unmistakable racking of his shotgun as he chambered a shell. I raised my hand to hold him off, not sure what I was going to do as an alternative if that did not stop him. I did not want to kill these creatures, who were now positioned for an imminent attack, about thirty feet in front of me. I quickly reached into their minds and could hear the same canine thoughts passing between them collectively as they were sizing up their opposition.

The lead coyote stared at me and sniffed the air, and I got the sense of some form of recognition. Then I saw the image of the former me standing on that back road, bald and afraid, as the pack of coyotes approached through the field. I guess that no matter what genetic changes I had gone through, my scent remained the same.

I did not see the huge white creature until it had passed over our heads from behind me and Lenny and landed on the earth with a thud that would have made Claire proud. It was the largest wolf I had ever seen, and three times the size of the Alpha coyote. It dropped something from its jaws on the earth in front of it and let out a howl that raised the newfound hair on my head like static electricity. The other coyotes instinctively began to back away, without turning their faces from the behemoth before them. The Alpha coyote held his ground. Lenny raised his shotgun and leveled it in its direction. I placed my hand on the barrel and forced it downward until Lenny relented.

I could sense the growing fear from within the pack as their canine thoughts flew amongst them. And then I recognized the distinct canine pattern I had picked up in the kitchen. Calm and powerful.

The wolf grabbed what I could now see was the large tenderloin from the kitchen and with a powerful flick of its head hurled it end-over-end over and beyond the Alpha, which stared for a second at its large white cousin and then turned and snatched the large piece of meat from where it landed. Without missing a step, it continued across the property and over the back fence with the remainder of its pack following closely on its tail.

"I have to apologize for my cousins," the White wolf said as it turned back to me and Lenny. "It's been a devastating year with the wildfires and a Chronic Waste Disease epidemic decimating the normal populations of elk, deer and rabbits in Northern Colorado."

"Many of the locals have been complaining about the loss of their farm animals to predation." Lenny added, "It's a hell of a thing; can't blame either side."

I just traveled trillions of miles on a spacecraft through a wormhole and back, conjured up a dead mule and yet, here I was more stunned by the talking wolf than Lenny appeared to be. The wolf's voice was unmistakable. Before I could respond, Helen and Bobbi appeared from behind us, breathing heavily from their run from the house, and tossed a large sack of clothing into the high grass over by the pond. The wolf leapt into the grass where it landed. I could hear suppressed moans coming from the area, like a creature consumed by pain.

"I was about to tell you at the dinner table," Bobbi said sheepishly, as Whitey now reappeared upright and fully clothed in his human form, from the tall grass by the pond.

*That we now have a werewolf in our group?* I groaned telepathically.

*We call ourselves hamløper; shapeshifters in your language.* Whitey interjected telepathically. If this kept up, I could drop my cell phone service.

"I'll fill you in on the way back to the house," Helen said with a smile. "I still have to feed Claire, who is still a little dizzy from the ride Everett and Michelle gave her."

I looked back anxiously toward the gulley one last time.

"Don't worry, they're not coming back," Whitey said. "I told them I would leave a full elk carcass for them later tonight, and then one every other week thereafter, as long as they stayed in their territory beyond the foothills."

"He keeps a whole refrigerated storehouse full of them on his property right down the road," Bobbi added, back to anticipating my thoughts.

We all turned back and proceeded towards the house.

*Welcome home, Jimmy.* I could hear Claire suddenly chime into my head. *And thanks for the hook-up with Mr. Rogers. I think I can do it now on my own.*

# CHAPTER THIRTY-SIX
# (RESTORING UNNATURAL ORDER)

The rest of the group were anxiously waiting on the back deck as we approached, having witnessed the whole event. The younger humans looked the most worried, the two young women looked like they had been crying, and I could see that Lucian was struggling to maintain a brave face. Even with all I had been through over the past couple of years, this was a lot to take in, even for me. Gina was comforting each of them in turn and ushered them back inside as we drew close. I knew she would keep them grounded.

Everett and Michelle were in the yard with Claire, who looked befuddled.

"That was some trip!" Claire said out loud. "My head is still spinning."

"When am I going to get that ride?" Lenny shouted in response, giving Everett's shoulder a firm slap.

I could not help myself. Before I even realized what I was doing, I grabbed Lenny's outstretched arm, hoisted him into a fireman's carry and took him around the property at my full speed. When we arrived back in the yard, literally in the blink of an eye, everything about him was disheveled, and he would not release his inverted grip on my waist. Everett carefully maneuvered him upright, raised him off my shoulders and placed him back onto his shaky legs. It looked like Bam Bam Rubble lifting Fred Flintstone.

"Careful what you wish for, Lenny." Everett said, with a laugh. "Isn't that right, Jimmy."

"If I could make you all stop spinning," Lenny replied, with a weak chuckle, "I'd shoot the whole lot of you."

Gina reappeared on the back deck carrying an oversized salad bowl filled with savory garlic vegetables for Claire. Michelle transported them back to the yard before Gina realized they had left her hands. Claire was thrilled and dug right in.

"Anyone for dessert?" Gina called.

"C'mon," Eddie said, appearing beside Lenny and gently guiding him through the sliding glass doors, "I've made a *Galaktoboureko* that will melt in your mouth."

Helen and Bobbi followed them in.

"You guys go ahead," Claire said. "I'm okay, really."

I looked out onto the back pasture and spotted the glow from Mr. Rogers. No one else seemed to notice him. The rest of us walked at a leisurely pace around the outside of the house, onto the side deck and into the dining room.

As we took our seats around the table, Helen appeared with a large, honey cake with the inscription 'Welcome Home Jimmy and Everett' across its top. She started to dole out the slices on plates while Eddie scooped generous portions of the custardy *galaktoboureko* into bowls for Lenny and the youngsters. Gina played mother with the coffee for the grownups and milk for Lucian and soon we all were immersed in a post memorial celebration of Mr. Rogers' passing like a true Irish clan. My grandfather, Spaghetti, would have been proud. The food tasted exceptional, bolstered no doubt from the love I felt flowing around this table.

"Are you afraid of dying, Bobbi?" Lucian asked suddenly. The table fell quiet.

"No sweetheart," she said sincerely, "some of my best friends are dead."

"Does it hurt to die?" He followed up.

I thought hard about that question. In my situation, it all happened so fast -- a bullet through the heart -- that I really did not feel any pain, until they brought me back from the dead and my body had to finish healing that wound. But the passage itself to the other side of the veil was painless.

"No, Lucian," I responded gently, "it doesn't hurt to die."

"Well, then I'm not afraid of dying." Lucian asserted.

*Out of the mouth of babes.* Everett winked from across the table.

"And you won't have to worry about that for a long, long, time!" Gina intervened firmly but with maternal gentleness. "C'mon, sweetheart, finish your desert. We have to get you back home."

"Oh, we can drop him," Scarlett volunteered. "We need to head back soon anyway."

"We have classes in the morning." Savanna chimed in, getting up from the table and removing her plate to the sink. Scarlett and Lucian followed suit. Gina had trained them well.

I could see how fond Gina was of Lucian, and of Scarlett and Savanna, who both openly doted on Lucian like he was their little brother. For the first time in years, I felt a pang of guilt for not providing Gina with a child, but I drew some solace from the fact she had found an outlet for her maternal love among this growing band of rag-tag misfits that kept pulling new members into our orbit.

Once the youth had left, we all adjourned onto the back deck for drinks. I was happy to see that Michelle, Gina and Bobbi were still enjoying their wine. Lenny, Helen, Whitey and Eddie were sipping from their first tumblers of Macallan single malt, neat, and were quickly advancing on cracking the second. Everett was rolling an exceptionally large joint from the plastic baggie of grass and Zig Zag rolling papers he had foraged from Michelle's purse. That was strange in itself because I had never seen Michelle carry a purse. Gina's proclivity for accessorizing was obviously rubbing off on the female Centaurian during my year in space.

I was a little worried about introducing alcohol into this new body of mine. While the food on Centauri was close enough to pass for our own, I never saw any alcohol or any other intoxicant during my time there. Then again, Everett and Michelle did not seem to suffer any negative side effects from the vast amount they consumed here on earth. I settled for a bottle of Coors, making sure to tip a drop or two over the deck rail and onto the earth below in memory of BJ Delaney, the first one from the neighborhood to bring the distinct brand back from Colorado to the Bronx in the early seventies. It tasted delicious.

Whitey came over and sat in the open chaise lounge next to mine.

"You did an amazing job on the house." I observed.

"Gina paid an amazing price for the work." He confirmed with a smile.

Given my abrupt departure, I did not have time to show Gina her way around the accounts.

01000100 01101111 01101110 00100111 01110100 00100000
01110111 01101111 01110010 01110010 01111001 00100000
01100001 01100010 01101111 01110101 01110100 00100000
01100001 00100000 01110100 01101000 01101001 01101110
01100111 00101110 00100000 01001001 00100000 01100011
01110010 01100001 01100011 01101011 01100101 01100100
00100000 01111001 01101111 01110101 01110010 00100000
01100011 01101111 01101101 01110000 01110101 01110100
01100101 01110010 00100000 01110011 01100101 01100011
01110101 01110010 01101001 01110100 01111001 00100000
01101001 01101110 00100000 01100001 00100000 01100110
01100101 01110111 00100000 01110011 01100101 01100011
01101111 01101110 01100100 01110011 00100000 01100001
01101110 01100100 00100000 01110100 01100001 01110101
01100111 01101000 01110100 00100000 01000111 01101001
01101110 01100001 00100000 01100101 01110110 01100101
01110010 01111001 01110100 01101000 01101001 01101110
01100111 00100000 01110011 01101000 01100101 00100000
01101110 01100101 01100101 01100100 01110011 00100000
01110100 01101111 00100000 01101011 01101110 01101111
01110111 00100000 01100001 01100010 01101111 01110101
01110100 00100000 01111001 01101111 01110101 01110010
00100000 01100001 01100011 01100011 01101111 01110101
01101110 01110100 01110011 00101110 00100000 01010011
01101000 01100101 00100000 01101000 01100001 01110011
00100000 01100001 01100011 01110100 01110101 01100001
01101100 01101100 01111001 00100000 01101101 01100001
01100100 01100101 00100000 01111001 01101111 01110101
00100000 01100001 00100000 01100010 01110101 01101110
01100100 01101100 01100101 00100000 01101001 01101110
00100000 01111001 01101111 01110101 01110010 00100000
01101001 01101110 01110110 01100101 01110011 01110100

01101101 01100101 01101110 01110100 00100000 01100001
01100011 01100011 01101111 01110101 01101110 01110100
01110011 00100000 01100100 01110101 01110010 01101001
01101110 01100111 00100000 01111001 01101111 01110101
01110010 00100000 01100001 01100010 01110011 01100101
01101110 01100011 01100101 00101110 00100000 01001101
01101111 01110010 01100101 00100000 01110100 01101000
01100001 01101110 00100000 01100101 01101110 01101111
01110101 01100111 01101000 00100000 01110100 01101111
00100000 01100011 01101111 01110110 01100101 01110010
00100000 01110100 01101000 01100101 00100000 01110111
01101111 01110010 01101011 00100000 01101111 01101110
00100000 01110100 01101000 01100101 00100000 01101000
01101111 01110101 01110011 01100101 00101100 00100000
01110111 01101000 01101001 01100011 01101000 00100000
01101000 01100001 01110011 00100000 01100010 01100101
01100101 01101110 00100000 01110000 01100001 01101001
01100100 00100000 01101001 01101110 00100000 01100110
01110101 01101100 01101100 00101110

*Don't worry about a thing. I cracked your computer security in a few
seconds and taught Gina everything she needs to know about your accounts.
She has actually made you a bundle in your investment accounts during your
absence. More than enough to cover the work on the house, which has been
paid in full.*

I looked over as Michelle toasted her wine glass in my direction, and I returned
her salutation with a tip of my beer bottle. She then returned to her immediate
conversation and said something that drew a peal of laughter from Bobbi and
Gina. I did not dare listen in.

*So, tell me about these numbers?* Whitey popped into my head.

*It's a Centauri thing, I couldn't explain it to you if I wanted.* I replied.

"One day it was all a jumble of numbers," I continued, switching to aural communication, "and at some point during my trip to Centauri, a genetic switch was thrown and *voila*, I became a binary wizard."

"Fair enough," Whitey responded. "Similar thing happened to me. One day I was thinking in just English; the next, I'm listening into conversations between the two German Shepherds my family owned."

Whitey went over to where the others were seated, refilled his tumbler with Macallan and returned to the chaise lounge.

"So, since we are getting to know one another, tell me about this wolf thing," I said.

"Well, as my ancestors tell it, we are the descendants of the Norse wolf-god, Fenrisúlfr, who was the son of Loki and a female giant named Angrboða." Whitey recounted in the rehearsed way of someone who had their oral tradition drilled into them. "But to tell you the truth," he continued, "all I really know is that over the generations, some members of my family line have been given the gift of hamløper. Shapeshifting."

Having recently done a little shapeshifting of my own, on a much smaller level, I was fascinated.

"Could you do it from birth?" I asked, as Gina dropped off a second beer for me and then, after letting her hand casually drift across my shoulders, returned to Michelle and Bobbi. I could hear Lenny telling some story that had Eddie, Helen, and Everett in stitches.

"It didn't manifest itself in me until puberty." He responded softly.

"Can you control it?"

"Sure," he responded. "It's not like in the movies where I turn only during a full moon. I can do it anytime, but I have to be careful because I have to strip off my clothes before the change." He laughed. "When I was a teenager, I lost many pairs of my favorite jeans before I got a real handle on it."

"So, what brought you here?" I asked.

"Work, land, solitude, take your pick." He acknowledged. "It just felt like the right place to be."

I thought about his beautiful house and large property just down the road. He must be doing well.

"Plus, I can purchase all of the elk I need from the local hunters in the area." He added. "Saves me from having to go out hunting on my own."

I wondered what hunting like an apex predator must be like. Then I thought about Dan Pearsall and the night I died. A true human apex predator. I will never forget that smile. I sensed Whitey tuning into my thoughts, so I quickly changed them.

"So, which one of this crew figured out your secret?" I queried, then rolled out the usual suspects, "Bobbi? Michelle?"

"Believe it or not," he responded with a smile, "it was Claire."

He took a long sip from his scotch, then continued.

"I was finishing up here one evening, up on a scaffold, when I heard my Coyote cousins calling from the foothills." He replayed the scene in his head for a moment before proceeding. "It was their call to the hunt. It was intoxicating." He finished his scotch. "None of the other crew was around and Gina was over at Michelle's house, so I let off a responsive howl, which echoed in the distance. I almost fell off the scaffold when I heard someone call up from below 'nice lungs' and looked down and saw Claire standing there."

At that we both burst into laughter.

"I really didn't know what to do." He continued. "I'd never been caught outright like that, and I sure as shit never met a talking mule."

*Well, that's okay, I never met a shape shifter.* Now it was Claire who was telepathically intruding on both our thoughts.

"She's fucking amazing." He shot back aurally.

"You don't know the half of it." I confessed.

"Well, I leapt down off the scaffolding and engaged in one of the most interesting conversations I ever had." Whitey said. "I've been forced to be a loner all of my life for fear someone would learn my secret. I had no idea that you were sponsoring a crew of misfits right down the road from me."

*I reached out telepathically to Bobbi and Michelle and the rest, as they say, is history.* Claire chimed in.

I stood up and retrieved a half-finished bottle of Macallan from over by the others and returned with a clean tumbler of my own. I filled his first before mine and then held it in out a toast, and we clinked glasses.

"Welcome to the misfits club." I toasted. "One big happy family for those who have none."

We both tossed down our drinks in one shot.

*You're welcome!* Claire interjected. *Do I know how to pick 'em or what?*

# CHAPTER THIRTY-SEVEN
# (BE THE BEE)

Whitey called it a night and headed off on foot down the road towards his home. A moment later I heard the calls of the coyotes from the foothills in the distance. Then a deep and mournful howl rose in response from the direction of Whitey's property. It was the sound of loneliness.

Lenny had fallen asleep in one of the chaise lounges, snoring happily. Eddie retrieved a blanket from the living room couch and draped it over his friend, then went inside to finish filling the dishwasher. Helen was helping Gina clear the remnants of our drinking fest from the deck. I was feeling pretty lit and was sipping the last of my scotch as I stared out over the back fields. The moonless panoply of stars overhead did little to encroach on the darkness of the lower property, and I strained to locate Claire, who had retreated into the blackness. A moment later, my eyes fixed upon the glowing hologram of Mr. Rogers out by his gravesite. The large silhouette of Claire's body soon passed between us, momentarily eclipsing him.

"She's going to be fine." I heard Bobbi's say from the spot she had quietly assumed off my right shoulder.

"Is that an official prediction of the future, or just a human consolation?"

"A little of both," she replied, reaching around my waist, and giving me a comforting squeeze. "My spirit guide assures me Claire will adapt as she always does. With our help."

"Do you see that?" I asked, pointing out towards where Mr. Rogers' glowing figure reappeared and slowly guided Claire on a parallel course towards the rise at the far end of the pond.

"What?" She responded. "Wait." I could feel her tapping into my mind. It reminded me of when I was a kid and talking on a landline phone and someone in the house picked up the receiver on the same line. If you were not listening for it, you may not even notice.

"Holy shit!" She exclaimed, once engaged. "That's so weird."

Given all of the paranormal experiences I had been introduced to through Bobbi over the past couple of years, I could not begin to fathom her concept of 'weird.' She was the first authentic witch I had ever met, and I had seen her do amazing things, including acting as a repeated conduit to my dead brothers and seeing the future.

"What's the matter," I said jokingly, "never seen a ghost before?"

"That's just it," Bobbi responded, "that's not a ghost. At least, not any kind of ghost I've ever experienced."

Despite my recent crash induction into the Fantastic Friends club, I remained an intuitive novice who needed to be gently led through the alternate reality maze of the paranormal.

"Looks like a ghost to me." I offered.

"Now look," she instructed, pointing, "you see how they are physically nuzzling each other?"

I could see them gently rubbing their necks together and nuzzling each other's ears in the soft glow from Mr. Rogers.

"Ghosts can't usually manifest that kind of energy. Not enough for a physical presence." Bobbi explained, like I was a first-year student at Hogwarts. "As a matter of fact, I couldn't even see Mr. Rogers out there until I tapped into your mind."

*He's a hologram.* Claire said, joining both Bobbi and I telepathically. *Jimmy did it for me earlier today. Now I can do it.*

"Well, that's certainly a first for me." Bobbi said excitedly. "Look at you," she teased, "coming back from outer space with a new kind of power."

"But I didn't!" I exclaimed.

*Yeah, you did.* Claire insisted. *You tapped into my head as I was mourning at the graveside earlier, visualizing him in spirit, a trick I had already picked up from Bobbi - thank you Bobbi - and the next thing I knew, he appeared to me like this.*

Bobbi and I stared out at the two of them as Claire gave him a more aggressive nuzzle. She was definitely physically engaging with something solid.

"Hold on," Bobbi said, "let me try something."

I could feel her delicately disengage from my mind, again, like someone softly returning that land-line phone receiver to its cradle, so as to not let you know they have been listening.

"Wow!" Bobbi exclaimed, "I can still see him."

"See who?" Helen asked as she exited the house onto the deck.

"Mr. Rogers," Bobbi pointed, "out there with Claire."

Helen stared out into the darkness. "Sorry, I got nothing," she said with a nonchalance of someone who had been down this road many times before.

"Shit," Bobbi shouted, "we're cross-pollinating!"

"Now what are we talking about?" Eddie asked as he joined us out in the darkness of the deck.

"I knew there was some transference the night of the storm," Bobbi said, ignoring the others while working it out for us in her outside voice, "when we were all tapped into each other, and as Claire mentioned, she can now see the dead."

*Spaghetti dropped by when you two were lost in space!* Claire interjected. *And what exactly is a 'wee idjit'?*

"This is full blown morphic resonance!" Bobbi declared excitedly.

Now Everett and Michelle appeared on the deck.

"What's this about morphic resonance?" Everett asked. "Is our telepathy spreading?"

"We're going to head out." Michelle said, cutting him off. "Everett and I have some catching up to do."

01001010 01110101 01110011 01110100 00100000 01101100
01101001 01101011 01100101 00100000 01110010 01100001
01100010 01100010 01101001 01110100 01110011 00101110

*Just like rabbits.*

Everett winked at me just as Michelle gave him a shot in the arm that sent him skidding across the deck, where he landed on the still sleeping Lenny and the two rolled off the chaise lounge together.

"What the fuck!" Lenny shouted, surprised, as everyone broke into laughter.

Gina appeared at the doorway at the sound of the fracas and flicked on the outdoor lights. "Lenny, stop acting like a clown and get off poor Everett. You are going to wake the dogs."

Everett leaned up and planted a kiss on the still groggy Lenny's lips.

That sent us all into a second wave of laughter. It felt cathartic.

01000011 00100111 01101101 01101111 01101110 00100000
01000101 01110110 00101100 00100000 01101100 01100101
01110100 00100111 01110011 00100000 01100111 01100101
01110100 00100000 01100111 01101111 01101001 01101110
01100111 00101110

*C'mon Ev, let's get going.*

"Wait, wait, wait!" Bobbi shrieked, holding both hands outstretched above her head for effect. "Your binary message to Everett is still just numbers to me."

"That's because it wasn't meant for you." Michelle said aurally for the benefit of the telepathically challenged.

"But I knew what you said." I responded.

"Yes," she said, "I'm still getting used to that." Michelle said. "I'll have to be a bit more discrete in the future."

01001100 01101001 01101011 01100101 00100000 01001001
00100000 01110011 01100001 01101001 01100100 00101100
00100000 01101010 01110101 01110011 01110100 00100000
01101100 01101001 01101011 01100101 00100000 01110010
01100001 01100010 01100010 01101001 01110100 01110011
00101110

*Like I said, just like rabbits.*

I laughed, as Everett rolled Lenny off him and leapt to his feet. Michelle looked like she was blushing.

"Wait," Bobbi proposed, "can I try something?"

"What are you up to?" Helen asked.

"Jimmy," Bobbi continued, "can I tap into your mind again?"

"You better not be thinking any dirty thoughts!" Gina shouted playfully.

This time I blushed, recalling our encounter. "Sure, go ahead." There was that soft lift of the receiver again.

"Now Everett, send Jimmy a message in binary, slowly" Bobbi instructed.

*Wait, I want in on this.* Claire popped into our minds.

"Go ahead, Everett." Bobbi continued.

01110010

*r*

01100001

*a*

01100010

*b*

01100010

*b*

01101001

*i*

01110100

*t*

01110011

*s*

I laughed right away. Bobbi looked confused as she adapted. I could see her lips enunciating each letter.

"Rabbits!" Claire called out from the back yard.

"Rabbits!" Bobbi repeated excitedly. "I got it. Rabbits!"

Everett looked over at Michelle with a gleam in his eye and just like that, they both disappeared.

"It takes a little practice," I said to Bobbi.

She looked like a kid at Christmas. "Cross-pollination! And this time you're the flower."

"C'mon bumble bee," Eddie said to his sister as he helped Lenny to his feet. "Time to go."

"You can stay at our place tonight." Helen said to Lenny, ushering him along. "I'll drive your car." She flipped Eddie her car keys. "You drive Bobbi."

"Goodnight all," Claire called from below. "Thanks for coming today."

*You okay?* I asked her telepathically.

*A little tired, but better.* She responded. *We can do a proper catch up tomorrow.*

I watched her disappear through the backyard gate and head off towards the gravesite.

*Welcome home, Jimmy. I've missed you.*

As we locked the front door after the crowd pulled out of the driveway, Gina slowly turned and leaned against the door.

"So now you read minds." She purred seductively, "what am I thinking?"

By the time she completed her gleeful shriek I had transported her up the stairs and onto the bed.

# CHAPTER THIRTY-EIGHT
# (WISE ASS *REDUX*)

Despite a rigorous and repetitive sexual encounter, this new body of mine still was not tired, so I could not join Gina in post-coital slumber. Blue had worked her way under the covers between us and was sound asleep. I waited until I heard their syncopated snores before slipping out of bed and down to the kitchen, where I indulged what remained my still very human addiction to caffeine.

Mr. Rogers' passing had affected me more than I would care to admit. My equally restless mind kept going back to Aldor's final threat: *"Beware the law of unintended consequences."* My new and improved body and all these wonderful mental and physical powers fell certainly on the positive side of the ledger book. But the prospect of watching my life-long companion, the woman I just made love to and left sleeping peacefully upstairs, grow old and die long before me, cancelled everything else out. Even with the love I was sharing with my growing family of magical misfits, Gina would always be my first and foremost.

*Your mind never shuts down, does it Jimmy?* Even Claire's thoughts were now taking on a sultry sound.

*Sorry, I hope I didn't wake you.* I responded, sheepishly.

*Not at all, I've been suffering from a bout of insomnia myself,* she replied. *Grab a cup of coffee and a few carrots and meet me in the barn.*

Having not yet mastered Everett and Michelle's grace in motion, I arrived at the barn moments later with an empty coffee cup and a handful of soaked, caffeinated carrots. Claire did not seem to mind the latter and munched them down in one mouthful. That did not keep her from talking.

*So, what's troubling you my friend?* She finished her carrots in a large swallow and then switched to speaking aurally. "Unless, you just want me to forage around inside your head until I figure it out myself."

"I'm not sure where to begin," I admitted, struggling.

"Oh, don't make me start singing 'Do-Re-Me' from *The Sound of Music*, I'll never get it out of my head. I once had to carry a fat music teacher on a trip through the mountains and she could never stop singing that song while she rode. It took me a month to clear it from my consciousness." Claire paused to inflict her Lurchy laugh, then sang the first line, "Let's start at the very beginning . . ."

I was surprised that she was in such good spirits after just losing the love of her life. She suddenly quieted as she intercepted that thought.

*I haven't lost him, Jimmy. Thanks to you and Bobbi, I can see him anytime I want.* She professed, a bit more somberly.

"But he's still dead," I said, thinking about it all, "sure, the magic tricks lessen the pain, but it doesn't change the outcome."

Claire stared at me for a moment in silence, digesting my statement with the caffeinated carrots.

*Why don't you tell me all about your trip?* She thought. *You can even tell me in binary, I could use the practice.*

Over the next few minutes, I took Claire through every moment of my trip to Centauri and back again at the speed of binary. I left out no detail, including Petrichor. It felt good sharing the experience with someone. Every once in a while, Claire nuzzled me in a comforting manner.

"So, this law of unintended consequences, that prick Aldor mentioned," Claire switched to aural. "How does it play out with you?"

"Everett said that I'm going to live the lifetime of a Centaurian." I replied.

"That's not too bad." Claire mused. "Hasn't done them any harm."

"But that will be five times longer than Gina will live." I said, softly. I could feel the tears welling up in my eyes. I had never vocalized that thought before. The sound of those words made it very real.

Claire fell silent for a few moments and I could sense her thoughts returning to Mr. Rogers. I could actually feel her heart ache with my own. The pain in my chest was just as intense as when I returned from the dead.

"No," Claire said tenderly, "I wouldn't want that. Not without Mr. Rogers."

"What am I going to do?" I asked.

Claire thought for a moment. Her eyes lit up. "Zap her! I mean, have Everett zap her with his Hadron thingy."

I thought back to Everett and my last conversation on Jayney.

"He didn't seem too keen," I countered, "and I don't blame him. He dodged a bullet up there."

Claire went into my mind and replayed my memory.

*He didn't say no. Not definitively.* Claire observed.

She was right. Everett did not say no, but he clearly was not feeling it.

"Go back and ask him again." Claire instructed. "You're a lawyer, go after it. Jimmy Moran does not do half-measures!" She walked over and grabbed a mouthful of hay from the wall rack, clearly thinking about how it would play out.

"Have you mentioned any of this to Gina?" She asked, after swallowing.

I shook my head. "No, I haven't gotten that far, this is the first time I've openly talked it through."

"Well, you better get your ass back up to the house and talk to her," Claire said with a flair, "while I take this ass, with its ass, out for its morning constitutional. Those caffeinated carrots really moved things along this morning."

With that, she trotted out the barn door and off into the back field in a cantor. I turned and looked up at the third-floor window at the back of the house and thought of the beautiful woman who slept peacefully inside. I was not sure how I was going to handle this next conversation. Suddenly I heard my sister's voice in my head. This was not a memory; it was a sentient, although cleverly cribbed, thought.

*Leap and the net will appear.*

# CHAPTER THIRTY-NINE
# (CHOICE OF A LIFETIME)

I sat quietly in the rocker in the corner of our bedroom, sipping a steaming cup of coffee and staring at the outlines of two figures under the blanket, realizing that over the past year Blue had grown to almost Gina's size. My mind unintentionally drifted into a replay of a host of memories of Gina's and my life together, in no particular order. There were many jubilant triumphs and some painful disappointments, with just the right measure of laughter and tears. And there was an eclectic soundtrack of songs from different genres, that punctuated these moments, which now played in the background of these memories. And that is when it hit me, there was no music on Centauri, or art for that matter. Their aesthetic appreciation or indulgence of art and culture began and ended with the mastering of their own physical beauty and mental perfection. Nothing else mattered.

But then I remembered that image of the floating child and the sound of Petrichor humming that familiar melody. It was haunting, but I could not place it.

Blue must have sensed my presence because I began to pick up indecipherable canine thoughts a moment before the covers toward the foot of the bed began to quickly rise and fall in a syncopated fashion while the muffled drumbeat of her powerful tail against the mattress increased in intensity.

"Bbbllluuuueeee!" Gina moaned softly but firmly from under the covers at the far side of the bed. "Knock it off!"

With that command, all movement and sound ceased. The lack of any follow-up to Blue's early morning stirrings created a vacuum that caused Gina's mind to wake into full consciousness, leaving her pleasant dreams in Morpheus' world. I realized then that I could not read Gina's dreams. However, her conscious thoughts were coming in loud and clear.

*Fucking dog!*

With that, Blue's tail resumed its reveille paradiddle under the blanket, and I discerned that Blue could sense and respond to human thought. Given our ubiquitously creative and prolific New Yorker use of the word "fucking" in my household, and the unconditional loving nature of dogs, it was no surprise that Blue associated the word only with its positive connotations.

Gina's head slowly rose from somewhere between the top of the covers and the king-sized pillow on her side of the bed, and Blue's thunderous tail beat returned with a vengeance. Gina did a double take when her eyes focused on me in the chair, as her thoughts wove the connection between the images of my old and new self. Whatever image you may have of yourself, it is how others perceive you that really matters. Gina's mental juxtapositioning of my two images brought home how much I had physically changed.

Gina smiled and pulled herself up into a sitting position at the head of the bed. I could not help but fixate on her still full breasts and perky nipples as the upper part of her naked form surfaced from beneath the covers. She had aged so much better than I had over our decades together, and as I stared at her body, I realized she had remained as fit as any athlete in their early forties. She did not need to be Centaurian to read my mind. Her smile grew larger, and she scooted over, shoving a grunting Blue beneath the covers to my side of the bed with her curvy hips, and raised her side of the blanket in an offering for me to join her.

*Tell her!*

Claire's mental instructions literally snapped me out of my rising libido. I needed to pay more attention to regularly blocking entry to my mind, especially with all the mental pickpockets gravitating to my ever-expanding family of mystical misfits. I felt like my mother just caught me masturbating.

"C'mon lover," Gina cooed, "I want to take that new sports car out for a joy ride."

I bit the bullet. "We need to talk."

Throughout our marriage, neither one of us had ever used that line to the other. We were always far more creative in our approaches to the more serious issues in life. Misplaced comedy was often the inappropriate but more palatable substitute for introduction of the painful discussions. I could find no comical entre into the discussion I was initiating. Gina's face registered instant concern.

She raised the covers defensively over her upper body. "Is everything all right?" she asked, with a worried tone.

"I'm fine," I said, my gentle smile offering its assurances. "In fact, I'm almost perfect."

The sparkle came back to her eyes.

"And that's the problem," I said.

"I don't understand." The concern resurrected in her voice.

"Whatever happened the night of the storm, the night Everett brought me back from the dead, has slowly genetically transformed me in a way that makes me more Centaurian than human."

"Well, you sure seemed pretty damn human last night," Gina said.

I sensed her images of our sexual marathon from her point of view, and I felt myself blushing.

"The last time I felt like that was our first night together."

Now I was treated to her remarkably clear memories of that night in my Bronx attic apartment when she first gave herself to me. We had been dating for a couple of months, and this was her first time back at my place, a poor man's version of a Parisian writer's loft, dark, cold, and drafty. We were sharing Chinese take-out and drinking cheap wine and talking about our future plans, as individuals. Over the course of the alcohol fueled conversation, those plans morphed into possibilities as a couple. We knew we had nothing but dreams, and that was enough. When we finally made love, it was truly magical. In that moment I was thrilled by her attention to detail. I was also deeply in love all over again.

"It's time to talk of different dreams," I said softly. I walked over and sat down on the foot end of her side of the bed, safely distancing my reach from her body. "My dreams are now going to extend for over five hundred years."

The sexiest part of Gina was her mind. She always caught the direction of a conversation on the first bounce. She had not lost a step.

"Oh," she uttered, "I see." Her mind was filled with funereal images. Without discernible movement, I was now embracing her. But it was me who was weeping. She was comforting.

"Shoosh, shoosh, darling, you'll be alright."

It took me a moment to understand what she was saying and when I delved into her thoughts, they confirmed the worst. She was accepting her mortality and my extended life without her.

"No!" I almost shouted, the volume causing Blue to gyrate wildly under the blankets as she fought to free herself and come to Gina's aid. Gina reached over and with one touch, calmed the dog.

"Look," she said softly, "we always knew that someday, one of us would pass first, leaving the other to survive, hopefully with enough fond memories to make it palatable."

I thought of how in my family, the elders were quite competent at anniversary deaths, and how my grandmother, Posey, passed within a year of Spaghetti. The same for my parents, my mother gratefully followed my father to the grave within a relatively brief time. But every one of those days in the interim was a heartbreaking reminder of their spouse's absence. I was facing almost five hundred years of that painful purgatory.

"And with your newfound talents," she offered hopefully, "we can still communicate, even touch. Look what you've done for Claire and Mr. Rogers?"

I thought back to Claire's response earlier that morning: *"I wouldn't want that. Not without Mr. Rogers."*

"But what if I can change that?" I sputtered desperately, lifting my head from her shoulder, and gazing wildly into her eyes.

"Change what?" She asked anxiously.

"You," I continued, "what if I can make you like me?"

She released me and withdrew herself farther back towards the head of the bed, the distance both physical and emotional. I could feel her response before she said it.

"I'm sorry," she whispered, "I just don't know how I feel about it."

My mind was flooded with rapidly morphing images portraying her deeply ingrained but buried religious beliefs. When I left high school, I had shed the shackles of our common Catholic dogma, but despite her own lapsed religious practices, she always maintained one foot back in mother church, casually attending religious services on and off over the years, just to pay her union dues. It brought home the fact that it was now far easier for me to distance myself from the fears instilled by lifelong religious indoctrination because I had crossed and could now see beyond the veil. This unexpected journey revealed to me that the universal power that controlled everything there and here, was pure love. Gina had yet to experience that luxury.

Gina stood and went into the *en suite*, and I could hear the shower rushing. Before I could follow her, I heard Claire in my head.

*That wasn't a 'no', Jimmy. Leave her alone for now.*

# CHAPTER FORTY
# (ADRIFT ON EARTH)

I imprudently underestimated the immediate fallout from my conversation with Gina. For the first time in over forty years, joy and laughter disappeared from our home. Gina made me promise that first day that I would not eavesdrop on her thoughts, and I kept it. But the estrangement was killing me. Long periods of silence replaced our constant witty, often double entendre banter.

I filled my time doing chores around the property, at human speed. I repaired what needed to be repaired, painted the interior of the house, and upgraded what needed to be upgraded, all with the hope that it would coax Gina out of her funk. It did not. Then I began replacing all of the wooden fencing around my property just so I would not have to be inside the house, passing Gina in silence.

Gina spent most days out and about by herself; day trips to distant stores and curiosity shops, often even leaving behind a very confused Blue. The dog sought solace down with Claire in the barn. I was not even second choice. Gina continued to go out every morning for her runs, which remained the only emotional and physical respite for Blue. But I was no longer invited. Out of desperation, I began running by myself along the back roads outside of our estate at full speed, and before I realized it, I had expanded my route to the northern and western borders of Colorado, all within the same time frame it used to take me to do our local loop. It proved an invigorating but brief distraction from my growing despair.

During an otherwise volatile world-wide market, I jumped back into my day-trading with a fanatical zeal, using my advanced sensory perception to my full advantage, and soon my extensive off-shore holdings had doubled again. I tried to lure Gina back into emotional contact by setting up her own trading accounts, but she remained disinterested and let them perform based solely on programmed algorithms without any intervention.

Our family of misfits immediately sensed the dramatic shift in the energy within our home and respectfully kept their distance, which only added to my growing isolation. Lenny limited his contact to the occasional phone call asking if we were okay and was there anything he could do. There was not. Everett and Michelle avoided any contact, and I had seen them only once as they passed the front of the house in their truck, both with forlorn looks on their faces as they tentatively waved at me. This loss of their fellowship hit me harder than I expected, which must have had to do with our Centauri bond. I could hear the lonely howl from Whitey some nights as I sat awake in the living room, sleep having all but abandoned me since my return. Even Scarlett and Savanna limited their visits to quick pop-ins to see and talk with Claire, often not even stopping into the house to say hello. Only Lucian kept coming around on a regular basis to offer his help with the chores, but even this young human child could sense that something was amiss, despite my and Gina's best efforts to shield him from our pain. Still, he was wise enough in his youth to not ask any uncomfortable questions.

Days turned into weeks, and then into months. My sixty-fourth birthday came and went in the middle of November, with only a card from Gina left on the kitchen counter. "I love you" was all that was written.

One day, during one of my runs, I found myself in the town of Hygiene, standing in front of the Oracle of Pythia. It was a Tuesday, so I knew the restaurant would be closed, but I felt drawn to it anyway. I had not reached out to any of our crew because I did not want to put them in the position of having to choose sides in the matter. I had even blocked my mind from them all, even Claire, who demonstrated her increasing displeasure with the situation by upping her daily manure production and delivering it in new and unexpected places, including right outside the window of my office.

She did not say anything aurally, just showed up every day with a determined look on her face and as she stared angrily through the window, her face appearing directly above my computer screen, she mouthed the words, 'Fix this Jimmy,' before turning her ass to me, raising her tail straight in the air like a salute, and releasing a cascade of ten pounds of steamy, dark brown mule muffins. She repeated this assault four times a day. The rest of the time she spent off in the back, walking and nuzzling with the holographic Mr. Rogers, or hanging out with Lucian in the barn.

Suddenly Bobbi appeared through the double doors of the restaurant and stood defiantly on its porch furiously wagging her finger in my direction.

"Jimmy, you prick, just because I can't reach into your head, doesn't mean I can't sense your presence. Get your ass in here!" This clearly was not a request, and she turned and went back inside without waiting for any response. I despondently trudged up the long wooden steps in human fashion and followed her inside.

I could hear Helen and Bobbi arguing in the formal dining room of the restaurant off to my immediate right. Eddie could be heard intermittently, unsuccessfully trying to referee the exchange.

"Stay out of it, Bobbi," Helen shouted, "this is not your prerogative!"

"Bobbi," Eddie added, "Helen's right, they need to work it out themselves."

"I'm telling you," Bobbi shouted back with equal fervor, "he needs to know! I've seen the future, and they're not together!"

I was home, sobbing in the hot shower by my office before the restaurant door had swung closed behind me.

# CHAPTER FORTY-ONE
## (AIN'T NO MOUNTAIN HIGH ENOUGH)

Over the next two weeks I could not get Bobbi's words out of my mind. I tried to approach Gina a few times to broach the subject, but she rejected all advances. When home, she spent most of her time isolated in the Tower, up in our bedroom suite, with the door closed. I retreated to the dungeon and started sleeping on the pull-out sofa in the living area outside of my office. Reflexively, I looked each morning at the large whiteboard calendar on the wall opposite the doorway to my office as I entered. On this particular morning, I noticed 'Thanksgiving' entered and circled on Thursday, November 26th, two days from now. In a fit of anger, I obliterated the word from the board with the palm of my hand.

I went upstairs to the first-floor kitchen, poured a cup of coffee, and went out on the beautiful new back deck. The sun was rising in the east but had not yet touched the Three Witches on the western horizon. In my human form, my acrophobia caused me to avoid all things taller than I was. But this morning, Longs Peak, the tallest of the three, seemed to be calling to me.

I covered the thirty miles distance to its base in what seemed like a minute, using the visual of the tallest mountain as my North Star, the last few miles following highway 7 to a large parking area. The sun was just reaching the peak when I arrived. I was surprised to see a number of hikers and climbers already funneling quietly from their cars and some tents onto a well-worn trail that brought them closer to the vertical ascent staging area. I ran the next nine miles alongside the trail using the sporadic groups of hikers with their head lamps as my mileposts to make sure I was heading in the right direction. One sign for Goblins Forest caught my eye, and I was half expecting to see one of these magical creatures lurking in the woodlands. I easily leap-frogged a number of brooks that I encountered, although when I crossed the Alpine Brook, I was almost spotted by one of the hikers that had taken a moment to rest on the bridge. By the time he had performed his double take in my direction, I was gone. When I reached the granite ridge that the other hikers kept referring to in their minds as "the Keyhole," I already passed the leaders and had it all to myself. The rocky formation did not really look like a keyhole to me. It looked more like an old-fashioned, U-shaped bottle opener among a sea of boulders. As I passed through the Keyhole, I was almost blown back onto the field from a fierce windshear that ambushed me at its entrance.

My new body took to the climb like it was built for it, and the ascent itself was invigorating. I was thrilled to be able to gaze outward without any vertigo. I also did not notice any impact of the increased elevation on my breathing. There was more than enough oxygen in the thinner air to sustain me.

With no one before me I just followed my instincts up along whatever paths through the mountainside looked traversable. There were helpful little signs along the way that told me that I was heading in the right direction. Did I mention that I loved my new body, I felt like a mountain goat.

By the time the sun was warming my skin, I had reached a point a few hundred feet below the summit. I was able to scramble up this last stretch by bounding from one outcrop to another with the ease of a hopscotch game. As I propelled onto the surprisingly level peak, I spotted a small circular disk embedded in the stone, the words "Colorado State A&M College B.M." engraved on its circumference. I also spotted Michelle.

"Took your time getting up here." She said, gazing off into the distance with her back to me.

"What the fuck—"

"—am I doing here?" She turned to me and smiled. "Early on Tuesday mornings, Everett likes to go to the Walmart in Longmont to do some shopping. No crowds or prying eyes. I use that opportunity to come up here and spend some 'me' time gazing out over your world."

I tried to reach into her mind but was blocked.

"Now, now, newbie," she continued aurally, "I think we should conduct this conversation the old-fashioned way. Human problems need to be discussed like humans."

She walked over to a large boulder and leapt up on it, invitingly tapping a spot next to her. I crossed the gap in one vault.

"By the way, Jimmy, that was me calling for you to come here this morning." She continued to stare at the beautiful country that stretched out before us. "Another little trick you'll probably pick-up before long."

She then turned to me and in that instant transformed into her radiant Centauri form and her eyes instantly mesmerized me. She was far more beautiful than the other Centauri women I had seen during my recent trip, a close second to Petrichor.

"Why the summoning?" I whispered, trying to maintain focus. "You could have just popped in across the road."

She smiled, amused at the effect she seemed to be having. "I needed to talk to you about what's happening between you and Gina."

That reminder of reality hit me like a cold slap in the face. I had been able to put it out of my mind during the ascent. It now came rushing back into my consciousness.

"There's really nothing to talk about." I volunteered. "She's made her decision."

"I'm truly sorry about that," Michelle replied. Everything human in me recognized the authenticity in her statement.

"You see," Michelle continued, "as I have watched the two of you over these past few years, I have marveled at the connection between you. So fucking human."

I stared at her profile as she said it, almost laughing at the expletive.

"You must feel the same way towards Everett." I offered.

She thought about it for a moment, her mind still blocked from my reach.

"I do . . . . We do," Michelle responded, "but our bond formed out of necessity and friendship. It took many, many years. We were in what some humans refer to as an 'arranged marriage.' After all, we were paired up and shipped out here right out of the academy."

She looked back into my eyes. "Although the sex was always good."

We both laughed at that.

"But you two came together by choice," she continued, "there was nothing beyond the two of you that kept you together, and that has always been fascinating to me."

I thought about all of the struggles that Gina and I had been through over the past forty years, and, during those many episodes where other women would have taken a hike, she stayed with me. When I felt Michelle eavesdropping on those memories, I shut my mind down.

"Well," I whispered, "there now is something outside the two of us that is tearing us apart."

"And that's on me," Michelle said softly, "I'm sorry about that."

"What do you mean?" I asked.

"If I hadn't ordered Everett to use the Hadron Distributor on you –"

"We wouldn't be having this conversation." I finished her sentence.

"But Gina would be still feeling the pain of your loss if we had not brought you back." Michelle said wistfully. "Hobson's choice."

Her words summoned a preview of the pain I would feel when Gina's now human life would end. I started to sob at the thought of it. Michelle reached over and gently caressed my shoulder in consolation.

"I wish I could help you." Michelle said softly, her own pain evident.

"I know," I said. "Everett said as much on the way home."

"They would never forgive a second breach of the Prime Directive." Michelle responded. "Especially, premeditated, as you lawyers like to say."

"Not even I could get you guys off a second time," I said, trying to inject a little levity. But my heart was not in it.

"No," Michelle responded, "there'd be no second-chances. They would probably turn us all back into earth monkeys."

"So, what am I going to do?" I asked, after a moment, now fully serious. "I can't live without her."

Michelle's arm reached around my shoulders and pulled me into a hug. Despite my own evolving physical prowess, her strength was disconcerting. But there was an equal tenderness to it. I could feel the tears welling up in my eyes and looked away so I could wipe them clear.

"C'mon, my Centaurian-Terrian hybrid," Michelle said suddenly, "we need to get off this rock before those lesser mortals start arriving at the edge."

She lifted me off the boulder and carried me to the edge where I had arrived. We both gazed down along the mountain side and I could spot the tiny little human figures slowly making their way towards the top. She reached over and grabbed my hand firmly in her own and I was drawn into a funnel of energy that transported me through space and time, but before I could call out to her, we were both standing before her house on Beverly.

"That's another trick you still need to learn, newbie," Michelle said as she instantly reverted to her human form and turned and headed in towards her house.

*Don't give up hope, Jimmy, if my time here on earth has taught me nothing, it has taught me that the universe always sorts itself out.*

As I watched her disappear through her doorway, I thought to myself how lucky Everett was to have a woman like that for five human lifetimes.

# CHAPTER FORTY-TWO
# (ON THE ROAD AGAIN)

I spent the next day petulantly increasing my offshore wealth exponentially by unfairly capitalizing on a mild form of prognostication, just slightly north of intuition, I must have picked up from Bobbi during our last cross-pollination session. Within seconds of opening up an account, I knew which way each market was moving moments before every fluctuation and began trading across the board with Centaurian speed. The money kept piling up in Mark Wallen's fictitious overseas accounts, but it gave me no joy. I was emotionally moribund.

By the end of the day, I needed to get out of the house and away from everything that reminded me of Gina. It was already dark, so I jumped into my used and weathered looking pick-up truck and drove east along county roads that led me past the A&W, through Berthoud and out beyond the roundabout at the end of town. It actually took me two loops around its perimeter before I exited the far side and left my newly adopted community behind me. It felt different than during my recent runs throughout the state at Centauri speed, where I knew no one could see me pass. Here I was banging along in my truck at the state speed limit, which made me feel exposed and anxious. Despite my celestial travels, I still felt a little agoraphobic.

I continued east and turned on the truck's radio to fill the silence, which just happened to be set on a Colorado classical station. Music that I first experienced in Bugs Bunny cartoons and on the Odd Couple television show from the 70s, now played in their grown-up versions, and soothed my mind. I turned onto Colorado Interstate Highway I-25 and headed north with no particular destination in mind.

It was cold, so I threw on the heater, which proved temperamental for the first few miles, before begrudgingly offering me enough heat to allow my hands to relax their grip on the steering wheel. I had a full tank of gas and nowhere to go. I just wanted to forget about these past few years and feel uncomplicatedly human again. I started to sing sporadically along with the Cadet Glee Club of West Point in their choral rendition of William Blake's *Jerusalem*. I realized that Centaurians could not sing any better than humans. Truth be told, I may have sounded worse than during any shower concert I had randomly performed during my earlier life. No wonder there was no music up there.

I was surprised at how few vehicles were on the road, and then remembered that most people usually traveled during the early part of the day before Thanksgiving and were probably now all happily arrived at their destinations, in the arms of their loving families. I kept the speedometer at 65 and stayed vigilant, actively scanning the roadside to make sure I would not accidently hit some frightened animal seeking safe passage across the highway. Then it started to snow.

Just above Fort Collins I spotted some movement up ahead just a few feet off the right side of the road. It was a couple of back-packers walking single file on the right-hand shoulder. The young man in the lead was carrying what I recognized to be a folded tent on his back and the young woman walking behind him struggled with a large knapsack on hers. A stunning young Alaskan Malamute, attached by a chain lead to the woman's knapsack, cautiously followed up in the rear, its thick, impenetrable coat quickly covering with snow. While this caravan seemed dressed appropriately for the season, they looked like they spent most of their recent time roughing it outdoors. As I got within fifty feet of them, I saw a hand emerge with the universal hitchhikers' 'thumbs up' sign.

The wretched part of me just wanted to continue along alone, stewing in my misery. But then the dog, startled by the approach of my large truck, bolted off to the side, pulling the poor girl down hard as they collapsed into a tangled mess. I suddenly remembered my father referring to hitchhikers as strays, and yet, he always picked them up. That was the time before serial killers had emptied the nation's highways of hitchhikers. At that moment, the baritone radio announcer heralded the midnight hour and wished his audience a Happy Thanksgiving. I was another hundred feet beyond them before I finally pulled over, wondering the whole time, what I was thinking. I backed the truck up along the shoulder until I almost reached them.

"You guys okay?" I called to the young man as he worked to disentangle the woman and beast. I could hear the distress in her voice as she rubbed her right ankle. The dog, still attached to the backpack, panted nervously, and stared protectively in my direction, ignoring the steady increase in the snow fall's intensity.

The young man ceased his efforts and turned to face me. He was a decent-sized kid with a fairly thin beard that betrayed his youth, and he was rightfully nervous at the approach of a stranger. I saw him reach back and place his hand on a hunting knife in a sheath on his right hip. I stopped a safe distance away and held up both hands to show my peaceful intentions. He could see in my parking lights, that I was unarmed.

"Where are you kids going?" I asked. I scanned their minds and sensed the name of the town Cody, Wyoming, moments before he answered. I could also sense that neither one of these kids was a serial killer, even though that was something the new me had nothing to worry about.

"Wyoming, Cody, Wyoming." He responded, cautiously.

I had no idea where Cody, Wyoming was, but I did not give a shit, because I had nowhere else to be. Thanks to my evolution, I was not feeling the least bit tired.

"This is your lucky day," I said with a smile. "I just happen to be heading in that direction. If you want a lift, hop in."

The young man leaned in and whispered to the woman, who nodded her head vigorously.

"Sure," he responded, "do you mind taking the dog? We could load her into the truck bed in the back."

"No," I said, rejecting any distinction between the comfort of these life forms, "There's plenty of room for you all in the cab. Do you need a hand with your stuff?"

The girl had allowed the knapsack to slide off her shoulders and the young man helped her to her feet. She was limping on that right ankle. I walked over and detached the dog's lead and then helped the woman and dog into the back seat of the truck's cab. It was then that I realized that she was a few months pregnant, when the thought 'love' emanated from the fetal girl within her womb. I could feel the young woman's relief as she settled into the warm compartment, and the dog happily clambered onto her lap.

The young man had returned for his tent and was stowing it in the truck bed, while I retrieved the woman's back-pack. He had taken his spot in the shotgun seat by the time I reached the driver's side and was warming his hands on the now rocking heater vents. The snow on his clothes had already melted.

Looking at the two of them as I slid back into the seat, I would have guessed they were not even twenty years old. They reminded me of Gina and me back in the day.

"My name is Jimmy Moran," I said without looking, as I got situated and accelerated onto the roadway. It was more a general introductory statement, than directed at either of the passengers.

When neither of them responded, I dipped into their thoughts. He was named Sean, and the girl, Bekki. He was an artist who worked with metals, and a sometime blacksmith to supplement their income, and she was a waitress to make the rent. They were traveling North together from Tucson, Arizona to visit her folks and tell them about their baby, and they were carrying their entire world on their backs. Within a few miles they had all fallen asleep, including the dog, whose name was Chloé. I lowered the radio to a whisper and continued on my way.

I was frustrated by the fact that I could not read their dreams, to get some sort of directions, so instead I focused on reading dimly lit road signs for the next four hours while daydreaming about Gina and our life together. We were not much different when we started out than these two, and I wondered if they were going to make it.

*As Emerson once said, it's not the destination, it is the journey.*

I finally saw signs telling me I needed to take US Hwy 20 West for Cody, Wyoming. By the time I reached the town an hour later, I knew what I had to do, but first I pulled into the parking lot of a Best Western hotel. I removed the title for the truck from the center console, included the notation "gift" on the sale price line and signed and dated the back. I jotted down the following note on the envelope that contained it:

*The truck is yours to keep. Good luck with your little girl.*

I removed what amounted to just over a thousand dollars from my wallet and stuffed it into the envelope, which I left positioned carefully on the steering wheel. As I slowly opened the door and slid out of my seat, I felt a warm tongue on the back of my right hand, which was still clutching the steering wheel for balance. I turned and saw Chloé now sitting proprietarily in the driver's seat. The others were still deeply asleep. I put my finger to my lips and gently closed the door behind me until I heard it catch. Chloé watched as I disappeared into the night. The steam from her breath fogged up the driver's side window.

I have never felt more human than at that moment in time.

I retraced my path from Cody back to Berthoud. At first, I moved at human walking speed, which allowed snow to accumulate on my clothing and which made me cold. But once I found my way back onto the highway, I kicked it into Centauri gear and ran along the shoulders fast enough where I could not be spotted by vehicles as I passed them. At one point, just as I reached the Colorado border, I came upon a trooper about to hand an older woman a speeding ticket. I slowed down just long enough to visually appear beside them like the Road Runner and wish them both a Happy Thanksgiving. I almost did the "*Beep, Beep,*" just for good measure. As I kicked it back into high gear, I looked back and saw the extremely confused officer shaking his head and tearing up the ticket.

The endorphins I was feeling from my random acts of kindness while carving through the cold night air with this extremely warm body provided me with astonishing mental clarity. I would not make Gina choose. I would reset the table and just live our lives as best we can, as long as we can. Whatever happens, happens. I had learned the hard way that there were no guarantees.

When I finally arrived back at my home, I was shocked to see the driveway filled with vehicles, all but one, a rented blue Audi, I recognized as belonging to the various members of the group. The fine layer of snow that had accumulated on them told me they had been there long enough for their engines to cool. Before I could scan the airwaves to see what was happening, I spotted Claire arriving at the side gate.

"C'mon Jimmy, we're all in the back waiting for you."

# CHAPTER FORTY-THREE
## (THE GATHERING *REDUX*)

As I rounded the back corner of the house, I spotted the members of my crew under our huge back deck, sitting or standing around the large farmhouse table sampling various forms of breakfast, some complete with eggs and bacon, some just toast or bagels, and some with just a juice or coffee. Despite the bone-chilling, snowy weather outside, they were all *sans* coats and comfortable thanks to a pair of premium Patio Bromic Tungsten Heaters at each end of the patio, which kept the area a balmy sixty-degrees. It was warm enough to keep the fountain flowing, and its background gurgling sound, amongst the wall of ivy that Gina had planted in my absence, made this space even more inviting. Claire parked under one of the heaters and shook off the snow.

*I think it's time to put on that new coat Pam Ervin left for me.* She thought to herself.

Helen came out through the sliding doors with a large platter of additional food which she served to those who wanted and then left the remainder in the center on top of a plate warmer.

"Come sit and eat," she called to me.

I surveyed the gathering for Gina but did not see her.

"She is upstairs getting dressed," Bobbi said, appearing out of nowhere at my side, "she just got back from her run, although I cannot fathom why anyone would want to run in the snow." She took inventory from around the table and continued, "Eddie and Whitey are upstairs cooking and Everett and Michelle will be over in a minute. The sisters and Lucian are home with their blood families."

Lenny gave me a hard once over from his chair at the nearest end of the table. "You look like you could use a little sprucing up yourself." Blue and Maeve came out of the house and excitedly sniffed at Chloé's scent on my hand, then took their places under the table so they could mooch whatever scraps were made available.

"That's a great idea," I acknowledged, then entered the house and proceeded to the ground floor *en suite* off of my office, where I had been recently keeping some extra clean clothes, so I did not have to go up to my bedroom. I could hear Claire's voice following me through the sliding doors, thumping the concrete with her hoof for emphasis.

"Don't take too long, Jimmy, there's family business to attend to."

I showered and shaved at human speed, letting the assuasive water cascade over me until it raised my core temperature back to a comfortable level. I felt unexpectedly nervous at the prospect of facing Gina in front of the group. I hoped she did not think I was behind their coming here today.

When I reappeared on the patio, everyone else had arrived, and then some. To my amazement, down across the far end of the table, over by where Claire was still soaking up the heat, stood my sister, Bonnie and her spouse Tessa, chatting with Bobbi and Helen. They oozed upper class English society donning matching ensembles of rag & bone tweed jackets with leather elbow patches, J. McLaughlin cashmere turtlenecks and Eileen Fisher wool trousers. Bonnie's ensemble was grey, Tessa's was tan. I watched as Bobbi and Bonnie stared silently at each other before bursting into laughter while Helen and Tessa stood to the side shaking their head in common human commiseration. When Bonnie looked over, it took her another long moment to recognize me. She politely excused herself from the others and quickly closed the distance. I easily lifted her in my arms and spun her around, forgetting my own strength.

"Whoa, Samson," she gasped, as I realized what I was doing and gently set her down.

I gave her another once over and pulled her back in for an extended hug. I had not realized until that moment how much I needed my tiny, big sister.

"Relax," she whispered in my ear, "you're going to squish the girls."

Being a man, I automatically understood her reference as a euphemism for her breasts, and being my sister, this made me instantly uncomfortable.

*No, you clown, not those 'girls.'*

Of course, now I was doubly embarrassed that my sister had understood that I was even thinking about her breasts, so I emphatically shook my head with Centaurian speed to cast out the whole thought pattern, and I am sure I said, "Nah, nah, nah, nah, nah, nah," as I did so. Instant childhood regression.

"That's quite a trick," she said when I stopped, obviously reveling in my embarrassment, as only a big sister can, "so, everything I've been hearing is true."

"You don't know the half of it," I responded, happy to change the subject.

"Well, you can tell me the whole story later," she teased. "But back to the girls."

With that, she unbuttoned her jacket and opened the left side to expose the inside breast pocket. She reached in with her right hand and gave the pocket a gentle prod with her fingertips. Suddenly, something in the pocket started to stir and out popped three tiny creatures as if they had been fired from a sling shot. After tumbling through the air for almost a foot in the space between us, they righted themselves and hovered. Bonnie opened her palm and the three tiny figures gently landed and each one bent a knee in a curtsey to me, tucking their gossamer wings behind them as they did.

"*These* are the girls." Bonnie said with just enough emphasis to make me blush again, "Alieki, Brentisa, and Cirrha."

Each of the tiny creatures bowed their head upon hearing their names.

They were certainly similar in size and appearance to the three Sprites I met back in London, in what seemed like ages ago.

"How did you get them past the airport security?" I asked, while still studying the figures.

"They exist at a different energy level," Bonnie responded, matter-of-factly, "they don't show up on x-rays. And if anyone else reached into my pocket, they would find nothing. Their appearance in our reality is totally within their control."

With that, Bonnie tossed the three into the air, and they immediately proceeded to investigate the offerings on the table, grabbing bits and bobs of buttered toast and sipping collectively from an abandoned glass of orange juice, much to the obvious delight of the other members of the crew, while Tessa made their respective introductions.

"Aren't they amazing," Bonnie declared, proudly.

"I'm thrilled you bought them to visit," I said, watching as one, I believe it was Brentisa, landed on Claire's muzzle. Claire almost went cross-eyed trying to fix on her, while Whitey laughed until Alieki landed on his portentous proboscis, which caused Lenny to now laugh, while covering his even larger nose with his two hands. Lucky for him, Cirrha was over by the fountain, investigating the surrounding wall of English ivy.

"Oh, they are not visiting," Bonnie said, "they are a belated birthday present, they are here to stay."

I thought about that, and given my recent ostracization, worried how the distant separation from their own kind may make them feel.

Bonnie was well into my thoughts.

*They volunteered to come. Their cousins spoke very highly of you and knew there was magic in your blood.*

"And for me, this is my belt and braces effort to keep all lines of communications open to you," Bonnie continued aurally, "because God forbid anything should happen to either one of us, where we could not communicate physically or mentally, the Sprites will be across the pond with word in the literal blink of an eye."

All three of the Sprites were now taking turns diving into the fountain's water like Olympic divers, to everyone's amusement. I scanned this content group of my extended family and reached over and pulled Bonnie close into my side. Then Bobbi abruptly turned towards the sliding glass doors and stared, while Blue bounded out from under the table in that direction, leading the others to look over. I felt Gina before I saw her. And when I actually saw her, my heart skipped a beat.

"I'm glad you're home," she whispered as she pecked my cheek, her hand on my closest arm to prevent it from reaching for her.

"And you must be Bonnie," she said politely as she leaned in for a hug, which my sister engaged fully. Bonnie gazed over her shoulder at me, and I could see the angst in her eyes.

"Ladies and Gentlemen," I heard Claire suddenly declare, stomping her hoof on the cement patio like a gavel to bring the crew to order, "to paraphrase another famously loquacious, but nowhere near as charming, large creature, 'the time has come for all of us to talk of many things.'"

# CHAPTER FORTY-FOUR
# (THE GREAT DEBATE)

Helen and Eddie gathered the last of the food and drinks from the table and carried them inside while Whitey and Lenny rearranged the chairs so that there were two at either end of the long table and four spread out equidistant on the side closest to the house, and three on the other side where Claire was standing. When Whitey and Helen returned, Claire directed everyone to prearranged seats according to her instructions.

"Eddie, Helen, Bobbi, and Lenny" she began, "you are over there on the inside of the table."

"Bonnie, Tessa and Whitey," she continued, "you newbies are over here on my side, where I can keep a close eye on you."

"Where is Everett and Michelle?" Lenny interrupted, as the roll call took their assigned places, "and who the hell taught you Lewis Carroll?"

"I've just sent for them," Claire responded politely, "and yes, Scarlett has been reading to me again. She's getting her masters at CU in Comparative Literature," Claire added proudly.

"Did somebody call our names?" Michelle shouted as her and Everett appeared from the ether.

"Finally, the band is back together!" Everett cheered, as he broke into an air guitar solo.

My mind began to buzz as silent nods amongst the members were belied by a flurry of telepathic introductions amongst new and old.

"Tessa," Claire said in an official tone, "these are our extraterrestrial friends and neighbors, Everett and Michelle."

"Greetings, Earthlings," Michelle dead panned, while Everett bowed solemnly in her direction.

"And I thought the Fairies were full of shit!" Tessa retorted, setting the table alight in nervous laughter.

"You two aliens sit down at that end of the table." Claire continued. "Jimmy and Gina, down here on my end."

I offered Gina the lead and followed her to our assigned seats. I took the inner side of the table and Gina sat closer to Claire. Blue and Maeve exited the house and disappeared under the table. Claire looked around at everyone silently for a moment, before continuing.

"First of all," she began aurally, "thank you all for attending our Thanksgiving Day breakfast on such short notice."

The people around the table all murmured various versions of 'you're welcome' and 'happy to be together again after all this time.'

"And I want to officially welcome our newest members," Claire continued, "Whitey, our most recent local addition, and Bonnie and Tessa from Salisbury, near Stonehenge."

Whitey stood up and clumsily bowed to the rest of the members, and the two women did their best impression of the Queen's wave.

"Now if you all would stop trying to read my mind, which is closed, I will get to the dire matter that brings us here." Claire said, all levity gone from her voice.

"And on that note, all future communication around the table this morning shall be by voice only. No exceptions."

"Sorry," Bobbi said meekly, "force of habit."

"Well," Claire continued, "for the benefit of the newbies, let me present the issue that has caused such a maelstrom in our otherwise peaceful, familial community here at *Casa de Moran*. A little over a year ago, through no fault of his own, Jimmy was shot to death in front of this house."

All of the witnesses to the event, nodded in acknowledgement, and Whitey seemed undisturbed by the talk of death, but I could see Bonnie and Tessa slightly recoil at the nonchalance of the others' visual response to their brother's demise.

"I'm fine," I interjected to calm them.

"And that's the other thing," Claire replied sharply, "no one speaks until I formally recognize them to do so. Is that understood?"

Everyone briefly mumbled their agreement and she continued.

"And as most of us who were there know, Everett brought Jimmy back to life that night using a proprietary form of energy reanimation that is far beyond any existing human technology. Everett, would you place the Hadron Distributor on the table in front of you so we can all see it?"

Everett paused. Michelle leaned over and said, "do what she says."

Everett complied and stood and removed the tiny silver tube from his pocket and gently laid it on the table before him. The others stood and leaned forward to get a better look at it.

"I thought it would be bigger," Lenny suggested. The others broke into laughter to lessen the increasing tension. Claire recovered the floor by stomping her hoof on the concrete.

"Now as most of us know, Everett was recalled to Centauri, to answer for his purported misuse of their technology and violation of their Prime Directive." Claire continued, "and we also know that Jimmy returned to Centauri with Everett to defend his friend before their High Council."

"I didn't get a chance to formally thank you for that, Jimmy." Michelle said somberly.

I nodded, appreciatively.

"While I love this leisurely stroll down memory lane while I digest my hearty breakfast," Lenny interjected, "is anyone going to get to a point here?"

"The point, Lenny," Claire responded sternly, "is that the tradeoff for all of these recounted events, is that Jimmy is now more Centauri than human."

"Well, I figured that out the night of Mr. Rogers' funeral when he disappeared with the wonder twins down to face down the coyotes," Lenny retorted, "but with all due respect, for this group, right now, that's really just another day on the farm."

"Yes, Lenny," Claire responded patiently, "Jimmy's physical and mental change, in and of itself, may not be all that exciting to our arguably jaded fellowship." Claire began to pace, Perry Mason style, along her side of the table as she gathered her thoughts. "But one of the unexpected side effects is that Jimmy will now live as long as our alien brethren."

"And how long is that?" Whitey asked.

"Well over half a millennium," Everett replied softly.

Lenny whistled. Bonnie and Tessa whispered to each other.

"Sign me up!" Eddie said.

Everyone started to speak over each other, except Gina and me. Claire brought the table to order with another forceful bang of her hoof.

"If you would all just wait a moment longer for me to finish," Claire commanded, "you will all have a chance to share your thoughts on the real issue."

"Which is?" Lenny asked.

"Whether or not you believe Everett should do the same thing to Gina." Claire stated boldly.

Gina shot up from her chair, her deep brown eyes incandescent in anger.

"As much as I love you all, this is not an issue to be publicly debated. This is between Jimmy and me."

"We understand that, Gina," Helen piped in unexpectedly, "but we all consider you to be our family now, and as a family, we want you to understand our feelings as you make whatever decision you ultimately come to," Helen said, her voice lowering in force and volume, "because at the end of the day, and I know this is selfish of me, it is the two of you, *as* the two of you, that have bound us all together."

"And in all fairness," Bobbi followed up, "you haven't tried to resolve this on your own, have you?"

"If you don't mind me saying so," Whitey offered politely, "I've only been around this group for about a year now, first just observing as an outsider on the perimeter, and then being authentically and warmly welcomed inside your circle by you, Gina, in particular. Up until a month ago, I believed this lone wolf had finally found his forever pack."

"Whitey's right, Gina," Eddie offered, "things have not been the same around her since Everett and Jimmy returned from Centauri."

"That's not my fault!" Gina retorted. "I'm not the one who has changed."

"It's not Jimmy's fault, either." Everett responded apologetically. "He didn't ask to be brought back from the dead."

"What exactly is the issue, here?" Tessa asked.

"Jimmy is now faced with suffering five or more additional human lifetimes without the love of his life." Bonnie answered her. "Isn't that right little brother?"

"Can't you do something for Gina?" Tessa asked practically, staring directly at Everett and Michelle.

"Look," I interjected, not wanting Everett and Michelle to be taking the heat, "Everett was just dragged across this galaxy to answer for breaking his world's Prime Directive, for bringing me back from the dead. It's not fair to put this on them," I continued, "and I don't blame him for what's happened to me, because if I have learned anything from my most unusual life, sometimes shit happens, and you just have to deal with it."

"Well, I can tell you all one thing," Lenny spoke up, "having seen many people die, and indeed, having happily helped a few of them along, I don't fear death, especially after listening to Bobbi, here, drone on and on and on about the wonders on the other side of the veil."

Lenny stopped what he was saying and looked around the table, "can't a man get a decent drink around here?"

Michelle disappeared and instantly returned with the half empty bottle of Macallan and a glass tumbler, which she filled and slid down the length of the table with a SOHO bartender's expertise. Lenny snatched the glass and downed the liquid in one gulp and wiped his lips on his sleeve.

"That's better," he said, examining the empty glass. "But after watching the pain I saw from the rest of you, hell, the pain I personally felt when we lay Mr. Rogers' to rest," Lenny now acknowledged Claire with a condoling look, "I can just promise you one thing, that I pray I am the first to go among you." He paused for a moment and sniffed hard to repel the tears that were forming in his eyes and pursed his lips to still the quiver that appeared, "because I don't want to watch any of you die."

Without any apparent movement, Michelle refilled his tumbler and returned to her seat.

"Well," Tessa interjected, "speaking for us humans, assuming that there are some other humans amongst this crowd, I am relatively old, in human years, and I have lived a wonderful life, with the love of my life," she reached over and gave Bonnie's hand an affectionate squeeze, "so whenever fate takes me, I will have no regrets."

"It's always easiest for the first loved one to cross the veil," Bobbi responded, "there's no pain, no regrets, in fact, you are back to being an energy form of your best self. They do not even operate under our concept of linear time." She looked over at Bonnie. "But for those of you that must remain here on this plane, the pain is real and palpable, and time here moves slowly."

"I've watched a number of my friends die in the Middle East," Eddie piped in, "and I can say without reservation that not one of them went peacefully. They each fought till their last breath to stay alive. There was fear in their eyes, not of death, but for the pain that would be inflicted on those they were leaving behind."

"I'm with Bobbi on this one," Helen chimed in. "As another one of us who has returned from the other side of the veil, it is a wonderful place, and I would have gladly stayed there with my uncle Gus if I could have." She paused for a few moments to collect her thoughts, then turned directly towards Gina. "But I wasn't leaving any loved ones behind. And if I had the choice right now, I would want to share this life with Bobbi for as long as I could."

Gina reached under the table and touched my hand for just a moment, and then pulled it away.

"What do you think, Claire?" Bonnie asked.

"Jimmy and I have already discussed my feelings on the matter," Claire responded thoughtfully, "but since we are all sharing here, I can say without qualification, that if I were Jimmy, I would not want to live another five minutes on this side of the veil without Gina."

Everett now chimed in. "I cannot tell you all how sorry I am for putting everyone in this situation." He gazed down each side of the table and met everyone's eyes long enough to make a connection. "But I am not sorry for one moment that I brought Jimmy back from the dead, or that I broke the Prime Directive to do it." He looked across the table at me and I saw a gentle smile form on his lips. "At the same time, the law of unintended consequences is a bitch, and I see now the pain I have unintentionally caused between my two dearest friends."

Now I could see tears forming along the lids of Gina's eyes.

"So even if Gina wanted me to," Everett said softly, "I'm not sure I could do it."

The whole time everyone was voicing their feelings, Michelle sat stoned faced. She now stood up from her seat and racked her shoulders back as she pulled herself to her full height and best posture. Then she disappeared for a moment and when she reappeared, she was in her true Centauri form. Everyone around the table but me and Claire gasped with some escaped aural exclamation of surprise and awe. Michelle looked more striking than most of the angelic females I saw up in the galleries during the trial. She looked less androgenous, more feminine. I actually felt the slightest stirring as I gazed at her. A moment later, Everett changed into his natural Centauri form as well. Then Michelle addressed us with an unexpected tone of formality in her voice.

"I've listened here quietly while you've all expressed your feelings about life and death. And on a purely, human, emotional level, I completely understand how each of you feels. Indeed, I empathize with all of you. Death sucks, no matter what waits for any of us on the other side." Now Michelle was pacing in a small circle directly behind her chair. "But what I'm not hearing from any of you, is the human passion and the fight that I've become so enamored with, especially since I've met you all. What each of you displayed that night of the storm, over a year ago, where you all without question faced death, not for yourselves, but for each other. For Jimmy. Hell, listening to you now, I feel like I'm back on Centauri, with all of this rationalization of your feelings. And I'm not sorry to say, that I'm not a fan."

She stood staring silently at the group, allowing her words to sink in.

"But as Jimmy had mentioned earlier, sometimes shit happens. There are no guarantees in any life whether you are a Terrian, or Centaurian," Michelle now moved her chair away from the table and stood imposingly in its place beside her husband. "All you can do is pick yourself up and deal with it. No regrets or recriminations."

Michelle placed her left hand on Everett's shoulder, and he reached up and covered her hand with his right hand.

"So," Michelle continued, her tone shifting to one of resolution and determination, "I've decided to make this easy on all of you."

Even with my advanced senses I could barely see Michelle move as she snatched the Hadron Distributor from the table and pointed it at Gina, its golden beam firing across the length of the table and striking Gina directly center-mass, its force driving her back from the table and against the wall. I had to move at full Centauri speed to prevent Gina's head from striking the concrete and then gently lowered her limp body onto the floor before the others fully comprehended what had taken place.

I looked over at Michelle, who appeared totally pleased with herself.

"She didn't want this!" I shouted.

"And you didn't *want* to be alone," Michelle said, defiantly. "So instead, you both got what you *need*."

Michelle now turned in the direction of the back property and effortlessly hurled the Hadron Distributor end over end through the air and into the deepest part of the pond.

"There," Michelle said, "it is done."

Everett appeared on the other side of Gina, checking her vitals, while the others started shouting their own scrambled instructions to one another on resuscitation techniques. Tessa asked if anyone called an ambulance and was ferreting her phone from her purse to do so, just as Gina started to stir, her moan reminding me of my own on the night of the storm. She pushed our helping hands away as she slowly lifted herself into a sitting position.

*What the fuck just happened?* Gina's voice simultaneously entered the minds of all who telepathically could receive it, and all began to respond in kind.

"Wait," Gina whispered, "did you just hear me?"

The others acknowledged her recovery with words of relief and love, both aurally and telepathically.

Gina slowly tilted her head upward and slowly opened her eyes. They were Nordic blue.

*I'm sorry Gina,* I shared. *I couldn't stop her.*

*It's okay, Jimmy.* Gina responded, staring into my eyes with a new sense of wonder. *We're okay.*

She grabbed my face with both her hands and pulled me into a passionate kiss, her strength already improved. I surrendered completely.

The moment invoked memories of when Gina and I exchanged that first kiss at the end of our wedding ceremony before our friends and family, so long ago. On telepathic cue, the others around the table applauded in much the same fashion, and Lenny added a whoop, whoop for good measure.

"Fuck the law of unintended consequences!" Michelle shouted like a warrior from behind us. "The Centauri High Council can kiss my ass."

Everett appeared beside her looking angrier than I had ever seen him before. He placed his hand on her shoulder and the two disappeared.

# CHAPTER FORTY-FIVE
# (RECOVERING SEA LEGS)

As was her way with every challenge the universe threw at Gina, she fully embraced her post-human life and turned it to her advantage.

Unlike my transformation, Gina's physical appearance did not change too dramatically but maybe that was because, at the time of my murder, I had pretty much let myself go. Her hair seemed fuller and more luxurious, and a revitalized layer of collagen had removed the faint crow's feet and smile lines from her face. Her radiant blue eyes were more sensitive to the bright Colorado sun than the brown of her Mediterranean ancestors had been, so she donned her sunglasses whenever she left the house. But her body looked the same it had always looked, totally fit and at least twenty years younger than the age on her driver's license.

Claire and Bobbi immediately began a crash course with Gina on everything telepathic, and she, as with everything she did as a human, picked it up on the first bounce. She took to it so quickly that it became her go-to form of communication between us, and I suddenly realized that the only way I could escape her constant attention was by blocking my mind from her. This usually resulted in her relatively quick manifestation at my office door with a very disapproving look.

"Don't be blocking my cell number." She would command playfully. I did not need to read her mind to know that she meant it.

Her enhanced physical abilities developed quicker than mine had. She rapidly went from breaking her own personal records on her runs to competitively staying with me as we crisscrossed the larger geographic areas, usually at night. And no matter how many miles we had logged overnight, she still would go for her morning run with Blue at her human speed.

Gina was soon outshooting Lenny at the gun range, which drove him crazy with jealousy and pride in equal measure. He soon began taking Lucian and the sisters out for their own lessons, because there was nothing more he could teach Gina. "Never too young to learn how to defend yourself," he would say as he packed the young ones off in his SUV.

The emotional distance that had developed between Gina and I since my return from Centauri evaporated with the transmogrification of her eye color. We had become best friends again and spent more free time doing things together around the property, which lessoned the workload, given her increased strength and speed. And we shared more day trips together, hiking effortlessly through the ubiquitous local mountain trails, including The Devils Backbone, my vertigo all but a memory.

Gina, too, was becoming less dependent on sleep, so we filled those newly acquired nocturnal hours like teenagers. All things again being equal, I was always the first to tire.

The passion and frequency of our love making required new and creative locations, given our shortened recovery times, and we often laughed about the time Claire caught us on top of the haystacks in her barn. Needless to say, Claire insisted we donate the remainder of the adulterated straw to the unsuspecting Colorado Horse Rescue and replenish the entire storeroom with a fresh batch. She could not face us for a week.

Michelle and Everett had made themselves scarce for those first couple of weeks. When they finally appeared at our front door, they waited outside until Gina formally came out to invite them in.

But before Everett would enter the doorway, he held up one hand and pointed to his partner with the other. "Say it."

Michelle stood defiant in her silence.

"Say it Michelle!" He commanded. I never saw this side of Everett before, especially around Michelle. I was actually a little worried that he was punching above his weight class in the match up.

Surprisingly, Michelle finally hung her head in surrender.

"I'm sorry, Gina," she whispered. "I just couldn't bare to see the two of you so unhappy."

Gina embraced Michelle tightly, giving her an extra powerful squeeze for good measure. "Apology accepted." Gina said. "I would have come around eventually; it was just a lot to process from my human perspective."

*Good*, Michelle shared telepathically, returning her own powerful squeeze. *Because I would probably do it again.*

The two amazons now broke their embrace and smiled at each other with a clear understanding that going forward, they were to treat each other with the respect of their newly forged equality. Gina looked over at me, smiled and took my hand. "And there's definitely been an upside."

*Like rabbits.* I shared telepathically, this time, without any blushing. The resulting laughter removed that last bit of tension from between the four of us.

After that, Michelle and Everett returned to the family of misfits with a vengeance. Michelle was no longer an unknowable alien to Gina. Michelle was now treating Gina like the true younger sibling she had become. Soon Gina was inviting Michelle out on hundred-mile runs, and they were always communicating telepathically. Indeed, Michelle taught Gina the art of binary, and in no time my wife could decipher or deliver it as fast as anyone. But I always insisted Gina and I communicate the important things using words, because they retained the emotional connection that was sacrificed with numbers.

Everett had developed a liking for fly fishing and often invited me along to watch him. While he was superb at the art of the cast, and even slowed his movements down to human speed, he never seemed to catch anything, and blamed my presence for scaring the fish away. But I enjoyed the time we spent together and used it to just talk about silly guy things, ideas for the property, and projects I hoped to begin or complete. It was my bro-time with someone who knew me better than most, including all of my secrets. We never spoke about our time on Centauri, or Petrichor, and that suited both of us.

Everett and Michelle also instituted group Driver's Ed Night. Once a week they took Gina and me up in Jayney to teach us all of the tricks to space travel. But we stayed in our solar system. Michelle turned out to be a far more daring instructor than Everett and had no reservations in toying with the government jets sent to investigate if we were a little careless when taking off or landing. Gina, of course, was a natural at the control panel and it never got old watching the excitement in her blue eyes.

And we entertained the rest of our mystical group more regularly than ever. There was always one or more of them appearing unannounced at our doorstep for a visit or chat, which always turned into a meal. Gina began taking the children along with her on regular shopping sprees, or out to eat, always spoiling them in the process. I loved listening to the sound of their laughter billowing through the hallways and reaching down to me in my office lair.

We continued to host our Saturday night group dinner, with someone new taking the lead as to the menu and drinks. Not everyone made it every time, but many appeared on most weekends and someone always showed up. Helen, Bobbi, and Eddie never missed it. And Claire always made her appearance, either physically or telepathically, depending on where we set our table.

We even started reaching out to some of the local neighbors with invitations for the occasional lunch or dinner out, sometimes at Grandpa's Café, sometimes at the Side Tracked Bar, both long time Berthoud establishments where we knew the customers were more interested in the service and food than the scenery. We were always careful not to tip our hands or do anything that would raise anyone's concerns or interests. Most of our neighbors had never taken too much of a notice of us before, and any questions that came up about our change in appearance were usually deflected by a wink and a reference to HGH, hair plugs and personal trainers.

However, only the extended family of misfits breached the walls of our home.

When Gina and I did venture out as a couple for an overnight trip beyond our town's borders, Lucian handled the Claire related chores around the property and Blue would stay over at Lenny's with Maeve. Whitey would always stop by the house during our absences just to check in with Claire. Sometimes, if we were traveling more than a couple of days, Lenahan would house sit and Whitey would take Blue and Maeve on midnight runs through the foothills in feral form, reintroducing the domesticated brutes to their wild side. He even taught them how to howl. And no matter where Gina and I were staying, Claire always reached out to us telepathically to say good night.

Bonnie and Tessa would visit us every other month, staying for just a week because they did not want to impose, but I always made sure that there were plenty of visitors every night during their stay, so they always enjoyed their time with us.

And the Sprites had quickly commandeered the full extent of the pond, and always spent some time each day chatting with Claire when she stopped by for a drink. They would come up to the house to visit for any group event, and spent their time flittering around the fountain and English ivy. Magic flowed as freely as the love we all shared, and a year passed before we knew it.

# EPILOGUE
## (AN EXPECTANT TWOFER)

On the rare occasion when one of us needed to actually sleep for any extended period of time, it was usually alone, while the other took care of some errand or caught up with a project, or a show they were interested in, or a book they wanted to read. If the two of us were in bed, there was no sleep to be had.

On the night before the second Christmas after Gina's evolution, I felt unusually tired, and decided to take a shot at getting some shuteye. I fell asleep quickly and soundly and I had no idea how long it lasted. But at some point, a telepathic message intruded into my subconscious like a bad dream:

01001010 01101001 01101101 01101101 01111001 00100000
01001101 01101111 01110010 01100001 01101110 00101100
00100000 01110100 01101000 01101001 01110011 00100000
01101001 01110011 00100000 01010000 01100101 01110100
01110010 01101001 01100011 01101000 01101111 01110010
00101110 00100000 00100000 01001001 00100000 01110111
01100001 01101110 01110100 00100000 01111001 01101111
01110101 00100000 01110100 01101111 00100000 01101011
01101110 01101111 01110111 00100000 01110111 01100101
00100000 01101000 01100001 01110110 01100101 00100000
01100001 00100000 01100100 01100001 01110101 01100111
01101000 01110100 01100101 01110010 00101110 00100000

01010011 01101000 01100101 00100111 01110011 00100000
01100010 01100101 01100001 01110101 01110100 01101001
01100110 01110101 01101100 00101110 00100000 00100000
01010100 01101000 01100001 01101110 01101011 00100000
01111001 01101111 01110101 00101110

*Jimmy Moran, this is Petrichor. I want you to know we have a daughter. She's beautiful. Thank you.*

The message jolted me awake from my sleep like I had been doused with ice water. Disoriented, it took me a moment to get my bearings in the darkness of my room. Once fully cognizant, I spotted Gina sitting quietly in the corner rocker. When I turned on the lights, I could see she was holding something in her hand, and she had a shimmering smile on her face. Before I could figure out what the small slender object was, her voice entered my mind with excitement and clarity.

*We're pregnant!*

01010100 01101000 01100001 01101110 01101011 00100000
01111001 01101111 01110101 00100000 01100110 01101111
01110010 00100000 01110010 01100101 01100001 01100100
01101001 01101110 01100111 00100000 01100010 01101111
01110100 01101000 00100000 01010100 01101000 01100101
00100000 01010111 01101001 01110011 01100101 00100000
01000001 01110011 01110011 00100000 01100001 01101110
01100100 00100000 01000001 01101110 00100000 01000001
01101100 01101001 01100101 01101110 00100000 01000001
01110000 01110000 01100101 01100001 01101100 00101110
00100000 01001001 00100000 01101000 01101111 01110000
01100101 00100000 01111001 01101111 01110101 00100000
01100101 01101110 01101010 01101111 01111001 01100101
01100100 00100000 01110100 01101000 01100101 00100000
01110011 01110100 01101111 01110010 01111001 00100000
01110011 01101111 00100000 01100110 01100001 01110010
00101110 00100000 01001001 01100110 00100000 01111001
01101111 01110101 00100000 01101000 01100001 01110110
01100101 00101100 00100000 01110000 01101100 01100101
01100001 01110011 01100101 00100000 01110011 01101000
01101111 01110111 00100000 01111001 01101111 01110101
01110010 00100000 01110011 01110101 01110000 01110000

ort for my writing by posting five-star reviews wherever you can. The next and final installment of The Claire Trilogy is called KMAG (an acronym). I promise you that I have given these wonderful characters one hell

01101111 01100110 00100000 01100001 00100000 01110011
01100101 01101110 01100100 00101101 01101111 01100110
01100110 00101110 00100000 01001011 01001101 01000001
01000111 00100000 01110111 01101001 01101100 01101100
00100000 01100010 01100101 00100000 01110000 01110101
01100010 01101100 01101001 01110011 01101000 01100101
01100100 00100000 01101111 01101110 00100000 01000001
01110000 01110010 01101001 01101100 00100000 00110010
00111000 00101100 00100000 00110010 00110000 00110010
00110010 00101110 00100000 01010100 01101000 01100001
01101110 01101011 00100000 01111001 01101111 01110101
00100000 01100001 01100111 01100001 01101001 01101110
00100000 01100110 01101111 01110010 00100000 01111001
01101111 01110101 01110010 00100000 01110000 01100001
01110100 01110010 01101111 01101110 01100001 01100111
01100101 00101110

*Thank you for reading both The Wise Ass and An Alien Appeal. I hope you enjoyed the story so far. If you have, please show your support for my writing by posting five-star reviews wherever you can. The next and final installment of The Claire Trilogy is called KMAG (an acronym). I promise you that I have given these wonderful characters one hell of a send-off. KMAG will be published on April 28, 2022. Thank you again for your patronage.*

# ACKNOWLEDGMENTS

To my wife, Lisa, who continues to amaze, support, and inspire me. I love you forever. This has been the kind of exciting year we used to imagine when we first shared future dreams in that drafty garret bedroom in Violet's Flop House on Tyndall Avenue in the Bronx. We were so young. We still are. Thanks for hanging in there. I know I am a pain in the ass.

To my children, their spouses, and their families: Luke, Georgie, Scarlett, Savanna and Stella; Jackie, Zack and Lucian (and his Dad, Matt); Mark, Sara (and fur-grandchildren Jackson and Ella). I am so proud of where this family is going. To the Morans, Jimmy, Liz, Dana, Kevin and Brooklyn James). I love you all.

To my siblings and their families: Veronica (never Ronni) and 'b' (my sisters and fairy godmothers and the basis for the characters Bonnie and Tessa – you really are magical); Eddie, Mary, Kathleen, Arthur and Hugo, Eddie and Danielle; Bernie (the "Ginger") and Denise, Eamon, Malachy (thanks for the insightful feedback on AAA and KMAG), Brendan and Nolan; Evan (and Nicole); and John, Tara, Taylor, John Michael (and Joyce). The Frawley Clan (RIP Aunt Chrissy & Uncle John). I did not have to imagine you into existence, you are always there for me. Thanks for keeping me grounded. To Ferd Beck, family sage, thanks for hanging with the Clan and for the generous sharing of all of your wisdom over the generations. Hi to your sister, Karen "Cruiser" Anderson, one of our New York Ex-Pats here in Colorado.

To Spaghetti and Posey McCaffrey, Tom and Bridey Burke, Ed and Vera McCaffrey. RIP. Thanks for not carrying through on your threats to drown me as a child (which I absolutely deserved). Must do better!

To the Wallen Witches, their spouses, children and grandchildren: Rachel and Gary, Adam, Julie, Paisley, Graham and Brynn; Brian (future anesthesiologist) and Matt; Cathleen (thanks for your valuable creative insights for AAA, especially Chapter 41, as well as the turning point in KMAG) and Beau (gave me excellent feedback for AAA and KMAG – you and Victor are the ultimate bad guys in the latter); Leslie and Madge; Michele, Terry and Tyler; Amy, Lori (say hi to your brother Joey), Ashley and Isaac; Jason, Amy and Blake Charles; Chad, Baylee and Ryleigh; Dina (the most mystical elf - thanks for reading the drafts of my novels ),

Randy, Randall and Julia. Love you all. I could not be Merlin without you. And of course, Norb and Mary (RIP).

To my brother from a different mother, Jimmy Fronsdahl (basis for Whitey in AAA and KMAG), and his lovely wife Kathy. Jimmy, I can openly share that you not only selflessly helped me whip TWA into final shape, but An Alien Appeal would not have been ready to hit the shelves this soon if not for your dedication and support as my Chief Editor and confidant. Kathy, your creative eye captured that iconic photo of Claire for the cover of TWA, which helped me manifest the brilliant cover for AAA by Richard Lamb. I miss you both terribly but wish you nothing but happiness in Idaho. Love you both.

To Colin Broderick, my literary brother from Riverdale (by way of Eire) and Lehman College. They will be mentioning us both in a course there some day. Thanks for all of your generous guidance, introductions, and great stories. Love to Rachel, Samuel., Bruce and Erica. You are truly blessed. Say hi to Billy Collins and Josh Brolin.

To Ricky Ginsberg and the NOCO Writers group. Wonderful group of talented bastards. Ricky you are a writing machine. Slow down or I will never be able to catch you.

To Dr. Nick Atlas, the brilliant modern-day mystic, who is doing so much to make this world a better place. Love you brother!

To Helen Lalousis (and Uncle Gus), my dearest friend, I love you forever. Let's make a movie.

To Bobbi and Eddie Roell, please tell me there are movie options coming! Love you both.

To the Collins Clan: my surrogate family, Terry, Jeanne, Michael, Eileen, Maureen, Anne, Billy, Mary, and Brian (Dutch, Mamma C, Denis, Kevin, John and Susan, RIP) – and their million spouses, significant others and offspring. Eileen, thanks for keeping me on course through the rest of the Claire Trilogy, your assistance as one of the inner circle readers was invaluable. Your character appears in KMAG. Damn the milk truck! I love you all.

To Dianne Rosenthal, my dear friend, one of my inner circle readers for AAA and KMAG, and the generous host of my first ever reading for TWA in your beautiful home and literary salon, you have been a blessing! Gertrude Stein could not have been more supportive, and Hemingway would have been so jealous, we would have had to finish it in the ring.

To my favorite extraterrestrials, and dear friends, Everett and Michelle. I would not have written the Claire Trilogy if I had not met you. Thank you for the continued inspiration and support. Everett, you are a genius, Michelle, a loveable bad ass. Love you both. Nanu, Nanu.

To all of my peeps on Beverly Drive and the remainder of Berthoud and Foothills Estates that I acknowledged in TWA, with special shout outs to Dick, Sue and Sally, Mike, Amy, Delaney and Charles Honaker, Pam (and Tique), Jill and Amy Ervin, Janice and Brian Erickson (Boston Still Sucks but your cousin WB was cool), and Darren, Silja and Anja (and April) Knolls, you guys are the best!

To Maureen, Jim and the staff at Side Tracked (Laurie, Courtney, Amanda, Haley, Eliza, Sammy and Cayle) and Jordan Polovina (Grim & Darling); the owner of Grandpa's Café, Carrie M, and staff, Malissa, Merry, Sara, Shay, Kirsten, Cedar and Angie, and the chef, Chrissy, and Grandpa's regulars, Carl F (my favorite physicist in the readers inner circle ), Dave S, Brian H, Neil O, Mike W, Jack [?], Dave H, Bill H, Don W, Chris G (voice like Wolfman Jack), "Cowboy" Billy and Nick "the Lid"; Jordan (and husband and parents), Rachel, Brittany, Brooke, Chloe and Tea (phon. Teya) at A&W (read my book!); and the families and staff that run Mr. Thrift, Hays Market and Berthoud Discount Liquor. To Berthoud Family Dentistry – Doc Carmen Beckwith ("are you telling me the truth?"), Tosha (thank God it is not a rectal thermometer behind that desk), Danielle (and your wonderful granddaughter, Neveah), Regina (and your family farm), Pamela, Sandy and Lindsay, thanks for keeping my teeth in my head, it makes it easier to smile in my photos. Amber McIver-Traywick and the Berthoud Surveyor, thanks for that first write up.

To my Riverdale crew, BC (and Nan), Mark ("Lenny" the Poet) Lenahan (and son Brian and family), thanks for the feedback on all three novels, Joe (and Donna) Serrano, Mike (and Delia) Augustyni, Jackie (and Sue) Vaughan, your names have already made it into the trilogy, but The Riverdale Chronicles are next on my list, so get ready. To my Clan cousins, "Brother" Mike Moulton, Donna Keenan, Michelle Moulton and John Argen, Pat and Cynthia Moulton (congrats on your wedding), you make our family far more interesting. Love you all. To Colonel Joe Dzikas and Lillian Martin (and Joe's wonderful family – RIP Erin) as promised, your character is an evil bastard in KMAG. To Pat Francis (and Michael), Tina and Franco, thanks for the insights on the sequels. To Steve Morley and family, including your Mom, thanks for the support and the Arthur Avenue cookies. To my lovely Riverdale neighbors Mae "Yin-Yin" Chin and Barbara Miller, miss you both.

To Ray Keane, my FLS best friend. To Michael ("always Mikey") Abramson, thanks for carefully reading the trilogy, you are a prince among men. To Emile "Bubba" Lafond (and his wonderful family – Hi Robin!), good luck with your book, *Father To Sons*. To the Honorable George Silver, my Jewish brother, it is so great to have a Judge in our family. To my dear friends Ralph and Debbie Droz and family, thanks for the feedback. To Chrissy and Cathy Tardibouno (you will always be family), thanks for the hometown marketing help, you are both amazing. To Gina Egan, thanks for Evan and the use of your name. Enzo Caltanissetta (Riverdale Bagels) and Flor and Sal (Dinos) thanks for posting the TWA flyers. Please ship me some food. Hi to Elaine Staltare and the Staltare Sisters. Thanks to all the rest of the PWWCs and Riverdale crews, you gave me a whole lot to work with, see you all in The Riverdale Chronicles. It's going to be a tome.

To my brilliant legal partner and dear friend, Robert "Bobby" Meloni, Adrienne (and family). Love you all! Hi Raff! Keep rocking.

To Dan Pearson, you are still the (scary) man! Much respect to you, your lovely spouse, Donna Hylton, and family.

To Margaret Reyes Dempsey for your blurb and suggested edits, and Richard Lamb for your amazing cover. To Christy Cooper Burnett (*No Way Home* & *Finding Home*) and Sharon Middleton (*McCarron's Corner* series) thanks for the blurbs.

To Kim Russo, dear friend and the most talented and gifted psychic to walk the earth, thanks for all of the support.

To Reagan and Minna Rothe and the entire production, sales, marketing and PR teams at Black Rose Writing, here goes number 2. Thanks for this opportunity and all of the support. KMAG is all teed up.

To all members of the Military, Police, Fire, and EMS departments throughout the country, thank you from the bottom of my heart for your selfless service. You are all loved.

Thank you Tommy "Rocky" O'Hagan, Bill McGinn, Orio Palmer, and all of those first responders and other men and women who sacrificed their lives twenty years ago on 9-11-01. It has been 20 years since your bravery and sacrifice. You will never be forgotten.

To Claire, you continue to inspire me to be that better human, and thankfully keep sharing your stories to publish under my byline. RIP Mr. Rogers, Maeve,

Lucky, Shorty, Phoebe, Stash, Cheeks and Duchess. Love to Honey, Blue and Jeter (pron. "Jeeta"). There, fini!

To Dr. Wayne Dyer (RIP), you are right. When you change the way you look at things, things really do change. Thank you.

# ABOUT THE AUTHOR

Photo courtesy of Georgina McCaffrey

Tom McCaffrey is a born-and-bred New Yorker who, after a successful career working as an entertainment attorney in Manhattan, relocated with his wife to a small town in Northern Colorado to follow a road less travelled and return to his first passion, writing. Despite the local rumors started by Claire the mule, he denies being in the Witness Protection Program.

# NOTE FROM THE AUTHOR

Word-of-mouth is crucial for any author to succeed. If you enjoyed *An Alien Appeal*, please leave a review online—anywhere you are able. Even if it's just a sentence or two. It would make all the difference and would be very much appreciated.

Thanks!
Tom McCaffrey

For fans of **Tom McCaffrey**, please check out our recommendation for your next great read!

*The Wise Ass*

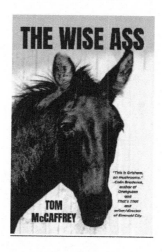

"...a story of abandonment, addiction, finding oneself—all mixed in with tear-jerking chapters next to laugh-out-loud chapters."

*– Tiff & Rich*

Made in the USA
Coppell, TX
05 April 2023

15282995R00142